BRUISED HEARTS

Books By Denise B. Henry

Bruised Hearts

UPCOMING

HEARTS IN BLOOM SERIES

Holiday Hearts

Staged Hearts

BRUISED HEARTS

DENISE B. HENRY

Manu House Press

For more information, please email authordenisehenry@gmail.com
Published by Manu House Press

ISBN: 978-1-9192534-0-4

10 9 8 7 6 5 4 3 2 1

First Edition Paperback- 2025

For the girlies who had their heart broken by the love of their life…..

THIS IS NOT YOUR SIGN TO GET BACK WITH THEM

Content Warning

Some readers may find the following topics distressing. Your wellbeing matters, please take care as you read.

Death & Grief
Accident
PTSD
Emotional Trauma
Anxiety
Panic attacks
Adult Content

Here's a playlist that inspired the story, it sets the mood for every twist and turn. Please enjoy.

1. Taylor Swift – Enchanted
2. Taylor Swift – August
3. Taylor Swift – Invisible String
4. Adele – When We Were Young
5. Selena Gomez – Lose You to Love Me.
6. Taylor Swift – Back to December
7. Taylor Swift – All Too Well (10 min)
8. Taylor Swift- My Tears Ricochet
9. Deborah Cox – All Cried Out
10. Fleetwood Mac – Silver Springs
11. Taylor Swift – Death by a Thousand Cuts
12. Taylor Swift – It's Time to Go
13. Fleetwood Mac – Dreams
14. Lana Del Rey – Young and Beautiful
15. SZA – Nobody Gets Me
16. Kehlani – Folded
17. Coldplay – Fix You
18. Jealous – Joe Jonas
19. Sabrina Carpenter – Man Child
20. Taylor Swift – Invisible String
21. Miguel – Adorn
22. Tonight- John Legend
23. Lady Gaga & Bruno Mars – Die with a Smile
24. James Arthur – Say You Won't Let Go
25. Taylor Swift – Long Live

Prologue

His name was the only thing my heart remembered when everything else began to fade. Everything was heavy. My body and my thoughts. Even the air I tried to breathe. Darkness pressed in on all sides, but it wasn't empty. It was crowded, stuffed with fragments and memories of every word I'd swallowed instead of spoken.

The silence around me pulsed with echoes I thought I'd buried. Our first kiss was clumsy, stolen beneath a sputtering streetlamp. His wide-eyed wonder, like he'd stumbled into something rare, maybe holy.

Dominic, Dom. My Dom.

Not the man who trained me to keep my walls up, not the man I had started to hate. No. It was the boy. The one who laughed until his voice cracked, he always smelled faintly of soap and fresh rain. He would look at me like I was both the beginning and the ending of every story he wanted to tell. I could almost hear him again, calling my name in that half-teasing, half-serious tone he saved only for me.

And then there was this ache. Not the ache of the body—that was gone now, too distant to cling to—but the sharper one that hollowed me from the inside. Regret. All the what-could-have-beens. Here, suspended between consciousness and nothingness, the excuses that once held me back seemed paper-thin. My walls? They were Fragile. Meaningless.

The darkness deepened, folding itself around me, softer than silk, deadly as a serpent. I felt it touch me like a lover, coaxing me towards rest. Towards peace.

And I almost gave in. Maybe soon.

But then came the thought; was this really the end of us? The grand finale of a story I never let myself finish. If this was where I stayed, then I would wait. Right here, inside the hush of the in-between, I'd wait for him. So that when he arrived, he would have me and not be alone. We'd have all the time we needed, time to laugh again, to forgive and to finally choose each other without hesitation.

But until then, I'll rest.

CHAPTER 1

Kelly

November 2008

The smell of pancakes should've made my stomach growl, but instead it just twisted into knots. I stabbed the pancake, like it had personally wronged me.

"Sweet sixteen," Dad announced proudly, hoisting his emotional support coffee mug like it was champagne. "Our Kelly is officially growing up."

My younger sister, Alexis clapped dramatically, while my older sister, Zara, rolled her eyes, all I could manage was a cracked smile. But the frustrated sigh I let out betrayed me because I could feel all their eyes darting towards me.

"Kelly?" Mum asked gently, tilting her head at me. "Are you feeling okay, sweetie?

"I'm fine," I lied quickly, my eyes darting to my phone, my party was tonight, and I still hadn't received an RSVP from him.

"You've barely touched your plate, darling." Dad chimed in gently, not wanting to make me more upset than I already seemed.

"I just didn't get much sleep, that's all," I replied, taking a sip of my juice.

I tossed and turned all night, staring at the ceiling while my birthday morning crept closer and closer. Every time I shut my eyes, one thought kept circling like a stubborn song stuck on repeat: Would Dominic show up tonight?

He'd only been in town a few months. Tall, a little mysterious, the kind of boy people whispered about in the hallways. I don't think I had met another boy as handsome as he was. We hadn't spoken, like properly spoken; until yesterday, when I'd done something totally reckless. I shoved a last-minute birthday invitation into his hand after school, mumbling something like; *You should come to my party tomorrow.*

What if he didn't come? What if he laughed about it later with Peter and the other guys? Or worse…what if he actually came, and I had no idea how to talk to him? I sighed, chewing on the edge of my lip more than my food.

"Too excited, huh? Can't blame you. Sixteen only comes once," Dad chuckled.

I smiled weakly, pretending that was the reason, but my insides were jittery for a whole different cause. My finally phone buzzed against the table, screen lighting up with a text from Mia. I grabbed it instantly, grateful for the distraction.

Happy birthday.

You're officially SIXTEEN, babe.

Don't freak out,

But skype me now!!!

My heart skipped. I shot a quick glance around the table. Mum was cutting pancakes for Alexis, Dad was refilling his coffee, and my older sister was scrolling on her phone. Perfect.

"Uh, can I be excused? I just need to take this really quick."

On your birthday breakfast?" dad glanced at me, his eyebrow raised and his forehead wrinkling.

"It's Mia," I said, which was enough explanation for all of them and Mum waved me off.

I slipped out of the dining room and padded up the stairs, phone clutched in my hand like it was about to burn through my skin. The second I reached my room, I ran to my computer, logged in, and skyped her.

Mia answered instantly, her face filled the screen, curls tied up in a messy bun, hazel eyes wide with the kind of excitement that made me want to jump through the screen. Her freckled honey toned skin was covered in a face mask, in the most hilarious shade of green. I cackled as soon as I saw her.

"Urgh, stop it. One day your gonna beg me for my skincare secrets," she said with fake irritation. "Anyway, Guess what?"

"What? What is it?" My own voice cracked, like I already knew where this was going but didn't dare hope.

"I just spoke to Peter."

"And?" My stomach flipped.

"And Dom's coming tonight!"

For a second I couldn't even breathe. The words echoed in my ears, bouncing around my skull like fireworks. Oh my God, he's coming to my party.

"Are you serious?" I whispered, bouncing in my chair.

"Dead serious," she said, practically squealing. "So, change of plans, forget the pink dress. You need to look hot tonight, wear the gold one."

I span round on my chair, excitement taking over and my legs suddenly feeling weak. All night I'd been imagining him ignoring my invitation, crumpling it up, maybe even laughing about it with his friends. And now, he was actually coming.

"Mia, I don't even know what I'm supposed to say to him," I confessed, pressing my hand to my cheeks. "What if I embarrass myself? What if it's weird?"

"Babe, relax," she said firmly, though I could hear the grin in her voice. "It's your party. He's the one stepping into your world, not the other way around. Just…be yourself. Trust me, he wouldn't be coming if he didn't want to."

I let out a shaky laugh, nerves buzzing in every vein.

After I shut down the computer, I couldn't help but finally feel *grown up*. The sound of birdsong filled my room, and the golden shimmer of sunlight spilled in through sheer lilac curtains. My bedroom smelled like strawberries and vanilla; a mix of my body mist collection and the cupcake scented candle Kennedy, my other bestie, had snuck into my room the night before.

I tried to run my fingers through my coils and regretted not wearing my bonnet to sleep last night. I scanned the room; my eyes settling on the polaroids of all the people I loved, pinned neatly along fairy lights.

"TODAY IS MY 16th BIRTHDAY" I let out a little screech and did my little happy two-step.

"Kelly? Can we come in?" Mum's voice came through my closed bedroom door, warm and soft.

"Yeah, come in." I grabbed the remote and quickly turned off the TV I had left on all night. I didn't want Dad telling me off on my birthday.

We had a little birthday tradition in our family, and I knew exactly what was coming. The door opened and in came Mum, holding the cutest little pink cake. Dad was close behind her with sixteen helium filled balloons. Alexis, my younger sister, ran straight in and jumped on my bed, then wrapped her arms around me giving me a hug. She handed me a card and finally smothered me in kisses. Whilst Zara, two years older than me, had her eyes glued to her phone as usual. She stood by the door and gave me a quick smirk before going back to texting.

"Happy Birthday to you, Happy Birthday to you. Happy Birthday dear Kelly, Happy Birthday to you!"

Mum placed the cake on the vanity, planted a quick peck on my forehead, then whispered with a sly wink "Don't worry, we saved the real cake for later tonight."

Dad set the balloons free, and they floated up covering my ceiling. That was always my favourite part of the tradition. Alexis and I screamed and jumped up trying to catch some of the spiral ribbons.

"Happy Birthday Princess. May this year bring you joy, happiness, growth, success, WISDOM. I hope you listen more and talk less, get good grades…."

"DAD," Zara shouted from the door, rolling her eyes at him.

"…oh, ha-ha, I hope you have a fantastic day princess, I love you," he said, looking sheepish and faked at being embarrassed.

"Thanks dad." and I mouth a thank you to Zara.

"You can borrow my Kurt Geiger shoes, Happy Birthday." Zara huffed before turning around and going back to her room.

"Thank You," I called in her direction.

"Right, we need to move quickly everyone. The caterer will be arriving soon, along with the decorators," Mum ordered, springing into action. She was always so good at planning events, so organised.

I jumped out of bed and ushered my over excited family out of the room, along with the cake. I drag a tangle teaser through my hair, hoping to get rid of the knots I could feel at the back of my head, I was unsuccessful. My afro was now in the messiest bun I'd ever seen, but I headed back downstairs to finish my breakfast. One of these days mum has *got* to let me have a cup of coffee.

Tonight, better be perfect, this needs to be the best party Amesbury has ever had. Everyone from school was going to be here, including Dominic Moretti!

Urgh, how could someone be so handsome?

After three months of just looking at each other and exchanging shy smiles, one of us had to make a move right? Maybe tonight, please God, let it happen tonight. What if this was all in my head? And he's just a genuine nice guy. Oh my God. What if he's not actually interested in me? If that's the case, then the floor might as well open up and swallow me whole. Great, now I feel miserable.

"Mum, can I please have some eggs with my pancakes?"

"Sure honey, two eggs for the birthday princess,"

I might as well eat something and try to get rid of this horrible pit I can feel in my stomach.

Dominic

My 8 a.m. alarm usually woke me up on weekends, but today I woke to the sound of traffic and angry horns outside my window. The hum of the fridge coming from the kitchen in the next room added to this experience.

I wiped away the tiredness from my heavy eyes and turned around, the creaking of my bed annoying me, as does the overburdened clothing rail standing in the corner of my room. I doubt I can even call it a room; it's literally five steps in each direction.

Damn, I need a wardrobe.

At least my room was tidy, I'd made sure of that. My clothes were organised as best as I could manage, trainers lined up neatly against a wall, posters pinned to perfection. It's the one space I had control over.

The flat was quiet, which meant Mum and Dad were already in the shop. I checked my phone. No messages as usual, but a reminder:

Kelly's Sweet 16th- 6 p.m.

Kelly Bamford. Even just seeing her name on the screen made my stomach flip a little. I'd noticed her the first week I started at school. How could I not? She was bubbly, charming and well…stunning. The kind of girl that walked into any room and completely changed the atmosphere with her presence, she had a sort of *light* about her.

I've never spoken to her though, I just…stare at her, like an idiot. The other day I gave her a smile, and she smiled back, but when I checked in the mirror later that evening I realised it looked like I desperately needed the toilet. To be honest, I didn't think she even knew who I was or my name. That was until she handed me the invitation yesterday.

"Hey, you should come to my party tomorrow."

That's how she asked me, just like that. Like we were already friends. Of course, I played it casual, but inside I was fighting the urge to grin like an idiot.

Oh my God, its 8:45a.m.! Dad's gonna kill me.

I jumped out of bed, pulled on my hoodie and jeans, splashed some water on my face in the bathroom and grabbed a banana before heading downstairs. No time to overthink right now, I had to be at the shop before nine. Thankfully, the shop was just below our flat.

Our shop Bella Gioielli was squished between the dry cleaners and the bakery—that smells way too good. It's a small shop, with an antique feel, I'm talking velvet trays and gold link chains. But my parents worked very hard for it, they worked every day, no holidays, and definitely no days off. Dad's brother, Uncle Antonio, helped with the accounting side of things. He lived on the outskirts of town, but we hardly saw him. My parents put their entire life savings into this business and had been making the best of it. They expected me to take over someday, so I've been working with them on the weekends, trying to learn the ropes.

The copper bell above the door jingled as I walked in.

"Oh! There he is the sleeping prince," Dad exclaimed, peering at me over the top of his wiry glasses that sat too low on the bridge of his nose. "Late."

"Dad, its 8:57."

"You should have been here at 8:30, tesoro," Mum chimed from behind the till.

I slipped behind the counter and gave her a peck on the cheek, then took over from her and began to clean the desk. Dad muttered some swear words in Italian, while mum rubbed his back softly, trying to calm him down.

The rest of the morning and most of the afternoon, I worked quietly and effectively; polishing jewellery, sweeping up, counting stock and attending to any customers that walked in. Every so often, Dad showed me how to appraise a piece and taught what kind of lighting worked best for different types of jewellery. I tried to focus but my mind kept drifting to tonight.

What do you even bring to a girl like Kelly?

I thought about taking her a piece of jewellery from the shop, a necklace or bracelet. Maybe a pair of earrings with a little diamond in it. But it didn't feel right, and I couldn't do that to my parents. But also, I wasn't sure exactly what she would like or if she even liked me like that.

By 4 p.m., I asked Dad if it was ok for me to leave early.

"Theres a birthday party tonight…for a friend from school."

"Alright. Remember you are a gentleman and don't stay out too late." He gave me a look but nodded, planting a kiss on my forehead and then shooed me away with a grunt.

"Wear proper shoes," Mum said, appearing from the back room. She gave me a hug and smothered me in kisses, "Domenico…. for goodness sake boy, have a shower."

An hour and a half later, I was showered and staring at my reflection. Clean shirt, with a sweater over my top, jeans, clean trainers—sorry mum not *proper* shoes, because it's a part, not church. I was meeting up with Peter, a new friend from school, and I felt much more confident knowing I won't be going alone. I stopped by the corner shop and picked up bought a birthday card and a single rose. It felt small, but better than turning up empty handed. Then, I start to feel the first tingle of nerves as I think of seeing Kelly.

Alright, Dom. Don't mess this up.

CHAPTER 2

Kelly

Our living room had been completely transformed. There was a pastel balloon arch stretching across the fireplace and some rose gold foil letters that said:

"HAPPY SWEET 16th KELLY"

The smell of cupcakes and a multitude of different perfumes and aftershaves filled the air, along with my mum's favourite lavender scented candles. The atmosphere was breathtaking; I made a mental note to thank my mum for all her hard work and expertise.

It had only been forty-five minutes since the party started, and already the room was buzzing with energy, people were huddled in little groups chatting away, some were dancing, and others were nibbling away by the snack table. My older cousins were sat at the dining table playing a game of cards with my dad and a few friends from school, whilst mum was doing that awkward *trying to be cool* two-step shuffle in the corner with Alexis. It didn't surprise me to see Alexis was dressed like the sugar plum fairy from her favourite Barbie movie. The sight made me giggle, and I couldn't help but roll my eyes; she did look super cute though.

I hovered near the stairs with Kennedy and Mia, trying to catch my breath and not completely freak out. I'd spent hours getting ready; finally managing to get my afro into a slick bun, and Zara helped me with my nails & lashes. My outfit was perfect.

I wore a short sparkly gold dress: it was strapless, and tailored to perfection, the fabric shimmered delicately under the chandeliers. Resting delicately just above my collarbone, was my birthday present from my parents: diamond earrings and a diamond studded necklace. On my feet were Zara's open toe Kurt Geiger wedgies. I felt so grown up, but also a bit nervous; like everyone was watching me; all of a sudden I don't know what to do with my arms.

"Kelly!" Mum called. "Come here, baby girl! We're about to sing!"

I smiled shyly and headed over, heart starting to race. It's not the singing that's got my nerves jumping, but I had a feeling tonight was about to change my entire life. Like something major was going to happen. Before I reached the middle of the room, I caught a glimpse of movement near the front door; it's Zara, black leather mini skirt, oversized bomber jacket, lips painted deep burgundy like she's about to film a music video. She caught my eyes and winked at me before stealthily slipping out. She was probably on her way to meet one of her secret guys that dad knows nothing about.

I raised my brows and recalled her telling mum and dad she'd "*be around all night*," but here she was, clearly on a secret mission. I made a mental note to blackmail her later. Right now, I've got bigger things to focus on. Like the fact that everyone had started to gather around the cake, ready to belt out the birthday classic. I stepped into the middle and smiled at all the faces present; I looked at my besties; the three of us have been friends since year seven, we knew all each other's secrets, and I trusted them with my life. I soaked up all the love I was feeling, closed my eyes, made my wish and blew out the candles.

Please let this night be special.

Like magical special. But not in a cringey way.

Just…something I'll remember forever.

I opened my eyes and then—I saw him.

Dominic. My heart fluttered and I started to flush a little under the warmth of the chandeliers. He walked through the door with Peter from our year group. I watched as he ran his hands through his hair and his fringe flopped across his face, my heart skipped. He tried to fix it and messed it up even more, but it looked better that way. He seemed a little nervous, which surprised me as although he's usually so quiet at school, he always seemed to carry himself with so much confidence.

Peter leaned over to say something to him, and he scanned the room until his eyes landed on me. I nearly forgot how to breathe. Kennedy and Mia were at my side in flash, both of them smirking like cartoon villains. I took a deep breath, threw back my shoulder and walked up to him.

"Hey, you came."

Up close, he looked even cuter. His eyes were a mysterious shade of green, I felt like I could almost drown in them. His lips curved up into a smile that made my insides turn to mush.

He handed me a card and a single rose. "I couldn't miss your special day. Happy Birthday."

"Oh my gosh, thank you," I gasped, suddenly hyper-aware of every word leaving my mouth.

The rose wasn't wrapped or anything, it was just simple and delicate. He shrugged, with one hand still in his pocket.

"Yeah, I didn't want to come empty-handed."

"Ahem, Happy Birthday Kelly." I had completely forgotten Peter was stood beside us, and he quickly handed me a birthday card and walked towards the snack table.

"It's beautiful." My attention once again fully on Dominic.

"You…you can open the card later," He replied, rubbing the back of his neck.

I nodded, feeling a weird mix of excitement and disbelief. *Dominic Moretti*, the boy I've been obsessing over for the last three months, has just given me a card *and* a rose at my birthday.

How absolutely romantic.

Before I could open my mouth to reply, I saw Dominic's face drop slightly and I sensed a presence behind me. Dad.

"Hello, young man," he has this mean dad tone he uses when he's trying to suss someone out without seeming too obvious.

"I'm Ray, Kelly's Dad. But you can call me Raymond…or Mr Bamford."

"Nice to meet you Sir…Uh, Mr Bamford. I'm Dominic. Kelly and I go to school together."

Dad narrowed his eyes for a split second, then looked from Dominic to the rose and then slowly studied my face. He gave a slow nod and forced a smile.

"Well, I appreciate you coming. It's nice to meet you, you're the first boy that has ever given my daughter a rose. I'll make sure I remember your face." Dad gave him a handshake that looked way too firm, but to Dominic's credit he didn't flinch. Dad looked genuinely impressed.

"Understood Sir."

I felt like I was about to evaporate. Thankfully, mum called him away, scowling at him, but he doesn't leave before bending down to give me a peck on my head.

"Enjoy the rest of your night," he said pointedly at Dominic.

I led Dominic to the snacks table and offered him some drinks and a slice of cake. Kennedy and Mia appeared at my side in seconds, stealing me away to a side room, in a whirlwind of excitement.

"Did he just give you a rose?" Mia screamed.

"Open the card, open it, OPEN IT!" Kennedy said, jumping up and down, nearly ripping my arm off.

I slowly opened the envelope like it was holding the nation's top secrets. Inside the card was a soft watercolour painting of a ballerina with a party hat. I giggled and carefully opened the card, fingers trembling. On the left, was his messy but sort of cute handwriting.

Happy Birthday Kelly.

You light up the room when you walk in.

Hope today makes you feel as special as you are.

Can I take you to watch a movie next week Saturday?

Text me later and let me know.

Dom x

And underneath that was his phone number.

Mia let out a screech that was so loud the guests in the other room got silent.

"Shh!" Kennedy and I said in unison, covering her mouth and eyeing the door to make sure no one walked in.

"You better text him, No Excuses." Whispered Kennedy.

"Tonight!" Mia added, pulling our hands away from her mouth with a scowl.

I laughed, heart pounding, and my cheeks felt too warm from all the excitement.

"I will."

And I did. We texted back and forth all evening and a date was set in stone for next week Saturday. School this week was going to be so bloody interesting that's for sure.

Dominic

July 2009

The clock on the wall moved so slowly it felt like a personal vendetta against me. Like it was mocking me. Our teacher, Mr. Cartwright, droned on at the front of the classroom about atomic structures, but my mind had checked out at least ten minutes ago. My pen now hovered over my notebook, barely moving, the words on the whiteboard blurred into soft shapes.

I glanced at the clock again, fifteen minutes till school ended. If I timed it right, I could meet Kelly in the sports field exactly ten minutes later. There was a new ice cream shop in town by the bookstore, and I couldn't wait for us to finally try it out. She mentioned craving a bubble-gum swirl last week, apparently she hadn't had one since she was ten.

She always said things like that. Casual little memories that became engraved in my mind. The plan today was to enjoy some ice cream, have a browse around the bookstore, and then I had to rush back to the shop and be *Mr Junior Jewellery Apprentice* for Dad again. Don't get me wrong, I loved helping out at the shop. I really did. The business itself had been around for about thirteen years now, since we moved to the UK from Italy.

I was just three years old then, and we lived in a little village in the West Midlands, what we had now was much grander than what we started with. It wasn't as luxurious as the jewellery houses in Knightsbridge, no, it was tucked away on our little high street, with its slightly rusty gold lettering and the tiny bell above the door. It wasn't flashy, but it was ours. Dad called it our family legacy.

But sometimes, I just want to breathe before I was thrown behind the counter to scrub necklaces, weigh stones and listen to Dad rant about customer retention. Lately everything felt like a rush, or a countdown. School. Family. Kelly.

Especially Kelly. We had been together for eight months now, and sometimes it still felt unreal. Like I blinked and suddenly I had this smart, beautiful…hilarious girlfriend who somehow chose *me*. She was already part of the family, my parents even had a little nickname for her, 'Keller-Kels,' I had no idea what it even meant, but Kelly loved it. She made everything feel better, even when they weren't. But her dad… that man really hated me. He looked at me like I stole his favourite watch or something. I smiled at him, and he frowned back. I tried to speak to him, and he grunted back. The last time I said good evening, he replied, "Is it?"

Her mum and sisters were amazing though. They spoke to me like we'd known each other for years. I'd always felt welcome around them, and I could easily spend hours in their house. That is, until Mr Bamford got home. I just don't understand why he disliked me so much. I drop Kelly home on time after each date; even made sure we don't kiss or hold hands when he's there. But every time he's around, I feel like I'm in a courtroom where I'm already guilty.

The bell rang and I was out of my seat before Cartwright could finish his sentence. I sent a quick text to Kelly:

Ice cream date? Meet me at the field.

She replied with three heart emojis and a X, I smiled like a fool all the way to the field.

In less than five minutes, I caught sight of her leaning against a wall in her green blazer and pleated skirt. Her afro in a high bun, but a few strands had escaped and was now framing her face. She caught sight of me and immediately lit up, jogging over and hooking her arm into mine like she always did.

"Hi," she grinned, giving me a soft peck on the cheek.

"Hey," I brushed a curl from her forehead. "Still want that bubblegum swirl?"

"Thought you'd never ask."

CHAPTER 3

Kelly

The walk wasn't too far, plus it was enjoyable. I ended up talking the entire time about Mrs. Baker, my history teacher, spilling coffee down her shirt. Then I told him about Kennedy demanding to wear sunglasses indoors and how Mia tried to convince her mum to let her go to a uni rave this weekend.

He was so attentive, and he talked almost as much as I did. He spoke a lot about his parents and their shop; sharing stories of their old home before they moved to Amesbury. I could listen to him talk forever.

We reached the new ice cream parlour "Ella's Creamery," and headed straight to the counter. It smelled of waffle cones and vanilla. Yummy

"Two scoops of bubblegum swirl," he gave me a wink. "And one scoop of vanilla for me please."

"Boring," I teased, poking him playfully on his shoulder.

"No, it's a classic," he countered.

We took our cones and sat outside, under the striped awning; the sun was shining and our knees brushed under the tiny table. The street was quiet and for a moment, it felt like nothing else existed but us.

"I love days like this," I said, licking my ice cream. "Just me and you, No pressure. No..."

His phone started to buzz before I could finish. He answered, putting the speaker on.

"Domenico? I have called you 5 times Caro Nipote."

"Uncle Antonio? Uh, I'm sorry I missed…"

"Where are you? I've been driving around looking for you. I even stopped at your school."

"Looking for me? Why? I'm at the ice cream shop, Um… Ella's Creamery"?

"Ok., ok, wait for me there. Wait for me." He hung up.

My heart raced, and I stared at Dom, eyes wide. He stared back at me; worry etched on his face.

"Dom? What do you think has happened?"

"I'm not sure. Uncle Antonio doesn't usually call me."

"Oh? Did you forget some type of meeting or family gathering?" I stood up and started to gather my things.

"No, I mean, I don't think so." He stopped me and pulled me back down. "He's on his way here, so let's just wait and see what he says when he arrives."

"Hmm, ok then let's wait then …"

"Domenico!"

We both turned around, and Dom's uncle was parked on the corner with his windows down. His face looked pale, eyes wide. My mouth dried up, and my heart dropped. Something was definitely wrong.

"Uncle..." Dom jumped out of his seat, dropping his ice cream on the floor.

"We have to go. Now. Get in the car, your parents have been in an accident," Uncle Antonio shouted from the car.

I gasped on the other side of the bistro table. Heart raced as I watched Dom sprint to the car. I'm already in tears, whipping out my phone to call my dad.

"Kelly, go home, I'll text you. It'll be ok," Dom called back at me, then he jumped into the passenger seat, and his uncle drove off with a screech.

My dad picked up on the second ring.

"Dad," my voice breaks, and my sobs come in sharp gasps. "Dad, its Dom."

"Kelly? Sweetheart, what's happened."

"Dom's parents…they've been in an accident."

"Where are you, I'm on my way."

Dominic

God, please, please, please. Let them be ok, please I'll do anything.

"Uncle…" my voice wobbled, and I took a deep breath to compose myself. "Uncle…are they ok?"

He looked at me with sorrow and pity in his eyes. I stared back at him, unable to comprehend what he was trying to tell me without words. I don't really have a strong relationship with my uncle. I mean, I barely knew him, we saw him on the holidays, but he did a lot of work for the shop behind the scenes. He was ten years younger than my dad and I guess at one time they were close, back in Italy, I suppose. Until distance and time drove a wedge between them. Now they were more acquaintances than friends.

But as I looked at my uncle driving like a maniac to the hospital, secretly trying to wipe the tears that spilled down his cheek. Struggling to keep his breathing in check and how he continued to glance in my direction from time to time. I realise he was just a little brother that was scared of losing the older brother he loves dearly.

Something broke in me as fear and reality sunk in. We arrived at the hospital, and I noticed he never answered my question.

"Moretti…we are here for Mr & Mrs Moretti," Uncle Antonio informed the nurse at the reception, unable to keep his voice from shaking. "My brother; Nicolas Moretti and his wife; Lucia Moretti. They were in a car crash."

Her eyes softened. "Follow me."

The walk down the hallway felt like a dream I couldn't wake from. Every step made my stomach twist tighter; *I want to scream. I want to run away. I wish I could rewind time.*

The nurse stopped at a door with a sign that said, 'Meeting room.'

"Please wait in here. A doctor will be with your shortly."

"Can't we just go to see my parents?" My voice was sharp; my patience had started to wear thin..

"Domenico, I think its best we wait for a doctor." My uncle responded, his arm on my shoulder as he led me into the room and into a seat.

Then the doctor entered the room and just like that, my entire life turned inside out.

My dad was gone. My parents were gone. I didn't even get a chance to say goodbye to them. My mum, I'll never see her face again. I didn't cry, beg, scream or fight. I just felt numb. Something had broken in me, and I knew I was no longer the same person.

I walked out of that room and sat on the hallway floor. My uncle eventually followed, wrapping his arms around me and holding me steady. He whispered something in my ears, but all I heard was a high-pitched ringing.

"We will figure this out; I will be everything you need. I promise." He tried to reassure me, pulling me to my feet.

I nodded, unable to form any sentences. The word orphan swirled through my mind. but I shut it down immediately. *I can't face that yet.* We don't go home…my home; instead, we go to his house, but it didn't feel the same. Too quiet, too tidy, too everything and nothing at the same time.

I'm already homesick. I just want to go home to my parents. To normality. Uncle Antonio set me up in the guest room—my new room, telling me I can take some time off school and then he handed me a clean hoodie. I can't sleep so, I lay on the bed and stare at the ceiling.

My phone buzzed loudly on the side table. It's Kelly.

"Dom, where are you? I'm coming over," She sobbed into the phone.

"Don't, not tonight. I'm not...I'm not at home."

"I love you. I'm here. Whatever you need, I'm here. You are not alone." Her voice felt warm, soft and steady. But what she said wasn't true. I am alone and I don't think I'll ever feel *not alone.*

I laid in bed awake all night and I refused to cry; crying won't bring them back.

Their funeral was three days later. Closed caskets; I never got to see their faces again. We chose white lilies for the funeral flowers; those were mum's favourites. Too many people walked past me saying *"I'm sorry for your loss"* like it was going to change things. That phrase was starting to piss me off..

Kelly stood beside me the entire time, like an anchor. She held my hand, greeted guests on my behalf and occasionally wiped her tears. She glanced in my direction and tried to read my face, but I knew it was emotionless. It had been like that since I left the hospital.

Her family were here also; their support had been great these last few days. Her dad even came to visit me on his own and gave me some advice, but I don't remember what we spoke about. He walked past and gave me a stiff hug before taking a seat at the back of the church with the rest of his family.

After the service, Uncle Antonio called me aside. We sat on the steps outside the church, both still in black suits. He had an antique box with him; it belonged to my parents. He also held a letter in his hand.

"Your parents wanted me to give these to you," He said, placing both items beside me. "I don't know what's in them, but they said to make sure you received these."

"Thanks," I replied, not touching either item.

He let out a deep sigh.

"I need to know what you want to do."

I looked at him, understanding his question.

"I want us to keep it. The shop. Run it, just like they did. To carry on their Legacy."

"That's what I hoped you'd say." He smiled proudly, patting me on the back.

The next six weeks are a blur; it's now the school summer holiday and the day we reopen the shop. Just for a few hours, to sort out some paperwork, tidy up and get the pieces of jewellery shined.

Everyone from school had been excited about leaving after our GCSE's, they had finally settled on whether they would be staying on for sixth form or transferring to a college. Kelly had decided to remain at our school's sixth form, this meant could still be near each other every day.

I didn't realise how much I needed her, but I did. I would break without her.

The inside of the shop smelled of polish and Dad's aftershave; closing my eyes, I breathe in. My chin began to wobble but I quickly pushed that to the side and switched the lights on. I turn to the clock on the wall; 8 a.m., I chuckled under breath, *Dad would have been so proud.*

Kelly showed up just after ten, coffees and bagels in hand. She's actually so amazing.

"Wow, it feels great to see the shop open again," she said gently.

"It's not the same without them," I forced a smile and thanked her for breakfast.

She walked around, admiring the new displays Uncle Antonio and I spent five hours building last night. I watched as she grabbed a cloth from the back and some surface cleaner. Then she placed her handbag on a stool and got to work.

"Thank you."

"For what?" she replied, not stopping what she was doing.

"For everything. You have been…so amazing, and I wanted to make sure you know how grateful I am."

"Dom, I am so proud of you. You have been through the unthinkable and come out strong. I know your parents will be proud too." She placed the cloth down and wrapped her arms around my neck.

"And just think, in a few weeks we start our A-levels, then university. We…"

"I'm not going to sixth form…or university." I cut her off. "I've decided to work full time in the shop with my uncle."

She blinked at me, clearly taken aback.

"Whatever you decide to do I will support you and I just know you will be great, I can see it in you."

"I love you," I blurted out. It was my first time saying that to her and my palms started to sweat a little.

"Took you long enough," She smirked and gave me a peck on the cheek. "I love you too."

"Alright lovebirds, enough of that. We have jewellery to polish and surfaces to dust." Uncle Antonio bursts into the shop; he had about five ledgers in his arms and a very old laptop.

I started to empty the bin behind the counter when I come across a picture frame with a photograph of me, Mum and Dad—sitting by the till. It was taken nearly a year ago, outside the shop on opening day. I blew away the dust that had settled on the frame and for a few moments, I looked at our smiling faces. Then taking a deep breath, I opened the drawer and placed the picture frame upside down beneath some papers. I made a mental note to take it home and add it to the box my uncle gave me.

CHAPTER 4

Kelly

October 2024

I stood in front of the full-length mirror, staring at the woman who gazed back at me. For a moment, I didn't recognize her. The gown I wore was breathtaking; a rich emerald-green satin, that shimmered beneath the soft glow of my bedroom lamp. The corseted bodice hugged my waist perfectly, lifting my shoulders, lengthening my frame, and making me look every bit the strong, confident woman I was supposed to be tonight.

My bronze skin seemed to glow against the deep jewel tone, and my mother's precious pearl necklace graced my neck. I looked composed, and ready; tonight wasn't just another evening. It was the culmination of a year's worth of planning, stress, late nights, and most of all hope. My charity, Wings of Hope, was hosting its first ever major fundraiser. Investors from around the world were flying in, donors with pockets deeper than I could ever imagine were gathering in that grand ballroom tonight.

If things went well, if I could somehow persuade them of the importance of my mission, then we'd finally be able to open the first ever fully funded University in Tawenga. I thought of the children we had already supported there; their smiles, their eagerness to learn despite having very little. That University could be their ticket to changing not only their own lives but the generations that came after them.

It had to be perfect. I couldn't let anything, or anyone rattle me. But even as I thought it, my stomach twisted with unease. Because one person wasn't going to be there, and no matter how hard I tried to ignore the ache, it gnawed at me. Dom, My fiancé. The man I had loved for years, the one I imagined building a family with, the one I defended endlessly when others whispered that he was too focused on work to ever be present.

He was supposed to stand beside me tonight, to share in the moment we had worked so hard for. But he wasn't coming. I knew it before he called, before he even sent the text. I knew it because he always let work come first.

I tried to pin back a stray coil that had escaped my updo, but my hands trembled. I told myself to breathe, to focus on the evening, not on him. Yet I couldn't stop glancing at my phone on the vanity table, waiting for it to light up. And then it did.

My heart leapt, and I snatched it up so quickly I almost dropped it. Finally. Maybe he'd surprise me and say he'd finished early, that he was on his way, that he wouldn't dream of missing this night.

"Hey," I answered, forcing brightness into my tone.

"Kelly," His voice was clipped, flat. Already I knew he was about to let me down.

"Tell me you're calling to say you're on your way," I said, gripping the phone tighter. "Please, Dom. Just tonight. I need you here."

A sigh filled the line, weary and impatient.

"I can't. I told you already. We're finalising the quarter reports, and my staff need me here. You know Uncle Antonio has been on my back about my responsibilities. If everything goes well he can step back and finally give me the reins."

I left out a deep sigh and chuckled weakly.

"Dom, do you even hear yourself? You never have time for me anymore and all I do…all I've done all these years is be there for you and support you. You know how important this is for me; it's everything I've worked for. An entire year of planning, and fighting for this dream; and you can't even give me one night?"

"It's not that simple, Kelly. You know how important this is for my career."

"And what about me?" My voice cracked, it already felt difficult to take a breath and I hated it, hated how weak I sounded. "Every time I ask you to show up, you have some excuse. I've been patient, supportive, and understanding. But tonight…tonight I need you."

"Don't make this about me not being there for you, because you know that's not true." His voice was clipped.

"Then prove it," I whispered. "Just once, prove it. Be there for me instead of hiding behind your desk. I'm not asking for the moon, Dom. I'm just asking for you."

Another silence. This one colder.

"I can't talk about this right now. I don't have time for your guilt trips."

"Guilt trip?" The words hit me like a slap. "That's what you think this is?"

"Kelly…"

"No, you know what? Forget it." My chest heaved, tears burning my eyes though I blinked them back furiously. "Stay at your office. Drown in your reports. Clearly, that's the only relationship you care about."

Before I could say anything else, the line went dead. He had hung up. I stared at the phone, my reflection in the black screen blurred through unshed tears. The pearls at my neck suddenly felt heavy, suffocating. For a second, I thought about ripping them off, about throwing the phone across the room. But then I remembered why I was dressed up at all.

This night wasn't about him.

It was about those children and their futures. It was about proving to myself that I didn't need Dom, or anyone, to validate my purpose. I slipped the phone into my clutch, grabbed my heels, and forced myself to breathe. Deep, steady, practiced breaths. My face in the mirror looked composed, and with one last glance, I whispered.

"You can do this, Kelly. With or without him."

By the time I walked down the stairs and out the door, the Uber driver was already waiting at the curb. I offered him a small, polite smile, even as my chest ached like it had been carved open. Sliding into the back seat, I smoothed my gown across my knees, lifted my chin, and reminded myself: tonight was all about hope.

Dominic

I leaned back in my chair, staring blankly at the spreadsheets glowing on the screen, but my mind wasn't on numbers. It was on Kelly. That damn phone call we'd just had still rang in my ears. Usually, her voice was sweet, soft, the kind of tone that could calm me after the hardest days, but today it was sharp and disappointed. The fight escalated so quickly I wasn't even sure how we got there. I hung up on her before either of us said something we couldn't take back.

And now, all I could think about was how tired I was of this cycle. Every time she wanted me to show up, to smile, to be that supportive fiancé on her arm, I was chained here, to this desk, to these reports, to this company. She wasn't wrong, but she wasn't right either, this business, my parents legacy, is extremely important to me. She knows that, more than anyone.

The truth was, Kelly wasn't the same girl I fell in love with. When I met her, she was like sunshine, bubbly, spontaneous, always laughing at my terrible jokes. She was fire and softness at once, pulling me out of my grief driven haze. But now… now it felt like every conversation was another nag, another reminder of how I was letting her down. I still loved her, but life with her felt mundane these days, predictable in all the wrong ways.

And yet, the idea of losing her scared me. Because if I didn't have her, what did I have left outside of this? I rubbed my temples, trying to clear the storm in my head. Work? Work was safe, it never nagged, and it never judged.

I forced my focus back onto the spreadsheet. My uncle had done a good job leading the company but I'm thirty-three now and I'm more than capable of taking over. It was time for him to step aside. This company wasn't his legacy; it was my parents. They poured their entire life into it and built it from the ground up.

And when my parents died, the responsibility landed squarely on my shoulders. I'd let my uncle manage out of respect, but that respect was wearing thin. I clenched my jaw, scrolling through the reports again.

"Dominic?"

The gentle knock at the door pulled me out of my spiral. Mrs. Thomson's familiar voice floated in as she poked her head around the door. She'd been my rock in this company for a decade, and tonight was her last day. Fifteen years of loyalty, and maternal scolding when I needed it most, and now she was leaving for retirement with her husband. I wasn't ready for this.

"How's it going?" She asked with that kind, knowing smile.

"Good," I lied, sighing as I pushed the reports away. "Just going over these before the Zoom meeting."

She nodded, stepping inside. There was something about her presence that always steadied me, even now, when everything felt like it was cracking at the edges.

"I wanted to say a quick goodbye," she said softly. "And thank you for everything. It's been an honour working with you, Dominic. Seeing the man you've become…it's been a privilege. Your parents would be so proud."

The lump in my throat formed so fast I almost couldn't swallow. I turned in my chair to face her properly.

"No, I should be thanking you," I said, my voice rough. "You've been an asset to this company and an even better… friend."

Her eyes misted, though she tried to brush it off with a chuckle. "I'll miss you too. Don't forget, your new assistant starts in a week. She's young, but smart. She'll catch on."

I huffed, running a hand through my hair. "She's got some big shoes to fill. You set the bar too high."

She laughed, the sound warm and familiar.

"Don't worry, she'll do fine. And I'm only a phone call away."

"Thank you," I said, meaning it. I opened the drawer and pulled out the neatly wrapped gift box, sliding it across the desk. "This is for you. Don't open it now. Just… a token of my gratitude."

Her lips trembled as she accepted it.

"Oh, Dominic…"

I stood and hugged her tight, tighter than I'd meant to. For a second, I let myself sink into that comfort, the feeling of someone who'd always believed in me, even when I didn't believe in myself. As she pulled away, she wiped at her eyes, chuckling again.

"And for goodness' sake…" She wagged a finger at me, like the mother I'd lost too soon. "Set a wedding date. Kelly's waited long enough. So have I."

That made me laugh despite myself.

"Yes, ma'am."

She blew me a kiss before closing the door behind her, and just like that, the office felt colder.

I sat back down, staring at her now empty desk outside my office. Another person leaving me behind.

My thoughts drifted back to Kelly. Her disappointed voice and sharp words. The way I'd felt my chest clench when she accused me of never being there. Maybe she was right. Maybe I wasn't there. But what choice did I have?

This company was my inheritance, my duty and my burden. My father's ghost haunted every decision I made. How could I walk away from that just to sip champagne at a fundraiser? No matter how noble the cause. And yet, I imagined her tonight. Standing in that emerald dress I helped pick out, her eyes scanning the room for me and finding only absence. Again.

I scrubbed a hand over my face. I was failing her, and I knew it. But I couldn't seem to stop. I pulled the reports back towards me, forcing my mind to harden again. Emotions were messy and I don't have the time or patience to dwell on this. I'd deal with Kelly later. She always forgive me; this time wouldn't be any different.

CHAPTER 5

Kelly

I stepped through the grand double doors, and felt my breath catch. Standing in the doorway, I scanned the crowded ballroom, my eyes dancing across the sea of glittering gowns and tuxedos. Crystal chandeliers shimmered above us, scattering light like diamonds, and the air buzzed with chatter and clinking glasses.

My fundraiser was alive. Not just alive, thriving. I felt a spark of pride pulse through me. We had already hit our fundraising goal, and there were still hours left in the evening. It was more than I had hoped for.

Clutching a glass of champagne, I wove through the crowd, smiling, greeting guests and thanking donors. Every time someone said, *"Congratulations, Kelly, this is incredible,"* my heart swelled. This was what I had worked for: all the long nights, endless calls and month upon month of constant stress. And it was worth every second.

"Kelly!" Kennedy's familiar voice rang out. I turned to see her waving at me from near the cocktail table. She wore a red dress which really complimented her blonde hair. Beside her was Mia, already grinning ear to ear, she looked stunning in a navy-blue sparkly number. I made my way over, heels clicking against the polished floor.

"Look at you," Mia said, giving me a once-over. "Emerald really was the move. You look like a goddess."

"Stop," I laughed, but the compliment warmed me. "I'm so glad you both came."

"Of course," Kennedy said, pulling me into a quick hug. "We wouldn't miss this for the world. You've outdone yourself."

"It feels surreal. I can't believe we've actually raised enough to start the project," I sighed happily.

We chatted for a while, catching up in between interruptions from guests who wanted to congratulate me. It felt good, grounding, to have my girls here. But as I glanced over Kennedy's shoulder, something caught my eye…well someone, a man standing by the bar. Tall, broad shoulders, golden hair brushing just past them. His tailored suit hugged a muscular frame, and when he turned slightly, I saw the piercing blue of his eyes.

My breath hitched. His presence was magnetic, commanding. He laughed at something a guest said, and the sound carried over the crowd, deep and warm. My stomach fluttered before I even realised I was staring.

"Earth to Kelly?" Mia teased, nudging me. "Oh my…Who's Mr. Tall, Blond and Dangerous over there?"

"I don't know. Probably just another guest," I shook my head quickly, cheeks heating.

But then I heard him introduce himself to someone near the bar. *"Erik Andersson. From Sweden."*

My eyes widened. No way. Erik Andersson…*the* Erik Andersson? He was one of my top investors, someone I'd been trying to get to an event for months. He had always declined…that is, until tonight. I never imagined he'd look like *that*. Young. Handsome, and bloody charismatic. My stomach twisted with nerves and something else I didn't want to name.

Before I could gather myself, he caught my eyes and started moving towards me, stopping to greet people along the way. Each time he laughed, heads turned. Each time he smiled, it felt like the room leaned in closer. And then suddenly, he was in front of me.

"Good evening," he said, voice smooth and low, his accent wrapping around the words. "I'm Erik, you must be Kelly. I must say, this is a gorgeous event."

I forced myself to smile, ignoring the flutter in my chest.

"Yes, I'm Kelly. And thank you…I'm glad you were able to join us tonight." My voice sounded a little too soft, too nervous, even to my own ears.

"It's a pleasure to finally meet you, Kelly." His eyes locked with mine, twinkling in the dim light. "I've heard so much about you."

"Oh? What have you heard?" My brows lifted slightly.

"That you're beautiful, intelligent, and passionate about your work. And I must say, I agree with all those things." He took a slow sip of his drink, never breaking eye contact.

"Well, thank you. That's very kind of you to say." Heat crept up my neck, and I let out an awkward laugh.

"It's only the truth," He replied easily. The way he said it, like it was a simple fact, not a compliment; it made my heart stumble.

We spoke for a few minutes about the fundraiser. I explained the vision for Wings of Hope, the work we were doing in Tawenga and the plans for the university. He listened intently, asking thoughtful questions…he seemed genuinely interested. And with every second, I felt myself relaxing and enjoying his company more than I should have.

"So," he said after a pause, tilting his head. "Tell me about you. Not just your work. What do you love? What drives you?"

I hesitated, my champagne glass trembling slightly in my hand. My instinct was to mention Dom… my fiancé, to ground myself in reality. But the words stuck in my throat. And for reasons I couldn't explain, I didn't bring him up.

Instead, I said softly, "I love… seeing change. Real change. Knowing that the work I do doesn't just look good on paper but actually transforms lives. That's what keeps me going."

"That's rare, Kelly. Most people chase success for themselves." His stared at me, eyes locked on mine. "You chase it for others. It's… inspiring."

I laughed lightly, trying to wave off the sudden warmth in my chest.

"You flatter me too much."

"Or maybe not enough," He leaned in slightly, eyes glinting with mischief.

I knew I should put distance between us, keep things strictly professional. But I couldn't help it, I was laughing more than I had all night. My cheeks ached from smiling, my stomach flipping each time he said something charming. And though guilt pricked at the back of my mind, I pushed it down. It was just harmless conversation after all. Wasn't it?

Hours slipped by in what felt like minutes, and the crowd began to thin, guests drifting out into the night. Erik remained by my side, still asking questions, still interested in everything I had to say and still making me laugh.

As the last of the guests left, he leaned closer, voice low.

"I would love to continue this conversation. Can I take you to dinner sometime?"

The question hit me like a splash of cold water. I nearly choked on my drink, guilt pressing heavy. What about Dom? The man who wasn't here tonight, yet even though we had a horrible argument just hours ago, he still held my heart. I think I had let myself slip too far.

"Erik," I said quietly, lowering my eyes. "I'm with someone. I mean… I have a fiancé." The word felt heavy on my tongue, almost like a confession and shame burned in my cheeks.

He looked surprised, a flicker of disappointment in his eyes, though he covered it quickly with a polite smile.

"I understand. I respect your commitment. Forgive me if I overstepped."

"No, it's okay. I should've said something sooner," I nodded quickly, wishing the floor would swallow me whole.

"But" he continued smoothly, "I'd still love to take you to dinner...not like that, of course. Strictly professional. We could discuss more about your future plans for the charity, and how I might be able to assist. Think of it as a business meeting."

I hesitated. My instincts screamed to end it there and just walk away. But the logical part of me, the part that had fought so hard to secure investors, reminded me that this was Erik Andersson. One of my biggest backers. A dinner with him could open doors I could only ever dream of.

"Okay," I said finally. "Next Friday, at seven?"

"Perfect." His lips curved into a satisfied smile.

The ballroom had finally emptied, and I gave some last instructions to the event coordinator, Erik waited patiently by the door. He held it open for me, then followed to where my Uber was already waiting. Then he stepped forward and, with a gentlemanly ease, opened the car door for me.

"Thank you for your company tonight," he said, eyes warm. "You've built something extraordinary, Kelly. I'm glad I got to see it and be a part of it."

"Thank you for coming," I offered him a small, genuine smile. "Really, it means more than you know."

Sliding into the backseat, I adjusted my dress as the door closed and caught one last glimpse of Erik, standing under the golden glow of the entrance lights, waving and smiling as he watched me go.

I leaned back against the seat, exhaling hard. My thoughts immediately drifted to Dom. Where was he? How had his night gone? Did his meeting run late again, or was he already home? My heart ached with a mix of longing and guilt. I unlocked my phone and called his number. It rang once, then went straight to voicemail.

"Hey, it's me," I whispered after the beep, my throat tight. "The fundraiser was a success. I wish you'd been there. I'll see you tomorrow for dinner. Love you."

I ended the call, staring at my reflection in the dark window. For the first time all night, the glitter of the chandeliers, the laughter, the champagne, all of it felt distant…empty. I was left with only the heavy silence of the car, and the tangle of emotions twisting inside me.

Dominic

Walking out of my uncle's office, I felt like someone had shoved a knife straight into my back and twisted. The words still echoed in my head, sharp and cruel, though I knew he hadn't meant them to be cruel.

"You're not ready, Dominic. Not yet. You don't have the maturity. You don't connect with people, and it's costing us contracts."

I had never felt so humiliated in my life. After pouring years of my life—all my youth into this business; shadowing him, learning every aspect of it, preparing myself to take over one day. And yet, with a few carefully chosen words, my uncle had reduced me to nothing more than an entitled kid playing dress-up in a man's suit.

I clenched my fists as I walked down the hall, ignoring the sympathetic looks from a few employees who'd probably overheard the conversation. I didn't want their pity. I wanted respect.

By the time I reached my office, the walls felt too small, the air too thin. I couldn't stay here another second. If I did, I'd explode. Grabbing my coat, I stormed out, my shoes striking the polished floor harder than necessary.

The cool evening air hit me like a slap when I stepped outside, but it did little to cool the fire raging inside me. I didn't want to go home, not to the silence, and I definitely didn't plan on going to Kelly's tonight. Not after the last conversation we had.

The thought of her made me ache. She deserved a man…*a husband*, who was a leader, someone who had it all figured out. She deserved stability, not someone spiralling because his uncle had said he wasn't good enough.

I unlocked my car and slid into the driver's seat. The leather was cold beneath me and hand hovered over the ignition. Then I felt it. The hesitation, the trembling. Every damn time. How long would it take me to get over this.

"Pull it together, Dom," I muttered, jamming the key into the ignition.

The engine roared to life, and I gripped the wheel so tightly my knuckles whitened. I reminded myself to breathe, pressing on the accelerator a little too hard. I drove aimlessly, the town lights blurring as I sped past them. My anger warred with grief, with the guilt that never left me. My uncle's words replayed over and over. *Not ready. Not mature. Doesn't connect with people.*

Screw him. Screw them all.

I found myself at the edge of town. That's when I spotted a brand-new bar, sleek and modern, buzzing with life. People spilled out of it, laughing, carefree. They seemed to really be living, whilst I had given up a most of my life, trying to prove myself to everyone. To prove that I was capable.

I parked across the street; my eyes fixed on the glowing neon sign. Maybe a few drinks would dull the storm inside me. Maybe for once, I could stop thinking.

Inside, the bar was crowded, the air heavy with music, chatter, and the clink of glasses. People brushed past me, a blur of perfume and laughter. Women glanced my way; some boldly, some shyly. I ignored them. I always ignored them. Attention was easy to get, and I had no patience for it.

I found a spot at the bar, away from the crowd, and ordered a whiskey. Then another. By the fourth, the burn was familiar, almost comforting. The haze softened the sharp edges of my uncle's voice in my head.

That's when I noticed her.

She was standing at the other end of the bar, trying and failing to get the bartender's attention. She raised her hand, leaned over the counter, even called out, but the man was too busy with other patrons.

I leaned back, watching her. Long raven hair cascaded down her back, glossy under the dim lights. Her lips were painted a bold red, full and sensual. The strapless black dress she wore clung to every curve—her waist cinched tight, hips flaring. Her legs long and toned beneath the short hemline. She had the kind of body that could make a man forget his own name and for the first time in a long time, I couldn't look away.

I pushed off my stool and walked towards her, my six-foot frame cutting through the crowd. The bartender noticed me instantly.

"Hey," I said, irritation edging my voice. "The lady's been trying to get your attention for a while."

"Ah…sorry, man. It's crazy busy tonight," He replied, looking flustered.

"Give her whatever she wants. I'll pay for it."

I didn't wait for her reaction. I turned and walked back to my corner, lifting my glass to my lips.

A moment later, I felt a light tap on my shoulder.

I turned, and there she was. Up close she was even more stunning. Her eyes were a striking grey, almost silver, and for the first time in my life, words deserted me.

"I just wanted to say thank you," she said, her voice smooth and melodic. "You're such a gentleman."

I gave a curt nod and forced a small smile before turning back to my drink.

She didn't leave.

"I hope you don't mind," she said again, a playful lilt in her tone. "I ordered a bottle of champagne. Would you like to share it with me? You look like you could use some company."

I spun slightly, ready to dismiss her. I didn't do this. I didn't entertain random strangers. I had Kelly and I had responsibilities.

But then she smiled.

And damn it, my heart skipped a beat.

"Sure," I heard myself say, my voice lower than usual. "Why not."

We moved to a quieter corner, champagne between us.

"I'm Amber," She said, introducing herself, her hands stretched towards me waiting for a handshake.

"Dom…Dominic"

"Which is it?" she giggled, taking a sip of her drink, her eyes fixed on mine.

God she was mesmerising.

"Dom is fine." I felt heat creep up my neck and chuckled lightly.

"Ok. Hello Dom.," she said, shaking my hand.

We talked for a while, and to my surprise, it felt easy. Her laughter was light, infectious. She leaned in close when I spoke, squeezing my arm at my dry jokes. The warmth of her touch seeped into me, loosening knots I didn't know I carried.

"So, Dom," she said, tilting her head. "What brings you here tonight? You don't strike me as the type who spends his evenings in bars."

I chuckled bitterly.

"Maybe I'm not. Maybe I'm just… fed up. Needed a break."

"From what?" Her eyes searched mine.

"Life," I said simply, pouring another glass.

"Well, maybe tonight you don't have to think about all that. Just enjoy yourself." She reached over, brushing her fingers against mine.

Her lips hovered close, her breath warm against my cheek. The tension was electric, unbearable. My heart pounded in my chest as every rational thought screamed at me to stop.

But I didn't stop.

I kissed her.

The world fell away. The guilt, the frustration, the endless pressure, it all vanished under the heat of her lips, the way she melted into me. For the first time in years, I felt alive.

And then we left the bar, hand in hand, the night air cool against our flushed skin. My palms were slick with sweat as I drove us to my flat, the silence between us heavy with anticipation.

We got to my door, and I hesitated, but she didn't. Her body was already pressed against mine; her arms wrapped around my neck. Her lips hovered just above mine, taunting me with the smallest gap of air. My chest rose and fell, the weight of every wrong decision pressing down on me, but my body wasn't listening. My body already belonged to her.

"Dom," she whispered, her voice silken, daring, like she knew I was seconds away from breaking.

That was all it took. My restraint snapped like brittle glass. I crushed my mouth to hers, rough and hungry. Her gasp vibrated against my lips before she kissed me back with equal fire, her fingers twisting into my shirt, tugging at me like she wanted to tear it off.

"God, you don't waste time," Amber murmured, her lips dragging down my jaw as I pinned her against the wall.

"Neither do you," I growled, the sound gravelly, feral, even to my own ears.

Every kiss was reckless, every touch an explosion I couldn't contain. I pressed her against the door, and the thud that echoed was met with her breathless laugh, muffled when she yanked my head down for another searing kiss. She tasted of champagne and sin; sweet, dangerous, addictive.

"You taste like trouble," I muttered, lips skimming her throat, drinking in every tremor that escaped her.

Her laugh was wicked, low. "Maybe I am. But you still want me, right?"

I locked eyes with her, storm-grey, daring me to walk away. I couldn't. I didn't.

"Yes, more than I should."

That was all the permission she needed. She hooked a leg around me, pulling me flush against her, and the friction sent fire down my spine. I groaned into her mouth, my hands gripping her thighs, her body fitting against mine like temptation made flesh.

Her nails scraped my shoulders, sharp as hell, I was sure it left marks, the sting only pushed me further. My fingers sought her middle, and she bit down on my shoulder to muffle a moan. My pulse thundered, drowning out rational thought, drowning out Kelly's face flickering at the edges of my mind.

"Take me inside," Amber breathed against my ear, her voice a command wrapped in a plea. "Now."

I didn't hesitate. My keys clattered to the floor as I opened the door behind her, steadying her as we stumbled in. Her laughter spilled between ragged kisses, her lips never leaving mine for more than a heartbeat. She kissed me like she was starving, like every second wasted was a crime, and I matched her with the same wild hunger.

By the time we hit the bedroom, restraint was a ghost long forgotten. Clothes scattered; Ripped, pulled, and thrown aside. Each piece falling to the ground felt like another line crossed. But, I couldn't stop touching her, pulling her closer.

"Dom…" she gasped as I pressed her into the mattress, her back arching into me. Her fingers tangled in my hair, pulling me down, her lips finding mine in a frantic kiss. "Don't stop."

"I wasn't planning to," I rasped, my forehead pressed against hers, our breaths colliding, hot and uneven.

She writhed beneath me, every movement stealing the air from my lungs. Her body moved with mine like we'd done this a hundred times before, like this madness was inevitable. I trailed fire down her neck, her collarbone, her skin trembling beneath my lips.

"This feels incredible," I groaned, the words torn from me before I could stop them.

Her smile curved, slow and dangerous, her hand gliding over my chest. "Yes…yes, it does."

I kissed her harder, deeper, like I could devour the guilt clawing at my chest. Every moan, every sigh, every gasp from her lips fed the fire raging between us. She arched up, meeting me, her legs tightening around me, and I lost myself in the reckless rhythm of it all.

"Faster," she whispered against my ear, her voice breaking with need.

I obeyed, every ounce of control unravelling. The sounds filling the room, her breathless cries, the creak of the bed, the mingling of our voices, all of that now blurred into something primal. I couldn't think. Couldn't breathe. All I could do was chase the fire consuming me.

"Dom," she moaned, clutching at me, her nails digging deep into my skin. "Yes, just like that..."

Her words pushed me over the edge, each one striking something raw inside me. I gave her everything, every ounce of pent-up frustration, every drop of conflict, every piece of myself I'd sworn belonged only to Kelly. It was the most alive I'd ever felt.

Her lips found mine again, softer this time, slower, her tongue teasing against mine.

"You're so addictive," She whispered, her grey eyes burning into me.

And God help me, I believed her.

The world fell away until there was nothing, but her body tangled with mine, her voice urging me on, my own name spilling from her lips like a secret she'd been waiting to tell.

When it was over, when the fire dulled to embers, I collapsed beside her, my chest heaving. Her head rested against me, her hair spilling across me like dark silk.

For a fleeting second, I let myself sink into her warmth, the passion, and the illusion of escape. But as my heartbeat slowed, guilt crept in, slicing through the alcohol induced haze.

I thought of Kelly. I thought of the life we'd built, the promises I'd made, the future we were supposed to have. And I knew, with every pounding beat of regret, that I'd just set fire to it all.

Amber shifted, pressing a lingering kiss to my chest before slipping out of bed. She dressed quickly, gracefully, like she'd done this before.

"Thank you for tonight," She purred; her smile tinged with mystery. She scribbled something on a scrap of paper; her number and placed it on the bedside table. I lay there, staring at the ceiling, drowning in the weight of what I'd done.

The door clicked shut behind her, and the silence that followed was brutal. The room still smelled like her perfume, oudy and thick, coating the air like smoke after a fire. My chest heaved, but not from passion anymore but from the crushing weight of reality settling in.

The sheets tangled around my legs, sticky with sweat and shame. Then my phone buzzed on the nightstand. Kelly's name lit up the screen. My stomach twisted as bile crept up my throat. I couldn't even bring myself to look.

I'd just thrown everything away for a night of recklessness that I couldn't even justify. I pressed my palms into my eyes until I saw stars, trying to erase the image of Amber's lips, her skin…her voice gasping my name. But I couldn't.

This had to be the ultimate betrayal. And the worst part? A dark, disgusting piece of me already wanted more.

CHAPTER 6

Kelly

I sat curled up on the sofa, wrapped in a blanket that was a little too warm but comforting all the same, staring at the clock on the wall as if that would make it tick faster. I hated waiting. My stomach was knotted, and my hands wouldn't keep still; I kept adjusting the glasses on the coffee table, fiddling with the snack bowls, pouring and repouring the prosecco until the bubbles had gone flat. Kennedy and Mia were on their way, and for the first time all week, I felt like I could breathe knowing I'd be able to offload. Just us girls, a quick catch up with snacks, no masks, no pretence.

The knock finally came, light, quick taps on the door. I sprang up with a sigh of relief and pulled it open to the sight of Kennedy grinning like a cat with a secret, Mia right behind her balancing a bottle of rosé and a packet of crisps.

"About time!" I teased, pulling them both in for hugs. The smell of Kennedy's perfume, sharp and floral, filled the room instantly. She always announced her presence without saying a word.

"Don't be cheeky, Kel," Mia laughed, kicking off her boots. "Traffic was a nightmare. And Kennedy needed to stop for *emergency snacks*," She rolled her eyes, gesturing at the bag in Kennedy's hand.

"Listen, you never know when chocolate buttons might save a life," Kennedy said seriously, plopping down on the sofa like she owned it.

I giggled, shaking my head, already feeling lighter. "Alright, sit. I've got prosecco waiting."

Within minutes we were sprawled on the couch, glasses in hand, nibbles within reach. The chatter was easy at first—work gossip, Christmas plans, Mia's latest dating disaster that had us crying with laughter. Then Kennedy cleared her throat dramatically, raising her brows at me.

"Ahem. Did you have fun at the fundraiser last night?" she asked, her tone theatrical.

Heat crept into my cheeks. "Yeah. It was good. A lot of people turned up. I think it went well."

"Oh, come on," Mia cut in, her eyes sparkling. "You can't just say that after you spent the whole night chatting to that tall drink of water. My God, Kel, he looked like Thor."

Kennedy clapped her hands in delight. "Exactly! I said the same thing. God of Thunder vibes all over. Are you telling me you didn't notice?"

I groaned, pressing my face into my hands, though I couldn't hide my smile. "You two are ridiculous."

"Ridiculously right, you mean," Kennedy shot back, nudging me with her elbow. "He was glued to you, babe. All tall, broad-shouldered, and enticing. And you? Blushing and giggling like it was prom night."

"I was not!" I protested, though my nervous laugh betrayed me.

Mia tilted her head, her grin wicked. "So, when are you seeing him again, hmm?"

I hesitated, swirling the prosecco in my glass. "He… asked me to dinner. Next Friday. To talk about Wings of Hope."

Their jaws dropped in unison, like a rehearsed routine.

"Dinner?" Kennedy repeated, eyes wide. "Kel. You do realise what men mean when they say dinner, right?"

"It's business," I rushed out. "He's interested in supporting the charity. That's all."

Mia leaned in, smirking. "Sure, business. Except business doesn't usually come wrapped up like a Marvel superhero."

I burst out laughing, shaking my head. "Stop it! Honestly, it's nothing like that."

Kennedy's grin turned sly. "Dom would be pissed if he saw what Erik looks like."

The sound of Dom's name made my stomach flip, though I shoved it aside quickly. "Enough. I need you both for something more important. Outfit help."

"Ooo yes!" Kennedy shot up instantly, already storming into my bedroom. "Fashion emergency? I live for this."

Mia followed with her glass, laughing. "Here we go."

We spent the next hour in a whirl of fabric, shoes, and shrieking laughter. Kennedy pulled half my wardrobe onto the bed, Mia kept making sarcastic comments about my obsession with blazers, and I paraded up and down like a reluctant model. They rejected most of my choices with brutal honesty.

"That's too safe."

"Too boring."

"You look like you're going to a job interview, not dinner with Thor's cousin."

Eventually, we settled on a sleek navy jumpsuit paired with nude heels. Professional, but still chic. I admired myself in the mirror, though the smile that tugged at my lips faltered as soon as I sat down on the bed. The laughter drained out of me like air from a balloon.

The girls noticed instantly. Mia perched beside me, Kennedy standing with her arms crossed.

"Alright, what's really going on?" Kennedy asked, softer this time.

I sighed, staring at my reflection. "It's Dom. I just… I don't know what to do anymore."

Mia frowned. "What do you mean?"

"It's like we never connect these days," I whispered. "He's always working late, always distracted. He barely talks about the wedding, and when I try to bring it up, he just shuts me out. Makes me feel like I'm invisible. Like I don't matter," My voice cracked, and I clenched my hands in my lap. "Sometimes I'm scared he doesn't even want this anymore. Scared he might call it off. Or that he's chea—"

"Absolutely not," Mia cut me off firmly. "Kelly, no. Dom loves you. He would never."

Kennedy nodded quickly. "Remember how he fought tooth and nail to win your dad over? He didn't do that for fun. He did that because he's crazy about you."

I swallowed hard, trying to believe them. "I don't know… he's been like this for years. It's not just his work. He always keeps me at arm's length when things get tough. Shuts me out, ignores me, like it's easier to deal with everything alone. It hurts."

Mia rubbed my back gently. "Men are idiots, Kel. Sometimes they think shutting down is strength. He's probably just stressed. Didn't you say his project at work's been a nightmare?"

"Yeah…" I whispered, though it felt like an excuse I'd told myself too many times.

"Exactly. Give him space, let him breathe. He'll come back to you," Kennedy reassured. "He always does."

I nodded, forcing a small smile, though inside my chest the doubt lingered like a brewing storm. They were right, Dom loved me. He's always loved me. He's never given me a reason to doubt him. And yet… my gut twisted, whispering that something wasn't right. I would be seeing him later tonight, maybe that would calm this anxiety that was building..

The girls didn't notice the war behind my eyes. Kennedy was already back to rummaging through my jewellery, holding earrings up to my face, and Mia was pouring more prosecco. I let myself laugh with them again, grateful for their warmth, but the flicker of unease refused to die.

Dominic

It was 6 p.m., and I was sat in my favourite restaurant, though at that moment I barely registered the charm of the place. The autumn sunset slanted in through the large windows, still too bright for a man with the world's worst hangover. I shoved my dark shades further up my nose, hoping they'd act as some kind of barrier against reality. But there was nothing I could do to quiet my mind.

Last night replayed in my head like a cruel loop. My chest ached with shame. I couldn't believe I had let myself give in to another woman, a stranger, so easily. I thought of Kelly… she didn't deserve any of this. Her soft, gentle face, the way her nose scrunched when she laughed, the little crease in her forehead when she concentrated, it was all I could think about. And I had thrown it away, just for one foolish, fleeting moment.

"How could I be so stupid?" I muttered under my breath, disgust seeping in.

The questions came at me faster than I could manage. *How could I do this to her? What would her family think? What would her father say if he knew?*

Shame burned hotter as I remembered Amber, her intoxicating scent that lingered like a ghost. I couldn't shake it. I didn't keep her number though; it was best for me to never see her again. But even the thought of that brought a strange ache, a longing I wasn't supposed to feel.

"Kelly never has to know," I whispered to myself, almost as if saying it out loud could make it true. "Why should I lose everything over one stupid mistake?"

I'd decided, at least for now, to bury it. No one could know, especially not Kelly. But even as I made that mental vow, the weight in my chest pressed down harder, a dull pain that wouldn't let up.

I looked up just as Kelly's car rolled into the lot. My heart caught in my throat. I quickly straightened, drained the rest of my water, and tried to shake off the chaos inside me. Time to act normal, or as close to normal as I could manage.

Kelly stepped out of her car, and the sunlight caught her hair, her afro was like a crown around her head, she looked like she was glowing. She walked towards me, her face lighting up with that smile that had always made me weak.

"Hey gorgeous," I said, standing to pull out her chair and greet her with a kiss.

“Hey baby,” she replied, brushing a lock of hair from my forehead as she hugged me. She paused, brow furrowed. “Are you okay?”

I froze. She could always tell. My poker face was rubbish. I laughed nervously. “Uh, yeah. Everything’s fine.”

She didn’t look convinced, but she let it drop. I tried to focus on her, on us, but my mind kept slipping back to Amber, to the sticky mess of last night.

I decided to focus on her victory. “I wanted to say congratulations on your fundraiser. You really pulled that off, Kelly. I’m proud of you.”

Her smile widened, her eyes sparkling. “Thank you! That means a lot coming from you.”

I tried to smile genuinely back, but it felt hollow. We placed our orders, and Kelly bounced back into her usual self, chatty and bubbly. Normally, I loved her energy. Today, I just felt drained, disconnected.

She started talking about wedding plans again, showing me pictures of venues, flower arrangements, and catering options she’d pinned on Pinterest. Her voice was light, excited, but he words were all blurred. I nodded along, trying to focus, but I had tuned out. When I realized she was waiting for my response, panic hit me.

“Well, what do you think?” she said, leaning forward with a bright smile.

“About what?” I asked, my voice sharper than intended.

Kelly's smile faltered slightly. "Summer next year, for our wedding. We've been engaged a while now; we should set a date and start planning." Her laugh was nervous, almost unsure.

"I don't know, Kelly," I said, rubbing my eyes. "Don't you think we need a bit more time? Everything feels like such a rush."

"Such a rush?" Her voice wavered, tinged with confusion and hurt. "I've tried to give you time. I haven't pressured you. But you can't even talk about the wedding without looking like I'm forcing you into it."

"I don't see the big deal. It's just one day," I muttered, raising my voice a little more than I intended. "This is all too much, Kelly."

Her brow furrowed, concern deepening. "Dom, what's going on? Is everything ok? Are we ok?"

I sighed, the sound heavy with guilt. "I'm sorry. I guess I'm just feeling a bit… overwhelmed. There's a lot going on right now."

She reached across the table, taking my hands in hers. Her touch should have grounded me, but today it just felt like another weight pressing down. "Do you want to talk about it? Did the meeting go badly yesterday?"

I pulled my hands away, frustrated with myself for even considering telling her the truth. "Don't worry about it. I'll be okay. You wouldn't understand anyway." My tone was harsh, defensive, and I hated myself for it.

Her eyes softened, but the worry didn't leave them. "Okay… I'm here if you want to share, though."

I looked at her, at the warmth and trust in her gaze, and my chest twisted with guilt. "Thanks. I just… I need some time to process everything, that's all."

We tried to eat, tried to enjoy our meal, but I couldn't taste anything. Every bite felt meaningless. Kelly chatted away, telling me about a meeting with one of her investors. I nodded along, smiled at the right moments, but my mind was elsewhere, spinning with the memory of Amber, the shame of what I'd done, the fear of losing Kelly.

"…so, we have a business dinner next Friday."

"Ok, that's good." I barely heard was she was saying, and I definitely didn't care. I couldn't wait to go back home and get back into bed. I just needed some time away from everything. From everyone.

Finally, the meal ended, and I made my excuses whilst standing to leave, kissing her lightly on the lips. She stayed behind, finishing her dessert, happy to give me the space I needed.

As I walked out, shades back on, I looked back at her. The woman I loved sat there, radiant and blissfully unaware, chatting happily with the waiter who had become a familiar face over the years. And I felt like a shell of myself, hollow and empty.

I needed to come clean. I had to, eventually. The weight of my secret pressed down so heavily I thought I might collapse. But when? How?

"Dom?" Kelly's voice called softly from behind me. I turned slightly.

"I'll see you later," I said, my voice tight, trying to sound casual.

She frowned, her expression concerned. "Are you sure everything's okay?"

I gave a small, strained smile. "Yeah, yeah… I just… I'll speak to you later."

She didn't say anything more, but her eyes lingered on me, full of unspoken questions. I walked out into the street, my mind racing. The guilt gnawed at me, an endless loop of what-ifs and should-haves. I knew I had already fractured the trust she had in me, if not yet then inevitably.

I clenched my fists, trying to push down the ache, trying to pretend I could carry this secret and still be the man Kelly deserved.

But I couldn't. Not really.

I slid my hands into my pockets, took a deep breath, and whispered to myself, "I'll figure it out… somehow."

I had no idea how.

CHAPTER 7

Kelly

I had been looking forward to dinner with Erik all week, though if I was honest, I wasn't sure if it was excitement or nerves fluttering in my chest. By the time Friday evening rolled around, I'd already changed my outfit twice before settling on a fitted navy-blue dress. It hugged my waistline in just the right way, sleek but not overdone, and paired perfectly with my black Louboutin pumps. I ignored my friends' advice and wore made me feel comfortable and powerful instead. I smoothed my palms over the fabric, telling myself I looked like the woman I wanted to project; confident, polished, ready to talk business and nothing else.

I leaned towards the mirror, adjusting the curl of my afro where it framed my face. My makeup was simple but effective, winged eyeliner, warm bronzer, and a bold red lipstick that made me feel powerful. For a moment, I imagined walking into that restaurant and commanding the room like I had everything under control, even though deep down I felt like I was barely holding myself together.

"Focus on the charity, Kelly," I muttered under my breath. "Wings of Hope needs this."

By the time I reached the restaurant, my stomach was a mix of hunger and anxiety. The place was softly lit, tables dotted with glowing candles, and the low hum of conversation filled the air. My eyes immediately caught Erik across the room. He was already seated, tall even as he rose to stand. That same polished look I remembered from the fundraiser; tailored grey suit, ice-blue eyes, hair slicked back with just enough wave to make him look both professional and effortlessly relaxed.

When he saw me, his smile widened, and I caught a flash of admiration in his expression.

"You look beautiful," he said simply, the sincerity in his tone making me feel both flattered and on edge.

"Thank you," I replied, my lips curving in a polite smile as he stepped around to pull out my chair.

"Please, sit. Thank you for agreeing to meet with me tonight."

I placed my clutch on the table and settled into the chair, trying not to notice how close he stood for that brief moment before sliding back into his own seat.

The waiter appeared, menus in hand, and we ordered drinks; Prosecco for me, whiskey neat for him. While we scanned the menus, we made small talk about London traffic, the recent bout of chilly weather, and the impossibility of finding a decent parking spot in the city. I found myself laughing at his dry humour, his ability to spin a story about being stuck behind a double-decker bus into something genuinely funny.

Slowly, the knot of tension in my chest began to loosen.

When our meals arrived; grilled seabass for me, steak for him. I slipped naturally into business mode. I told him about the charity, the way it had grown since its modest beginnings, and the vision I had for its future. As I spoke, his attention didn't waver once. His nods, the occasional sharp question, the way he leaned in slightly with his forearms resting on the table, it all told me he was genuinely listening.

"…and that's why an annual fundraiser would be so beneficial," I explained, gesturing lightly with my fork. "Not just for donations, but for building awareness, creating momentum year after year."

"I agree," he said, his voice low but certain. "Consistency like that will keep people invested. It's smart. You're not just building a charity; you're building a brand… a legacy."

The way he phrased it made me pause. Legacy. I hadn't even dared use that word myself but hearing it from him made my chest swell with pride.

He cut into his steak and added, "We can go through some numbers later, maybe even run a projection. I'd love to assist with your next fundraiser, if you'll let me."

For a moment, I forgot to breathe. This was exactly what I needed; support, investment, belief in the work I was doing.

"Thank you," I said softly, meaning it more than I could put into words.

When I glanced up, I caught him watching me intently, his ice-blue eyes lingering on me in a way that felt almost too heavy, too personal. I felt heat creep into my cheeks.

"I have to say," he said slowly, "you have a remarkable combination of talent and beauty."

I gave a polite smile, forcing my tone to stay professional. "Thank you, Erik. That's kind of you to say. But tonight is really only about the charity."

He chuckled, leaning back slightly, as though giving me space. "Of course. I'll behave."

I picked up my glass, sipping the Prosecco to calm my nerves. Despite the undercurrent of flirtation, I had to admit; I respected him. He wasn't just another wealthy donor throwing money around; he was intelligent, strategic, and genuinely engaged in what I had to say.

The evening continued with easy conversation, and I almost forgot my initial nerves, until he tilted his head and asked casually, "So, your fiancé… what's he like?"

The question stopped me cold.

My fork hovered above my plate as my mind scrambled for an answer. It felt too intimate, too personal for this moment, and yet, avoiding it would only make things awkward.

"Dom is… wonderful," I said finally, my voice softer than I intended.

I forced a smile, but inside I felt something crack. "He's kind, caring, supportive. He's always been there for me.

He's the best." The words sounded rehearsed, like I was reminding myself instead of him.

He studied me quietly, his gaze steady.

"Is everything okay?" he asked gently.

I swallowed hard, placing my fork down. "We've just… been going through a rough patch," I admitted. The words felt dangerous, like opening a door I had been determined to keep shut. "But I know we'll get through it. We always do."

"I'm sorry," he said immediately, his voice full of genuine regret. "Forgive me for prying. It's clear you love him very much. I'm sure the two of you will work things out."

I nodded, but the embarrassment crept hot across my skin. Why did I disclose that to him? To someone I barely knew?

The rest of the meal passed in lighter tones; talk of travel, the best restaurants in Stockholm, his plans while he was in London. I found myself laughing again, the earlier tension dulled by his charm and the wine warming my bloodstream.

By the time dessert came, he mentioned he'd be in the city for a few months.

"Maybe we could catch up again before I leave?" he suggested. Then, with a playful grin, added, "Strictly business. I promise." He raised both hands in mock surrender.

I chuckled despite myself. "Of course. I'd like that."

When we finally stepped outside, the night air was cool against my skin. We lingered by the curb, the city lights washing the pavement in a golden glow. Then He leaned in and brushed a soft kiss against my cheek. His cologne was warm, woody, with a hint of spice. It clung to me even after he pulled back.

"Goodnight, Kelly," he whispered, before walking in the opposite direction.

I stood frozen for a moment; my car keys clutched in my hand. My heart thudded hard against my ribs, a rhythm I couldn't control.

Once inside the car, I gripped the steering wheel and closed my eyes, trying to steady my breathing. I'd kept my composure at dinner; I hadn't crossed any lines, but something about Erik lingered. The way he listened, the way he looked at me, the way he made me feel seen.

And for the first time in a long time, I questioned my relationship with Dom.

I shook my head sharply. No. It was normal to notice other people, to feel attraction now and then. It didn't mean anything. It didn't change the fact that I loved Dom, that we were engaged, that our future was already planned.

Still, the doubt whispered. The flicker of unease in my chest wouldn't quite die.

I started the car and drove home, repeating to myself that things would work out. They had before, and they would again.

Tomorrow was the garden party sponsored by Dom's company, and I couldn't afford to let my mind spiral. His colleagues would all be there, along with his uncle, Antonio; stern but hilarious and very opinionated, he was never shy to voice his disapproval. Dom and Antonio always clashed, and it would fall to me, as it usually did, to smooth over the tension, to smile, to charm, to keep everything light.

Dominic

My flat felt extra quiet this evening, the kind of quiet that weighed heavy on me. No TV, no music, just the low, nostalgic hum of the fridge and the distant sound of traffic outside. I sat on the edge of my sofa, phone in hand, staring at Kelly's photo on the lock screen for longer than I should've. She looked happy in that picture, carefree. She had no idea what I'd done, and God help me, I wanted to keep it that way.

My phone buzzed suddenly, snapping me out of it. Peter's name flashed on the screen. I exhaled slowly before answering.

"Hey, Peter," I said, trying to keep my tone casual.

"Dom, my guy!" Peter's voice came through, lively as ever. "You good?"

"Yeah, yeah. Can't complain. You?"

"I'm buzzing, man. Wedding's only a few months away now. It's starting to feel real."

I leaned back into the sofa, rubbing the bridge of my nose. "Excited?"

"Nervous as hell, but yeah, excited. Can't wait to marry her. Feels like I've been waiting forever." His voice carried this boyish energy, like he couldn't believe his luck. "You know what I mean?"

I swallowed hard. "Yeah. I know." My voice sounded flat, even to me.

Peter didn't notice. He kept talking, words tumbling over each other. "So, suits. I was thinking navy, maybe tailored Italian cut. Sharp but not stiff, you know? What d'you reckon?"

"Sounds good," I muttered, forcing some enthusiasm into my voice. "Navy suits you."

"And the shoes. Bro, I need your advice. Black or brown? She says black, but I feel like brown would pop more against navy."

I let out a small laugh, though it didn't quite reach my chest. "Go with black, mate. Classic. Less chance of looking back and cringing."

"True, true," He chuckled. "That's why I need you, man."

I closed my eyes briefly, guilt clawing at me. If only he knew.

"So…" He hesitated for a beat, then continued, "what are we doing for the stag night? I want something good, but not messy. No strippers, none of that. She'd kill me.

Just the boys, you know? Vegas-style energy, but… London edition."

I smirked despite myself. "We'll figure it out. Maybe Marbella, maybe stay local. I'll make sure it's good."

"See, that's why you're my best man," Peter laughed. "You've got it handled."

Best man. The words hit me like a weight to the chest. How the hell was I supposed to stand beside him on his wedding day, smiling, while I carried this rotten secret inside me?

Peter's voice softened then, shifting. "You and Kelly… have you guys set a date yet?"

My throat tightened. I forced myself to answer. "Not yet."

"Not yet?" He sounded surprised. "Dom, come on, you've been with Kelly since we were sixteen. Don't keep her waiting forever. She deserves that ring, the whole shebang."

"She's already got a ring," I said quickly, deflecting. "The rest… we're working on it."

Peter snorted. "Working on it? Mate, you've been engaged how long now?"

"Couple of years," I muttered.

"Exactly. You don't want her thinking you're dragging your feet." He paused. "She loves you, bro. I can see it every time she looks at you. Don't mess about with this. Lock it in. Give her the day she's dreaming about."

I forced out a laugh that felt hollow. "Yeah. You're right."

"Of course I'm right." His tone was light again, teasing. "Don't keep my girl Kelly waiting. She's basically family already. You'd be stupid to let that slip."

I gripped the phone tighter, my jaw clenched. If only he knew how much I had already slipped.

The memory of Amber hit me then, unbidden. Her laugh, the way she'd leaned into me that night. The alcohol had been flowing, my head cloudy, my judgment worse. One bad decision, one selfish moment. And now it sat on my chest like a boulder.

I thought about telling Peter right then, just blurting it out. He was my closest friend… my brother in all but blood. Maybe he'd understand, maybe he'd tell me what to do.

But the thought of it made bile rise in my throat. If I told Peter, it wouldn't stay secret for long. He'd look at Kelly, and it would be written all over his face. And Kelly… Christ. If she ever found out, she'd leave me. She should leave me.

And the truth was, I couldn't survive that. Kelly was everything. She believed in me when no one else did. Losing her wasn't an option. So, I swallowed the confession, burying it deeper where no one could touch it.

"Anyway," I said abruptly, cutting Peter off mid-thought, "I should get going."

"So soon?"

"Yeah, work's mad right now. We have the garden party tomorrow…you're coming right?"

"Of course, I wouldn't miss it, mate. And Dom?"

"Yeah?"

"Don't overthink it. She's the one. Always has been."

My throat tightened again. "Yeah. I know."

We said our goodbyes, and I ended the call. The silence of the flat pressed in again, heavier this time. I thought about Kelly, the way she fussed over details, how she always made people feel like they mattered. And me? I'd made her feel invisible. I'd ignored her when she reached out, shut her down when she wanted connection. She probably thought I didn't care anymore.

But God, I cared. Too much. I loved her so fiercely it terrified me. That's what made the guilt unbearable. I wanted to give Kelly the world. But how could I when this secret hung between us like thorns?

"She can't ever know. No one can ever know," I muttered, my voice barely above a whisper.

The words echoed in the quiet room, a vow as heavy as any I'd ever made. I would take it to my grave if I had to. Because losing Kelly wasn't an option. And if living with this guilt was the price I had to pay to keep her, then so be it.

CHAPTER 8

Kelly

I was at home, bustling around my bedroom, getting ready for the garden party. I had just slipped on my strappy yellow sundress, the fabric flowing softly around my calves. The dress was perfect for the sunny day, but I made sure to wear my knitted cardigan because it was autumn after all. Hopefully, they would have some firepits or blow heaters to keep the guests warm. I was smoothing down some creases on the dress, when my phone buzzed insistently on the dresser.

I glanced at the screen and smiled; it was Zara. I hadn't spoken to my older sister in nearly six months. She moved up to Scotland with her husband two years ago, it was always a treat to hear her voice. I picked up quickly, my voice bright.

"Hey, Zara!" I said, plopping down on my bed.

"Kelly! There you are, finally," she laughed warmly. "I was about to call the entire country to find you."

I laughed too, shaking my head. “I’m just getting ready for Dom’s Garden party. You know, the annual one sponsored by Bella Gioielli.”

“I bet you look gorgeous,” Zara said immediately.

“How’s Richard?”

“Uh…he’s…alright,” She chuckled awkwardly before correcting herself. “He’s well, he’s just at the gym. I’ll tell him you said hi.”

I smiled, brushing a stray curl from my face. “I miss you, Zara. I wish you were here. I haven’t seen you in months, and it feels like forever.”

“Same here,” she said softly, a tinge of longing in her voice. “Life just gets in the way, you know? But I’m so proud of you, Kelly. You’re out there, doing amazing things, and I swear you just get more beautiful every day.”

I blushed, feeling warm and loved. “Thanks, Zara. That means a lot. Honestly, I could use some of your Scottish calm right now. I’m a little nervous about today… with everyone, and… Dom.”

“Oh, hush! You’ll be fine. And everyone will be eating out of your hands at the party. You’ve got this, Hun.”

I chuckled, but there was a twinge of nerves in my chest. “I hope so. I just want everything to go smoothly. I don’t want to mess anything up.”

“You won’t. And hey, take lots of pictures so I can live vicariously through you.”

“I will. Promise.”

We chatted for another few minutes, the conversation was light, comforting, and made me feel grounded.

Eventually, we said our goodbyes with promises to video call soon.

No sooner had I put the phone down than there was a knock at the door. I practically skipped over, my nerves and excitement tangling into a fluttering mess in my stomach. I opened it, and there he was, beaming, dressed impeccably in a crisp white shirt and tailored grey suit. He was slightly early, but I didn't mind one bit.

"Wow," he said, eyes widening slightly as he took me in. "You look absolutely stunning, Kelly."

I felt heat rise in my cheeks. "Thank you," I said, leaning up to give him a quick kiss. "You look rather handsome yourself."

He grinned and stepped inside, holding my hand. "Not nearly as radiant as you, though."

I laughed, tucking a loose strand of hair behind my ear.

He shook his head, playful mischief in his eyes as he spun me around. "Let me just… appreciate what's mine."

I rolled my eyes, but I couldn't hide my smile. "Flattery will get you everywhere, you know."

"Good," he said, leaning down to whisper in my ear. "Because I intend to enjoy this day with you, fully and unapologetically."

I shivered at the intimacy, though it was innocent, and let him guide me towards the car. He was in particularly high spirits today, more than he had been in ages. And I lapped it up, I was desperate for the attention, longing for the tiniest amount of intimacy I could get from him. And today the cup was overflowing.

"You look like you're auditioning for the cover of a luxury magazine," he joked, sliding his hand along the small of my back as I entered the car. "I'm practically next to royalty right now."

I laughed, the sound ringing lightly in the crisp morning air. "And I suppose you should be bowing then, and calling me 'Your Majesty'?"

He feigned offense, getting into the driver's side. "Yes! About time someone recognised your elevated status."

I nudged him playfully.

The car accelerated and I began to feel relaxed, enjoying his attention and laughter. He reached for my hand, holding it as if it were a prize, and I felt the stress of the last few weeks fade slightly. At one point, he began humming our favourite song, and soon we were singing it at the top of our lungs, laughing as we stumbled over the lyrics and drew curious looks from a few early guests.

Finally, we stepped into the garden, and I felt my breath catch. The setting was breathtaking; a pristine white pavilion, adorned with delicate lanterns, stood as the centrepiece. The garden itself was awash with vibrant floral arrangements, custom topiary, and the sun glinting on crystal glasses. Thankfully, there were firepits scattered here and there, a few guests huddled around each one. A pocket philharmonic orchestra played classical music nearby, their notes drifting through the air with a serene and luxurious elegance.

Dom paraded me around the space proudly, his arm around my waist, introducing me to some new business partners and colleagues. Everyone seemed genuinely happy, laughter and conversation weaving around us like a gentle breeze. Champagne flutes were raised, canapés were being passed, and the atmosphere was light, convivial, and celebratory. Even Uncle Antonio, who was usually so stern, seemed to be enjoying himself. I could hear his booming laugh from across the garden, and the sound made me smile, easing the remaining tension in my chest.

"Dom, everything looks amazing," I said, glancing around. "I don't think I've ever seen anything quite like this."

He leaned down and whispered in my ear. "I told you, it's all about making a statement. And you, my love, are the crown jewel of the day."

I rolled my eyes at his dramatics but felt my heart swell. "Flattery again? You really do have a talent for it."

"I have to keep you happy, don't I?" he replied, his lips brushing my temple in a quick, affectionate kiss.

We moved together through the garden, greeting guests, exchanging pleasantries, and I began to feel more confident and in control. The early apprehension I had felt melted away, replaced with a quiet sense of pride. Dom's hand stayed on the small of my back, his presence a comforting anchor in the swirl of activity.

"Look over there," he said suddenly, pointing towards a cluster of men. "That's the group from the Manchester office. You should meet them; they've been dying to talk to you about your charity work."

I followed his gaze and smiled, feeling a little thrill of anticipation. Meeting influential colleagues and partners always made me a little nervous, but his presence steadied me.

As we approached the group, he squeezed my hand lightly. "You've got this," he said softly. "Just be yourself."

I exhaled audibly and nodded, then stepped forward to greet the guests. The conversation flowed smoothly, laughter was shared, and I felt like I belonged in this world just as much as he did. Champagne and canapés were passed, and I allowed myself a brief indulgence of a delicate smoked salmon canapé, savouring the flavours and the energy around me.

Later, I caught Dom's eye across the garden. He gave me a small wink, making his way over to me.

"I'm glad you're enjoying yourself," he said, slipping his arm around my waist as we found a quiet corner near the pavilion. "You've got that glow today, you know, the one that makes everyone else fade into the background."

I blushed, tucking a stray curl behind my ear again. "You're too much, Dom."

He leaned in, his lips brushing my ear. "Am I? Or am I just stating the obvious?"

I laughed, a genuine, carefree laugh that made him grin. "Maybe a bit of both."

"I can't believe you managed all this," I said, still marvelling at the setting. "It's absolutely spectacular."

"I'm shocked too," Dom replied, giving me a gentle squeeze. "I'm glad my uncle trusted me enough to let me plan this."

I smiled up at him, my nerves from earlier completely gone. "You certainly succeeded, hopefully you will get more opportunities to prove yourself."

I realized that, for the first time in weeks, I felt completely present and seen by Dom. I gave me sense of peace. Everything else—the stresses, the doubts, the small quarrels we had, felt distant and inconsequential. Today had to be proof that we could navigate the world together, gracefully and effortlessly.

Dominic

I watched Kelly move through the crowd, that yellow dress I loved so much, catching the sunlight just right. Every curve, every sway of her hips, made her look radiant, and I felt a familiar swell of pride at having her by my side. She was a natural at mingling, effortlessly charming everyone, making them laugh, making me look good.

"Dom, my boy! There you are!" a booming voice cut through my thoughts. Uncle Antonio emerged from the crowd, his presence as commanding as ever.

He turned to Kelly, eyes twinkling, and kissed her on both cheeks. "Kelly, my dear, looking ravishing as usual!"

Kelly beamed, her radiant smile somehow making my chest ache. "Uncle! It's so lovely to see you. How are you?"

"Better now that I've seen you," he said with a chuckle. "But Kelly, please could you excuse us? I need to quickly discuss some important private matters with my nephew."

He turned to me, hand on my shoulder, leading me towards a group of colleagues gathered near the pavilion. We settled with a group of associates, discussing plans to attract new business partners next year. I tried to contribute as much as possible, nodding at points, exchanging ideas, but my mind kept drifting.

And then I saw her.

A woman walked into the garden, her long black hair cascading in soft waves down her back, confidence radiating with every step. My stomach dropped.

It was Amber.

I froze in place, my mouth slightly agape as I watched her glide across the sun-dappled grass. She looked stunning, mesmerising, and for a moment, all I could think about was the passion, that reckless night, that mistakes I had made. My pulse quickened. *What the hell was she doing here?*

I scanned the garden for Kelly, but she was nowhere in sight. My mind was a whirlwind of guilt, fear, desire, all mixing into a heavy, suffocating tension. I drew in a shaky breath, trying to focus, but the memory of Amber's scent, her touch, came rushing back.

Peter leaned towards me, raising an eyebrow. "Dom? You alright?"

I clenched my jaw, trying to speak, but the words caught in my throat.

I lowered my voice, murmuring under my breath. "Look… I have to tell you something."

Peter's brow furrowed. "About what?"

"I've been keeping something from Kelly," I said, my voice low, tight with shame. "Something…stupid. It happened after my meeting a few weeks ago. I was in a bad place, and…" I swallowed hard, unable to meet his eyes. "I slept with someone. That woman over there…that's her, that's Amber. I need to find Kelly. Now. Before it's too late."

Peter's expression shifted from confusion to disbelief and finally settled into quiet disappointment. "Dom… I can't believe this. This is so out of character for you. I… I don't even know what to say."

"I know," I said, urgency creeping into my voice. "I know. Peter, I just need your help. Can we find her? Kelly…please. I need to make sure she and amber don't cross paths.

He sighed, running a hand through his hair. "Mate… this is huge. I'll help you, but you have to tell Kelly. You can't keep this a secret. She will find out eventually and your entire relationship with Kelly will be ruined."

"You're right. She deserves the truth. I can't keep lying to her, not anymore. But for now, help me find her so I can get her out of here." I forced myself to take a steadying breath.

Peter nodded reluctantly.

We started scanning the crowd, moving carefully through the throng of guests.

Peter leaned closer, his voice low. "There she is." His mouth dropped when he noticed she was walking towards Amber, led by Uncle Antonio.

My heart froze and my stomach dropped into my shoes.

I started towards them, each step heavy with tension, aware of every eye in the garden, every smile, every whisper. But even as I approached them, I couldn't stop myself from watching Kelly interact with Amber, with such ease and innocence.

"Dom!" Kelly called out, waving me over, her smile bright and full of life. Amber's face, though, was different; shock flickered in her eyes, and then she quickly masked it with a polite, almost indifferent expression. My heart slammed against my ribs. *Oh God. Please don't let her say anything.*

Kelly gestured towards Amber. "Here he is, this is Dominic, my fiancé I was just telling you about," she said, smiling warmly, pointing in my direction.

Amber raised an eyebrow. "Your fiancé?" she asked, clearly confused. Her eyes flicked to me, and the chill in her gaze sent a shiver down my spine.

"And your new boss," Uncle Antonio added quickly, stepping in. "We were expecting you on Monday, but it's so lovely that you could make it to the party."

Amber extended her hand, cool and composed. "Hi… nice to meet you," she said, her tone polite but distant. My stomach twisted at the memory of her warm, teasing voice from that night, a voice I hadn't heard in weeks.

I forced a smile, trying to keep my mouth from betraying the turmoil in my mind. "Uh… nice to meet you too," I managed, shaking her hand awkwardly. My palms were clammy, and my tongue felt like sandpaper.

Kelly nudged me gently with her elbow, brow furrowed. "Dom? You okay?"

I shook my head quickly, forcing a laugh that sounded hollow even to my own ears.

"Um… yeah, yeah. I think I've had one too many drinks," I lied, hoping she'd buy it. She gave me a sceptical look but didn't press, at least for now.

"Your desk is right next to his office," Uncle Antonio continued, oblivious to the tension coiling around me. "But let's not worry about all that for now. Come, I'll introduce you to some more people."

He ushered Amber away, and I felt the weight of my panic grow heavier with every step she took. I had to get a chance to speak with her privately. She could ruin everything; my life with Kelly, with just one word. And I couldn't let that happen.

As soon as they disappeared behind a cluster of guests, I excused myself from Kelly.

"I need some air," I muttered, forcing a smile that I knew didn't reach my eyes. She didn't protest, though her concerned gaze lingered on me.

I spotted Amber leaning against a pavilion post, the same seductive smirk curling at the edge of her lips. My stomach twisted again, but I squared my shoulders. *Focus, Dom.*

I grabbed her arm lightly and tugged her toward a hidden corner. She turned with a mock gasp.

"Ooo…where are you whisking me off to?" she said, voice low, teasing.

I fixed her with a hard look. "Amber, listen. Tonight...here, you say nothing. Not a word. Do you understand?"

Her eyes sparkled with mischief, but her tone was sharp. "Don't speak to me like that. I don't owe you any favours…and *I* haven't done anything wrong."

"I know…"

"…you could have told me you had a girlfriend. No…. a fiancé. But you didn't, did you?"

Shame swept over me, and I felt my forehead bead with sweat.

"You're right. I'm at fault here."

"So why should I do anything for you?"

I exhaled, jaw tight. "Because I love Kelly. What happened between us was …. just a one-night stand, a mistake. That woman over there deserves so much more, she can't find out about this. It would break her."

She stepped closer, her lips brushing mine lightly. "How about we make this a fun deal for both of us… one kiss, one more night, and no one would ever know," she whispered, her warmth a dangerous pull.

I recoiled, fury and guilt flaring. "No. Not happening. Do you understand? Kelly is the only person that matters right now. You don't get to…."

She laughed softly, a dangerous melody. "…oh whatever, Dom. I'm just trying to have some fun. You can't be so uptight especially when we are going to be working so close together."

I said nothing.

Her gaze softened slightly, though that edge remained.

"Fine. I'll say nothing," she said, holding up her hands in mock surrender. "But only because I enjoy seeing you squirm a little. Makes me feel alive."

I exhaled slowly, relief mingling with lingering panic.

She smirked and leaned forward impulsively, pressing a quick, soft kiss to my lips. My body froze, my mind screaming to pull away, but my lips moved slightly, almost involuntarily, returning the kiss for a brief, heated moment before I stepped back.

"See you on Monday," She whispered, smirking again.

I leaned back against the wall, exhaling heavily, my heart hammering. My palms were still damp, my stomach tight. I knew this wasn't the end but at least for today I had everything under control. I just had to figure out how I was going to compose myself at work.

CHAPTER 9

Kelly

I had lost sight of Dom in the crowd, my breathing accelerated as I began worry. Evening approached and the afternoon sun had begun to mellow into golden hues. Laughter still echoed across the garden, but I couldn't shake the unease creeping into me. He had been fine one moment, teasing, laughing; pulling me close while we sang like two carefree teenagers, and then he had vanished.

I convinced myself he was probably sitting in the car, feeling unwell. That had to be it. Maybe the champagne had caught up with him, maybe the pressure of entertaining his business partners. My heels clicked softly against the gravel as I walked down the winding path towards the parking area.

Then he appeared suddenly, walking briskly in my direction, his head slightly lowered, muttering under his breath as if fighting some private storm. His face was flushed, his shirt collar unbuttoned, and a bead of sweat clung stubbornly to his temple. He looked flustered.

My heart tugged with concern. "Dom?" I called softly, picking up my pace. When I reached him, I touched the back of my hand gently to his forehead. His skin was clammy and far too warm. "Darling, you don't look good at all."

He paused, forcing a smile that didn't reach his eyes. "Sorry I disappeared; I just needed a moment."

I searched his face, trying to read what he wasn't saying. He looked exhausted, drawn in a way I hadn't seen before.

"Don't apologise. You're obviously not well. Maybe we should call it a day and head back?" My voice was calm, but inside, I was already making a mental list of things; herbal tea, aspirin, maybe a cool cloth, anything to help ease him.

"Yes, that's a good idea." His tone was clipped, almost rushed. Without waiting, he walked ahead and opened the passenger door for me.

I slipped into the seat, smoothing down my yellow dress. I still felt light from the day; the party had been beautiful. When Dom slid into the driver's seat, I tried to keep that energy alive.

"You know the party went…,"

His hand hovered over the start button, "Put your seatbelt on. You know I don't…"

"Oh yes, I'm sorry. I was just so…"

He clenched and unclenched his hands, as if to release some anxiety.

"You know I need you to do that as soon as we get in the car."

"I know, I'm sorry," I replied, my seatbelt now fastened, "The party really was wonderful. Everything looked so elegant, the flowers, the pavilion, the orchestra. It all felt magical."

"Mmm." His eyes fixed on the road as he started the engine.

I pushed past the quiet response, hoping to draw him out.

"And Uncle Antonio," I added with a laugh, "he was in such high spirits! I don't think I've ever heard him laugh like that. He even tried to teach me a beautiful Italian proverb, but I've already forgotten half of it."

Dom gave a faint grunt of acknowledgment, his jaw tightening as he turned onto the main road.

I tried a final time, refusing to let the silence take over.

"And Amber…your new assistant. She seems absolutely lovely. So polite and professional. I really hope it all works out with her. She'll be such an asset to Bella Gioielli."

His hands gripped the steering wheel tighter. "Yeah," he muttered, nothing more.

The flatness of his reply caught me off guard. A flicker of confusion passed through me, but I ignored it, focusing instead on the positive. The day had been too good to unravel now. "I'm really proud of you, you know," I said softly. "Seeing you surrounded by all those people, all of them so impressed with you and your work…"

My voice trailed off when I noticed he wasn't paying attention to anything I was saying. His gaze stayed locked on the road, his expression unreadable, my words hadn't reached him at all.

The drive home felt like an entirely different world compared to the journey there. Earlier, we had been belting out our favourite song at the top of our lungs, windows rolled down, laughter spilling into the wind. Now, silence hung heavy between us, filling every corner of the car until it became suffocating.

I sat with my hands folded neatly on my lap, staring out the window as the city lights flickered past. The silence was uncomfortable, but I tried to convince myself it was nothing more than tiredness. I didn't want to push him, not tonight.

I let the hum of the engine, and the rhythm of the road fill the space. In my heart, I clung to the earlier moments of joy; the way he had looked at me with pride, the way he had held my hand as if nothing could come between us. That had to mean something. That had to matter.

We pulled up outside my apartment building, and I waited for him to reach over and open my door as he always did. But he didn't move. He sat there, staring straight ahead, his knuckles pale against the steering wheel.

I swallowed down the sting of disappointment. Forcing a small smile, I leaned over and pressed a light kiss to his cheek. "Thank you for today," I whispered. "I really did have a great time."

"Yeah," he said again, his voice barely above a murmur.

Then I turned to exit the car, but before I could open the door, his arm curved around my waist and held me for a second. Then he leaned in and kissed me. It wasn't hurried or distracted like I half expected—it was deliberate, deep, almost as if he was trying to reassure me in that moment. It felt like an apology, and I appreciated it. I needed it.

When he finally pulled away, his breath brushed against my ear. "Let's make a plan to discuss our wedding," he whispered, low and certain, the kind of tone that used to melt me. "You wanted next summer, right? I think we can work on that."

For a heartbeat, my chest lifted, warmth flooding through me. This was everything I had wanted to hear for so long, the next step, him choosing *us*. Finally, it was happening.

But as I searched his eyes in the dim glow of the dashboard, something tugged at me. The words were right, but the weight behind them felt off. His gaze didn't quite hold mine the way it used to. There was a flicker of hesitation, maybe even distraction; that I couldn't name.

Still, I forced a smile, nodding. "Yes. Next summer would be perfect." My voice came out steadier than I felt.

I wanted to believe him, I truly did. And yet, as his arm slipped away and I reached for the door handle, a small unease lingered in the pit of my stomach, like a thread pulled too tight but not yet snapping.

I had barely made it through the main door when the sharp screech of tyres split the air. I turned instinctively, but all I caught was the flash of Dom's car speeding down the street, vanishing into the night as if chased by ghosts.

Dominic

It had been two weeks since Amber started working as my assistant. Two weeks of clipped conversations, polite professionalism, and efficient organisation. On paper, it was going well. She was sharp, competent, and already easing into the rhythm of my business life, in a way that made me wonder how I'd ever managed before. But beneath the smooth surface, there was a current running strong. A dangerous one. Attraction.

I hated admitting it, even silently to myself, but it was there. Amber was beautiful in a quietly tantalizing way; it was impossible not to notice her. Flirtatious when she wanted to be and playful with her words. Still, I'd managed to keep myself in check, to remain composed, to stay faithful to Kelly. I reminded myself of that every morning. And yet, each day the line blurred more than I cared to admit.

I walked into the building that morning, nodding politely to the receptionist before heading straight for my office. My focus shifted the moment I saw her. Ever punctual, papers spread out neatly on her desk outside my office. She arranged them with an efficiency that impressed me more than I'd say aloud.

Her outfit gave me pause. A black pencil skirt, fitted just enough to emphasise her curves, paired with a soft white blouse that made her look both professional and—something else.

My eyes trailed down before I could stop myself, lingering on the sway of her hips and the roundness of her ass as she bent slightly over the desk.

I cleared my throat, deliberately loud. "Ahem."

She straightened immediately, turning to face me with a smile that bordered on mischievous.

"Good morning…" she said, drawing out the words, her gaze flicking from my face down to my suit and back up again.

The look was deliberate.

I smirked, masking the brief surge of heat. "Nice to see you here bright and early."

She tilted her head, that smile growing into something just shy of smug. "I could say the same, Mr. Moretti. Though I have a feeling you're more of a night owl than a morning person."

That earned her a chuckle from me. She wasn't wrong, but I didn't need her knowing how easily she could read me. I glanced around quickly, scanning the hallway to ensure no one else was nearby. The last thing I needed was whispers starting.

"You free later?" I asked, keeping my voice casual. "We should grab a work lunch. To go over this week's meetings and organise the calendar properly."

Her brows lifted, eyes sparking with something playful.

"A *work* lunch," She repeated, stressing the word *work* like she didn't entirely believe it.

I narrowed my eyes, amused despite myself. "Don't flatter yourself, Amber. Strictly professional."

She laughed lightly, shaking her head, but she didn't argue.

The workday began as usual after that. Colleagues started trickling in, doors opening, footsteps echoing in the corridor, snippets of conversation filling the once quiet space. The safety net of company forced me to retreat into my office, closing the door behind me as if that alone could drown out the temptation of the woman sitting just outside.

I should've felt relief, but I didn't.

Instead, I caught myself noticing things I shouldn't. The way her laugh carried faintly through the door when someone cracked a joke by the printer. The way her perfume lingered faintly when she walked past to drop off files. Small, ordinary things, magnified by the unspoken tension that had taken root between us.

And worse, she knew it.

We fell into a rhythm throughout the day. Meetings, emails, phone calls. She slipped in and out of my office with updates, efficient as ever. But it was the in-between moments that tested me.

A glance held a second too long. A brush of her fingers against mine when she passed me a folder. A smirk playing on her lips when she caught me looking.

It wasn't overt. It wasn't scandalous. But it was there.

At one point, she leaned over my desk to hand me a report, the gathered neckline of her blouse went slack, exposing her full bosom. My eyes immediately drawn to the succulent pair and I forgot how to speak.

"Here you go," she said, her tone perfectly even. Professional. But her eyes…her eyes lingered on me and stayed there until I met them. The air between us felt thick.

I forced myself to look back at the papers. "Thanks," I replied, struggling to keep my voice neutral.

She turned to leave, and I told myself not to look. Not to watch the confident sway of her steps as she walked back to her desk. Of course, I looked anyway.

By mid-afternoon, my restraint was starting to wear on me. Every glance, every smirk, every too-close moment pressed harder against the line I'd drawn for myself. I found myself leaning on sarcasm and dry humour just to keep the atmosphere manageable.

"Careful with those glances," I muttered at one point when she caught my eye in the staff kitchen.

She raised her brows innocently, mouthing a silent *what glances?* before returning to her desk.

I groaned under my breath, running a hand through my hair. She knew exactly what she was doing.

And the worst part? I wasn't entirely sure I wanted her to stop.

The restaurant was quiet, just as I'd hoped. It sat on the edge of town, a place where the food was good enough, but the draw was its emptiness. No one came here on a weekday afternoon. Which meant no one who mattered would see me sitting across from Amber.

I swirled the ice in my glass, the condensation dampening my palm, before taking a slow sip. I needed the coolness, something to steady the heat that had been rising in me all morning.

"Okay," I said, clearing my throat, pushing the thoughts down. "Let's go through this week's schedule. We've got three board meetings, two client dinners, and the zoom call with the branch in Manchester."

Amber was already flicking through her notes.

"I've blocked time for prep sessions before each board meeting. Also, don't forget you were meant to get back to Mr Rossi from Edmund & Co, to set up that presentation" She glanced up then, eyes sharp but playful, and then she smiled. "You're welcome."

I chuckled, shaking my head. "You're on the ball, I like it."

The conversation stuck to business for a while, deadlines, upcoming projects, the logistics of travel. I told myself it was just a lunch, nothing more. But every so often, I caught her watching me, the kind of look that burned even after she glanced away.

After the plates were cleared, she set her pen down and leaned back in her chair. "Can we talk about something else?"

I knew where this was going before the words left her mouth. "Amber…" I warned.

She tilted her head, lips quirking. "The atmosphere between us. You feel it too, don't deny it."

My jaw tightened. "Don't bring that up again."

"Why not?" she asked, calm, bold. "Pretending it's not there doesn't make it go away."

I forced a laugh, but it sounded hollow in my ears. "You're imagining things. This is a professional lunch, don't let it confuse you."

She arched a brow. "Is it? Because if this is what professionalism looks like, I need to adjust my definition."

The comment hit harder than I expected. Because she wasn't wrong. And no matter how many times I told myself I was committed to Kelly, I couldn't deny her pull.

I looked away, focusing on the smudge on the rim of my glass. "This is dangerous ground Amber," I muttered.

Amber leaned forward, her voice softer now. "Exactly. Which means you feel it too."

I didn't answer. Couldn't. My throat went dry. When I finally glanced back at her, the certainty in her eyes shook me.

I settled the bill in silence. The air between us thick, heavy, electric. I told myself I was still in control. That I hadn't crossed any lines. Outside, the sun was low, throwing long shadows across the street. I held the door open for her, as habit demanded, and that was when it happened.

As she walked past me, she turned, quick, impulsive, and threw her arm around my neck. Her lips crashing against mine.

For a moment, I froze. My body stiff, my mind screaming at me to push her away. But then—God help me, I kissed her back.

It was fire. Heat. Something raw, just like that first night.

And then clarity. Shame.

I shoved her back, my voice sharp. "What the hell do you think you're doing?"

She looked at me, lips swollen, eyes dark. "Admit it. You wanted that."

I clenched my fists, anger boiling. "Don't ever do that again."

Back at the office, the tension only grew. She stayed out of my way and refused to make eye contact with me. I knew I had to do something about this, before we really crossed the line—again. I waited until after closing, when I knew the office would be empty and surprisingly, she hung back also, as if waiting for me.

"You're fired," I said, standing by the open door to my office. My voice was sharp, startling her.

Her eyes widened. "What?"

"You heard me. Pack your things."

"You don't mean that," she snapped, stepping closer. "You don't get to pretend this is all on me, Dom. You kissed me back."

"I told you to stop!"

"No," she shot back, jabbing a finger into my chest. "Stop lying to yourself. Stop lying to *her*…Kelly, your precious fiancé. You think she deserves this half-hearted version of you? Because I don't."

Anger and desire collided, my emotions felt messy and uncontrollable. "You don't know what you're talking about."

She smirked bitterly. "Oh, I know exactly what I'm talking about."

She turned to grab her bag, but I caught her wrist. She spun, colliding into me. And then, it was chaos.

Our mouths crashed together, desperate, hungry. Papers scattered as I lifted her onto the desk, my hands roaming, tearing her blouse open. She tugged at my shirt, pulling it over my head.

Breathless, I muttered against her skin, "This is wrong."

"Then stop," She whispered, biting back a moan.

But I didn't stop. Couldn't. The sound of her voice, the heat of her body, it drowned out reason.

My office, my sanctuary, turned into something else entirely, as my naked torso pressed against hers. The desk creaked under us as if it too disapproved.

"Dom…" she gasped, breathless.

"Amber…"

The creak of the door opening didn't register at first. Not until a voice cut through the haze.

"What the hell going on here?"

I froze.

Uncle Antonio stood in the doorway, his face a mask of shock and disappointment.

I scrambled off the desk, fumbling for my shirt. Amber pulled down her skirt, shame written all over her face as she ducked to retrieve her blouse.

"Uncle, I can explain—"

"I don't want to hear it, Domenico," he snapped, voice low but dangerous. "This is unacceptable. It's bad enough in a professional setting. But you? Did you forget you were engaged?" His disgusted glance at Amber burned hotter than any slap.

The weight of his disappointment crushed me.

"You know better than this," he said, his voice quieter now, pained.

Amber looked between us, rolling her eyes at his comment, but said nothing.

"Miss," my uncle said firmly, "pack your belongings. Our brand is built on family values and respect. You're not a good fit here."

Her breath hitched, but she steeled herself, cleared her desk and walked out. She didn't even glance back at me. I clenched my jaw, staring at the floor.

"You're lucky I can't fire you," he said, approaching me.

I lifted my head, defiance burning despite the shame. "Uncle…"

"Domenico Nicolas Moretti," he thundered. The use of my full name made me flinch. He had never once used it. "You are engaged to a good woman. Kelly loves you. And I know you love her. What is this?"

"I…"

He cut me off again. "You are like a son to me. I only want what's best for you. But I won't watch you throw everything away for lust. My brother would be disappointed…as am I."

His words sliced deeper than any blade and then he walked out, leaving me stunned, hollow. I stared at the mess around me. Papers scattered, my shirt discarded on the ground, the scent of Amber and shame still lingering.

CHAPTER 10

Kelly

My phone buzzed, jolting me out of the comfort of an early evening cup of tea. When I glanced at the screen, I saw Mia's name flashing.

I smiled faintly and answered. "Hey, Mia. How are you?"

Her voice came out fast, trembling with urgency.

"Kelly, I'm with Kennedy. You're not going to believe what we just saw."

Immediately, my stomach tightened. "What's wrong, Mia? Is everything okay?"

She rambled, her words tripping over each other. "So, Kennedy and I met up for a coffee just outside town, across from the new restaurant—you know the nice one. What's it called, Kennedy?"

From the background, Kennedy's voice piped in. "The Hornbeam."

"That's it. The Hornbeam. Anyway, we were just sitting there, chatting, drinking coffee and…" Mia faltered, her tone changing to something I couldn't place. "Kelly, I don't even know how to say this, but before I do, I need you to know that we love you, okay? We'd never hurt you."

The knot in my stomach twisted into something sharper. "Mia, just say it."

Kennedy's voice cut through, impatient, blunt.

"We saw Dominic. With a woman. Coming out of The Hornbeam. And they were kissing."

For a moment, everything stopped, the ticking clock in the kitchen, the hum of the fridge, even the air felt frozen.

Mia's voice returned, softer now, like she was afraid I'd shatter. "I'm so sorry, Kelly. We know how much you love him. Urgh, men can be such dogs."

A gasp escaped me, unbidden. My hand flew to my mouth, but it couldn't stop the sharp sting that rushed to my chest. I had suspected a little, the distance in his eyes, and the tension he always seemed to have in his voice. Suspicion was one thing. Hearing it confirmed, no, witnessing it through my friends, was another.

"I can't believe it," I whispered, voice trembling. "How could he do this to me? After everything… after all I've given to him, all we've been through. I supported him in everything, and this is what he's been doing behind my back?"

Mia sniffled quietly on the line. Kennedy's tone softened. "I'm sorry, Kel. What are you going to do?"

"I… I don't know," I stammered. "I just… I need to think. I'll speak to you both later."

I hung up before they could respond, my hands trembling. The phone slipped onto the sofa beside me, and I stared across the room. A photo frame caught my eye; our first holiday together, in Portugal. We were so young, carefree, our skin sun-kissed and our smiles endless. That was us then. Was it all just a lie?

Numbness spread through me, but beneath it was a roaring ache. He was my first love, my only love. The boy I grew up with, we were meant to be planning our wedding. And now…

My body moved before my mind did. I stood, grabbed my coat and keys, and walked out.

The drive to his flat was a blur. My heart pounded so violently I thought it might split my chest open. When I pulled up, his car wasn't outside. For a fleeting second, I was relieved, maybe he wasn't home, I needed the time to compose myself.

I walked inside, the familiar scent of the building; wood polish and faint detergent, filled my lungs. The lift seemed to crawl upward, mocking me with each stop. When I finally reached his floor, I marched down the hall and rang his doorbell. Just in case he was in.

No answer.

I pressed again, longer. Still nothing. My fists clenched at my sides. So, I waited.

Leaning against the wall, tears pricking my eyes, I pulled out my phone and scrolled through our messages from the past few weeks. They were filled with love hearts, jokes, little plans for the future. How could he write such things and kiss someone else at the same time?

A thought stabbed me; he's probably with her right now.

The ding of the elevator snapped me back. My chest tightened. I turned, standing stiffly by the door, hands twisting the strap of my bag. The doors slid open and revealed him. He looked pale, tired; almost heavier in the way he carried himself, like guilt had weighed him down.

"Kelly," he said, his voice rough. "What are you doing here?"

I swallowed hard, summoning every ounce of strength. "Dom, I need you to tell me the truth. Are you cheating on me?"

He froze. The colour drained from his face, and his eyes dropped to the floor. "Kelly… I'm so sorry." His voice cracked, barely above a whisper.

My body shook. "So, Mia and Kennedy were right," I said, my voice breaking.

Confusion flickered in his eyes. "Mia and Kennedy?"

"They saw you," I hissed. "At The Hornbeam. Kissing someone. Don't bother lying, they told me everything."

His shoulders slumped. "I didn't mean for it to happen. It was… it was a mistake; it was meant to be a business meeting but she…"

I laughed bitterly, though it came out more like a sob. "A mistake?…just stop lying. They saw you kissing her, Dom. That's not a mistake. That's a betrayal."

"Ok, ok…you're right," he pleaded, stepping closer. "I had a moment of weakness, but I'm back to my senses. It won't happen again. Please believe me. I love you, Kelly. Only you."

He reached out, his arms open, but I stepped back, tears burning down my cheeks. "I don't know if I can believe you."

"Okay," he said quietly, looking defeated. "I'll do anything to make it right."

I looked down at my hand; the engagement ring glimmered under the hallway light. Slowly, my fingers slid it off. The weight of it, once comforting, now felt foreign. I held it out to him, my heart splintering with the gesture.

"I think we need time apart. I can't deal with this, Dom. Not knowing if you're truly happy… or if I'm enough for you anymore."

His face crumpled. "No, Kelly. Please. Forgive me. It was just a kiss, nothing else, I swear. A foolish moment."

Tears blurred my vision. "You don't get it. You've made me feel unwanted for months. Like I'm in the way. Like everything I do irritates you. Maybe… maybe it's time we call it a day."

I dropped the ring on the floor and turned, ready to leave, but his hand grabbed my arm, desperate.

"Counselling!" He shouted. His voice cracked with desperation.

"What?" I turned around, by brows furrowed.

"Let's try counselling. You've said it before, remember? I'll make the appointment. Please, Kelly. One last chance. We have to try."

His hands gripped my shoulders now, forcing me to look at him. His green eyes: those eyes I once adored, burned with regret.

But I couldn't meet them. My gaze drifted past him, through him, as memories clawed at me. I was there when he buried his parents. He was there when I fought to start my charity. We were partners, fighters, survivors. And now?

My knees buckled. And I started to heave, feeling that familiar pain in my chest. I crumbled into his chest, sobbing uncontrollably. His arms wrapped around me instantly, holding me tight, as if he could piece me back together with sheer force.

"I love you," He whispered again and again, his words a mantra, an anchor that steadied me and pulled me away from the brewing storm.

His lips brushing my hairline. "I'm sorry. I'll fix this. Please, forgive me."

Dominic

November 2024

It was the last Friday of November, and I was sat across from Kelly in the therapy room, trying to keep my breathing even while my insides were knotted tight. The walls were too white, too clean, like they'd been scrubbed free of every stain except the ones I carried in here with me.

Kelly's shoulders stiff, her eyes cast downward, she twisted one of her coils around her finger until it looked like it might snap. Her jaw was clenched; I knew she was holding back all the words she wanted to hurl at me.

I sat motionless, but inside I was restless. My leg bounced involuntarily, my fingers drummed against my knee, and I let out a long sigh that filled the silence. I couldn't look her in the eye. I told myself I was calm, but I knew it wasn't calmness; it was control, barely.

Ten minutes dragged before the door opened.

"So sorry for the delay," Dr. Grady said, gliding in like the ten minutes hadn't felt like a lifetime. She was small and sharp-eyed, her glasses slipping to the end of her nose as she settled into her chair. She gave us that practiced smile, the kind therapists give, when they're trying to convince you the room is safe.

Neither Kelly nor I returned it.

"So," she leaned forward, hands folded neatly, "what brings you both here today?"

I didn't move or speak. My tongue felt unnaturally heavy in my mouth.

Kelly exhaled sharply. "I recently found out...," she said, her voice tight but steady at first, "...Dom has been seeing another woman. We're engaged, and we should be planning a wedding, but instead..." Her voice cracked. She trailed off, eyes glistening as she looked away from me.

The shame burned in my chest. I lowered my head, staring at the watch strapped to my wrist as if it could rescue me. Dr. Grady's brow arched, lips pressing into a thin line of disappointment.

"How long has this been going on?" she asked.

Kelly's hand shook as she dabbed at her cheek with a tissue. She didn't answer.

I cleared my throat, my voice rough. "It was just once, we just met, flirted; it was one business...one date and we kissed." The lies tasted bitter even as I swallowed most of the truth. I didn't mention the one-night stand or even that the woman was Amber. Those details would destroy Kelly completely. I couldn't say them out loud.

Dr. Grady's face stayed neutral, though her eyes betrayed a flicker of judgment. "Why do you think you sought intimacy with another woman?"

"I was selfish," I snapped too quickly. "That's it. I was selfish."

Her gaze pinned me, unblinking. "Or perhaps there's more to it than selfishness. Why now? Why her?"

I shifted in my chair, heat rising in my face. "Because I'm flawed, alright? I don't need a diagnosis for why I can't keep my head straight."

Kelly turned to look at me then, her eyes red, her mouth trembling like she wanted to scream.

But Dr. Grady's voice stayed calm, even. "Dominic, this isn't our first time meeting. You act like I don't know you; its ok to admit your parents' deaths were traumatic. And growing up without them, with your uncle raising you, has left wounds you haven't addressed. Patterns. You've kept people at a distance. Even Kelly. From time to time, you push her away, don't you?"

Her words sliced deeper than I wanted to admit. I rubbed my temple, fighting the urge to bolt from the room.

"You've spent years seeking affection," Dr. Grady continued softly, "because deep down, you're still that boy who felt unloved. That boy who believed he was never enough."

I clenched my jaw. I hated how much it rang true.

Kelly spoke up then, her voice trembling but strong enough to carry. "We used to be best friends. Now everything I do irritates him. I try to connect, but it feels like he shuts me out on purpose."

The silence that followed was suffocating. Dr. Grady wrote a few notes, then looked back at us. "Let's try something different. A visualization exercise. Please take a pen and paper."

I reached across the table, my fingers brushing Kelly's by accident. She flinched away. We both closed our eyes, as instructed.

"Imagine the wedding has come and gone," Dr. Grady's voice softened, coaxing. "You're living together. Your dream life. What does it look like? Where are you?"

For a moment, I actually let myself see it. The skyline stretched out beneath me, glittering lights scattered across the city like diamonds. A penthouse suite, glass windows from floor to ceiling. The heartbeat of London below us, constant and alive. Kelly and I, together, untouchable in our own high-rise kingdom.

When I opened my eyes, I wrote it all down. My hand didn't shake.

"I see us in the city," I said, reading it aloud. "A penthouse with the whole skyline laid out in front of us. I love the energy, the excitement. It'll be just the two of us, living at the centre of everything," I smiled faintly.

Kelly unfolded her paper slowly. Her voice was a whisper, but it carried more weight than mine. "I see us in a beautiful old home. A garden, with space for kids. Family nearby. Stability."

She crushed the page in her hand as a tear slipped down her cheek. The difference was glaring, hanging in the air between us like smoke. Her eyes locked on mine. And in that look, I saw her realise what I had been trying to ignore: we weren't dreaming the same dream anymore.

Dr. Grady didn't need to say anything, and Kelly's silence said enough.

On the drive back, the air between us was unbearable. She stared out the window, her arms crossed tightly, while I gripped the steering wheel, for once there was something to distract me from the thought of being in this death trap.

Finally, she broke the silence. "You've changed since your parents died."

Her words hit like a sucker punch. My grip tightened, my throat burned.

"Don't…" I said, my voice low, dangerous.

But she didn't stop. "You shut down. You shut me out. I can't reach you anymore, Dom. You're not the boy I fell in love with."

The fury rose in me, uncontained. "Don't bring my parents into this," I snapped, my voice loud enough to shake the air in the car. My chest heaved. My jaw ached from clenching so hard.

Kelly's eyes widened, but she didn't flinch. She just looked at me with sadness—that was worse than anger. For the first time in years, I wasn't sure if we had anything left to save.

CHAPTER 11

Kelly

Retail therapy was meant to clear my head; that was the plan anyway. After Dom dropped me home, I paced my flat for ten whole minutes, replaying everything from the car ride and the therapy session before. My thoughts were heavy, like stones in my chest, and I couldn't sit still. If I didn't get out, I was going to combust.

So, I threw on my jacket, grabbed my bag, and decided to wander into town. Nothing major, just the usual high street, a few shops, maybe something sparkly or completely unnecessary to distract me from the weight pressing on my lungs.

The air was cold, sharp in a way that almost helped, like the November chill might numb me if I let it. I drifted aimlessly until I spotted a little boutique I'd never noticed before, tucked neatly between the florist with its blinding display of chrysanthemums and the cosy bookshop I sometimes ducked into.

The shop looked inviting, a warm light spilling out through the windows, scarves and delicate dresses hanging in carefully curated displays. I don't know what pulled me in exactly; maybe instinct, maybe chance. But when I stepped through the door, the bell chimed overhead, and I froze.

Because standing behind the counter, flipping through a stack of scarves like she owned the place, was Amber. The same Amber I'd met at the garden party. For half a second, I considered walking right back out. I wasn't in the mood for small talk or niceties, not today. But something inside me, call it curiosity, call it fate, made me pause. She was new in town, wasn't she? I remembered that much. Maybe checking in would give me something else to focus on.

I forced a weak smile onto my lips.

"Hey, Amber, how's it going? What are you doing here? I thought you worked at Bella Gioielli?" I asked as cheerfully as I could manage, stepping into the boutique.

Amber looked up sharply, her eyes flickering with shock before narrowing into something else, something cruel. A small, knowing chuckle slipped from her lips, low and mocking.

"So, Dom still hasn't told you," she said, almost gleeful.

Did she just call him Dom? My heart tripped in my chest. "Told me what?" I asked, the cheeriness in my voice cracking like glass.

Amber smirked, then sighed dramatically, as though she'd been waiting for this moment. She looked me dead in the eyes, her expression flat but her tone dripping with false sympathy.

"Kelly, I'm so sorry. I didn't know you and Dom were together when it happened. I thought he was single."

The words didn't land properly at first. They hovered, heavy and unformed, above my head. Then my skin prickled, and my heart started thundering so loud I could barely hear her.

"What do you mean?" My voice was small, almost trembling. "What happened between you and Dom?"

Amber tilted her head slightly, as if debating how much to reveal, then shrugged casually, like she was telling me about a bad coffee order, not detonating my entire life. "We slept together. About a month ago. We met at a bar; and he invited me back to his place."

I staggered back a step, clutching my bag tighter against my side. It felt like someone had punched the air out of me. The room tilted ever so slightly, and for a moment I thought I might actually faint.

They slept together.

It wasn't just a kiss. It wasn't just flirtation. It was betrayal in its most intimate form. A million images flashed through my head at once: Dom at the garden party, stiff and strange; Dom looking at her too long; Dom's restless energy these past few weeks. Everything suddenly clicked, and I hated that it made sense.

Amber must've noticed the change in me because she pressed on, her voice almost bored.

"But anyway, you don't have to worry about me. Antonio fired me when he caught us fooling around at work."

She said it so casually…*fooling around,* as if she wasn't shattering my engagement, my future and my sanity in the middle of a boutique surrounded by silk scarves and candles.

My hands felt clammy, and my chest was tight, every breath shallow. The edges of my vision blurred like I was underwater. Was this a panic attack? I didn't know. I just knew I couldn't breathe properly, and I definitely couldn't think or even form words. But then something else sparked inside me. A different kind of heat.

Anger.

It rose slowly, burning away the fog in my head, solidifying me again. I clenched my fists and forced my breathing to steady. Amber's smug, detached little expression was like fuel on the fire.

"You know what Amber," I finally said, my voice steadier than I felt. "Thank you for telling me the truth. It wasn't your duty; Dom should've been the one to tell me. But he's been too much of a coward."

Amber raised her brows slightly, almost impressed by my composure, then turned as the door chimed behind us. A new customer walked in, shaking the cold from their coat. Amber smiled sweetly and excused herself without another word, gliding over to greet them.

Just like that, she was done with me. Finished with her little revelation; she had tossed her grenade and now her job was complete.

I slipped out quietly, the bell above the door chiming again as I stepped back into the cold. My legs moved automatically, carrying me elsewhere, though I barely registered the street around me.

It felt like the ground had given way, like I was walking on nothing. My engagement to this man that was meant to be the love of my life; all of that was gone. Yet, underneath the raw hurt and the humiliation, one thing became crystal clear:

Dom and I were over.

There was no coming back from this. Not this time. Not ever.

Dominic

I pushed open the door to the bar, and the wave of warm air hit me. The atmosphere was buzzing with laughter, and that faint sticky smell of spilled beer, it was familiar and almost comforting. Therapy had left me raw earlier, and the last thing I wanted was to sit alone at home with my thoughts gnawing at me. I needed the guys, even if I knew they wouldn't go easy on me.

Peter had texted earlier: *Meet us at The Royal, 8 sharp. Drinks on me.* I knew what that meant. He was staging an intervention, his own way of making sure I didn't crawl back into avoidance.

I spotted them tucked into a booth near the window. Peter was nursing a pint, Aaron had his usual whiskey, and Liam, of course, was already halfway through his second beer and entertaining everyone like he was the main character of a west end show.

"Dom!" Liam called, his grin too wide. "The man of the hour."

I slid in beside Peter, already feeling annoyed. "Yeah, yeah. Keep it down, will you?"

Peter gave me a look, the kind that said *I warned you.*

"So, Dom, is what we heard about Amber true?" Liam's voice was laced with mischief, his eyebrows dancing as if this was just a story to laugh about. "Or is it just bar gossip?"

My jaw clenched. I wanted to deny it, but what was the point? The guys knew. Hell, Peter probably gave them the basics already. I stared down at the condensation dripping down my glass of water, before finally speaking.

"I guess Peter told you guys." My voice was low, heavy with shame. "Yeah. It's true. It happened; it was a mistake. And now I'm in a mess."

Aaron winced, running a hand through his hair. Liam, predictably, let out a whistle and leaned back like he was watching the drama unfold on TV.

"Classic excuse," Liam said, smirking. "But seriously, what were you thinking? You're engaged to Kelly, and you were fooling around with Amber? Wow…bit greedy, mate."

Peter shot him a look sharp enough to cut glass. "Not helping, Liam."

I let out a sigh, looking out the window at the neon reflection rippling across the glass. "I know, I'm an idiot. I don't even know what to do. I love Kelly; but you've all seen Amber, you know how…anyway that doesn't matter. I tried to resist and…I couldn't."

There. I'd said it, the ugliest truth.

"Dom, that's not fair on Kelly," Aaron said, his voice firm but not cruel. "Have you told her everything yet?"

The words made my stomach churn. I rubbed my temple and shook my head. "I haven't told her everything. She knows about the kiss. She gave me back the engagement ring." My throat tightened, the memory hitting like a blade. "But if she knew we also slept together…" My voice trailed off.

Liam smirked and raised his glass. "Well, then you're just out of luck, bro. But you're right, Amber is smoking hot. I can see why you were tempted."

"Jesus Christ, Liam," Peter groaned, pinching the bridge of his nose. "Do you ever think before you speak?"

"What? I'm just saying what we're all thinking!" Liam shrugged, unbothered.

Peter slammed his palm lightly against the table, making our drinks ripple. "This isn't a joke. This is Dom's life, his relationship. If he truly loves Kelly, then he needs to do everything he can to make it work."

"Exactly," Aaron nodded, looking in my direction. "Even if Amber is gorgeous, that doesn't mean she's the right person for you."

Liam leaned back in his chair with that smug grin plastered across his face. "I mean, come on, Dom. You've got Kelly at home, ring on her finger, she's bloody hot…stunning, and you still went and got tangled up with Amber? If that's not peak stupid, I don't know what is."

My jaw tightened. I'd been holding my tongue all night, but finally Liam's tone set me off. "You think I don't already know that? You think I need you sitting there acting like some damn comedian, rubbing it in?"

He shrugged, sipping his pint slow, like he had all the time in the world. "I'm just saying what everyone's thinking. Don't shoot the messenger."

I slammed my glass down harder than I meant to, the thud making Aaron flinch. "You're not a messenger, Liam, you're a wind-up merchant. Every time one of us screws up, you've got some slick little comment ready. You think that helps me? You think I don't already hate myself enough?"

Peter gave him a warning look, but Liam just laughed, egging me on. "Relax, mate. If you can't take the heat, maybe don't make dumb decisions. Nobody forced you in between Amber's thighs."

That was it. The heat rose straight up my neck. "Shut the hell up, Liam. You weren't there. You don't know what led up to it, what was going on in my head. It's easy for you to sit there and judge when you've never been in a serious relationship in your life!"

His grin dropped. "Don't come at me like that. Just because I'm not playing happy families doesn't mean I don't know what loyalty looks like. You cheated, Dom. End of. Don't spin it like you tripped and fell into her."

I leaned forward, voice low and sharp. "You think I don't get that? You think I don't replay that night over and over, wishing I could undo it? You act like you've got the moral high ground, but you've never had to carry the weight of someone trusting you completely, and you blowing it."

Aaron muttered, "Alright, calm down, both of you—"

But Liam cut back in, eyes narrowed now. "Don't try and flip this on me. You're the one hiding from Kelly. You're the one lying every day. And if you actually loved her the way you claim, you'd have told her the truth by now instead of sitting here crying into your glass."

My fist clenched on the table. For a second, I wanted to swing at him, just to shut him up.

But instead, I spat the words out: "You think it's that easy? You think I can just walk in, drop that bomb, and watch her walk out of my life? I'm not ready to lose her, Liam!"

He snorted, grabbing his pack of cigarettes. "Well, newsflash, mate…you already lost her the second you unzipped your trousers. You're just too cowardly to admit it."

The silence after that was thick. My chest was heaving, jaw aching from how tight I was clenching it.

Liam stood roughly, his chair scraping loudly against the floor. "I need a smoke before I say something worse." He shoved the chair back in and stalked towards the door, followed closely by Aaron. The entire exchange had left me feeling withered, I fought the urge to follow him out and finish the argument.

Peter sighed, rubbing a hand over his face. "Hot-headed as always. You two are gonna kill each other one day."

I slumped back, staring into my glass. "He doesn't get it. None of you do."

But deep down, I knew Liam wasn't wrong. That was what stung the most. Their words clashed in my head, all the teasing and judgment. Even the pity. None of it eased the weight crushing my chest.

Peter leaned forward, his eyes steady. "Dom, you've really got yourself in a mess."

I laughed bitterly. "Tell me something I don't know."

"Should I just tell her the truth?" I asked, my voice cracking despite me trying to sound casual. "What if she wants nothing to do with me after that? I can't live with that… I can't."

His eyebrows furrowed, disbelief etched across his face.

"So, you're just going to keep lying to her? How can you even think of marrying her when can't even be honest with her?"

The words cut deep, sharper than any insult. Because he was right. How could I even look at Kelly and talk about vows and forever when the foundation was already crumbling under lies?

I rubbed the back of my neck, heat rising. "I don't have an answer for you. I just… I can't picture losing her. She's my future. She's my everything. But I screwed it up. I screwed it up so bad."

He leaned in, lowering his voice. "Man to man, you can't keep lying to her. It's not right. It's not fair. Be a man and tell her the entire truth. You at least owe her that much."

I nodded, though the motion felt hollow. I wasn't sure I trusted myself to actually follow through.

"Look, we all make mistakes," he said, his voice softening. "But it's important we own up to them. Whatever happens, I'll be here to support you, bro."

I tipped back the rest of my water, wishing it was something stronger, something to block out the ache I was feeling..

CHAPTER 12

Kelly

Dom had tried to reach me multiple times over the past few days, but I had been ignoring him. He called, sent texts, and left voicemails—I'd left them all unanswered. Every time his name lit up on my screen, my chest felt like it was being squeezed in a vice. But the silence wasn't giving me peace either. My head was screaming with unanswered questions, and my heart was too heavy to carry all this by myself. So, on Saturday, against my better judgement, I sent the text: *Meet me at the park. By the pond, where we usually feed the ducks.*

When I reached the gates, my stomach churned with nerves. My legs felt like they weighed a hundred pounds each, but I kept walking, forcing myself forward.

Dom was already there, sitting on a bench like nothing in the world had gone wrong. When he spotted me, his face broke into a smile, like I was still his, like everything was normal. That smile almost broke me, because it reminded me of the boy I fell in love with.

He stood as I approached, hands twitching like he wanted to grab me, pull me into his arms. But before he could, I threw up my palm.

"Don't." My voice cracked, but I forced steel into it.

His hands fell back to his sides. "Kel…"

"Is it true about Amber?" My voice was tiny, trembling. The words almost didn't come out, but once they did, I couldn't take them back.

He blinked, playing dumb. "Huh? What are you talking about?" He kept his voice was low, careful.

My throat burned as I said it louder, firmer. "I know about you and Amber. Is it true, Dom?"

His mouth opened, then shut. He looked away, then back at me. His jaw flexed, like he was scrambling for the right lie. Finally, he sighed and said, "Kelly… yes. I didn't want to tell you it was Amber I kissed. I'm sorry, you know it meant nothing…"

"STOP LYING, DOM!" The scream ripped out of me before I could stop it, raw and ragged. A couple walking their dog turned to look, but I didn't care.

"Amber told me everything. This wasn't just a kiss. You *slept* with her. How could you do this to me?"

His face crumpled. "Kelly… Kel, please. Ok…hear me out."

My chest rose and fell as I glared at him. "No, Dom. I'm done listening to your excuses. You had every chance to come clean, but instead you chose to treat me like a fool.

Do you know how humiliating that is? Amber looked me in the eye and told me things *you* should have had the guts to admit!" My voice came out shaking with rage and heartbreak.

He stepped closer, but I stepped back. His eyes widened like I'd slapped him.

"I have given you *everything*," I spat, my fists clenched. "All I've ever done is love and support you. And this…" I jabbed my finger at him, trembling. "This is what I get in return? A cheat for a fiancé? A liar? Do you have any idea how much I trusted you?"

Dom's face fell, his voice breaking. "Kelly, I…God, I'm sorry. Please, just… let me explain. I swear, it was a mistake. It meant nothing. You're the one I love. You're the one I want to marry. Please believe me."

I shook my head so hard my vision blurred. "A mistake? Don't you dare! You have sacrificed sixteen years of loyalty; of building a future together, for …for a *mistake*. You knew exactly what you were doing when you touched her. When you kissed her. When you *fucked her in your bed*. You knew…and you still chose to betray me."

His lips parted, but no words came. Just this panicked, broken look.

"I can't trust you anymore, Dom," I whispered, though my voice was hard. "I can't even *look* at you without seeing her hands on you. Without hearing her voice mocking me as she told me what you couldn't."

He lurched forward and caught my wrist. "Kelly, please. Don't say that. Don't do this…."

I yanked my hand free like his touch burned me. "Don't you get it? You have ruined us. You killed everything we had…it's all ashes now."

Tears stung my eyes, but I blinked them back, my throat raw.

His knees buckled, and for a second I thought he was going to collapse right there. "I was stupid. Weak. I don't even know why I did it. She doesn't mean anything to me, please, you're all I have. My home, my future, my everything."

I stared at him, my chest aching like it was splitting in two.

"You're a stranger to me now," I said hoarsely. "I don't know who you are anymore."

His head snapped up, his eyes filled with hurt. "I'm still me. I'm still the man who loves you. Please, Kel, don't erase me from your life."

I wrapped my arms around myself, holding my ribs like they were all that was keeping me standing. My voice turned to ice. "It's too late, Dom. We're done"

Then, I turned and walked away, every step tearing at me. I didn't cry this time.; I'd cried enough today, yet my heart felt like it had shattered into a million jagged pieces.

Behind me, I heard him calling my name, his voice cracking, breaking. But I didn't look back. Not once.

Dominic

I stood by the pond and watched as Kelly walked away from me, her back rigid, her steps purposeful. Every stride she took felt like a knife twisting deeper into my chest. The sight of her disappearing through the park gates felt final, like she wasn't just leaving this place, she was leaving me…us…our life.

I had finally stopped calling out to her. My throat had closed up, raw from begging and hands trembled. My mind was on fire with words I should have said, truths I should have confessed earlier, risks I should have never taken.

God, I'd never seen her that angry before. Not Kelly. Not my Kelly. She was fire and heartbreak rolled into one, and I had put that look in her eyes. I sat down heavily on the bench. For the first time in years, I felt like a boy again. Lost. Small. Completely out of my depth. My hands fumbled for my phone before I could think better of it.

There was only one person I could call: Uncle Antonio. I searched his number, my thumb hovering before pressing call.

The line rang twice.

"Domenico, Buonasera," came his voice, warm and steady. He sounded in a good mood, and guilt immediately clawed through me.

"Ciao, Uncle. I need some advice, please," I said quickly before I lost my nerve.

"What's happened?" He knew me too well; he'd heard the strain in my voice instantly.

"Kelly… she broke up with me," I forced out, my throat burning. "Because of Amber."

Silence. Then, cautious: "What do you mean, because of Amber?"

I swallowed, my mouth dry. "Do you remember she found about the kiss? Well, I didn't… I didn't tell her everything."

"Everything?" His voice sharpened like a knife. "Domenico…what's everything?"

The shame rushed up so fast it nearly choked me. I dropped my head into my hands. "I slept with her. Before she started working for us. I didn't know she would ever… God, I didn't know. It just—it just happened, and I never told Kelly."

The silence on the line was worse than any shouting. Then came the sound of his heavy sigh, like the weight of my stupidity was pressing down on him too.

"Dio Mio," he said, disappointment dripping from every syllable.

"I messed up, Uncle," I said quickly, my words tumbling over each other. "I know I messed up. I don't know what to do. I don't know how to fix this. Please, just…just tell me what to do."

"You cannot always expect to fix things," he snapped back, voice suddenly firm. "Every time you make these stupid decisions, you think you can wave your hands and make it right. The world doesn't work this way,

Domenico. Sometimes you have to live with the consequences of your actions."

His words stung because I knew they were true. Still, anger flared hot in my chest. "So, what am I meant to do? Just accept it? Just let Kelly go?"

"You made your bed, now you must lie in it," he said, harsher this time. "If Kelly does not want to forgive you, you cannot force her. You need to learn from this. You cannot keep making bad decisions and expect people to bend over backwards to accommodate you. It is time to wake up, Son."

I pushed my fingers through my hair, tugging at the roots. My body buzzed with frustration, with self-hate. "Uncle, I'm reaching out for advice, for help. But all you're giving me is clichés. Just tell me what the hell I'm supposed to do!"

His voice rose, roaring through the phone. "What advice do you want from me? Should I tell you to cheat on her with her mother next, or maybe her sister? And then we pray she forgives you? Is that the advice you want?"

"Don't…"

"No! You dug this hole yourself, Domenico. Now you must climb out. You've been busy swinging your privates around town, and now you are surprised there are consequences?" His fury scorched through me. "Wake up. You are not a child anymore. Accept the consequences and learn from your mistakes."

I was shaking now, anger and shame colliding. "Uncle, I just…"

"I don't need to hear more," he cut me off, his voice dropping low, controlled. "I have never been more disappointed in you. Your parents didn't raise you this way. I did my best to instil our values into you. And you…" his voice broke slightly "…you have distorted their memory with your actions."

The mention of my parents sliced through me like glass. My grief was always there, always sharp. Now it was being used against me. Rage shot to the surface.

"DON'T YOU DARE BRING MY PARENTS INTO THIS!" I thundered, loud enough that everyone within earshot turned around.

"You're supposed to be a reflection of your parents, whether you like it or not," Antonio said calmly, almost too calmly. "You tell me you are a man, that you want to be treated like one. But you make childish mistakes. You say you're ready to take over the business, but you can't even hold together a relationship. I am not a blameless man, Domenico, but I accept my mistakes, learn from them, and do better. If I handed this business to you tomorrow, you'd run it into the ground, just like your relationship with Kelly."

His words knocked the air out of me. My chest burned, my pride was completely shredded.

"Thank you, Uncle," I spat, bitter and broken. "Thank you for your lack of confidence in me."

And before he could say another word, I hung up.

The screen of my phone went black, my reflection faint in the glass. I looked wrecked.

I leaned back on the bench and stared at the pond, its surface rippling with the evening breeze. For years, Kelly and I had walked here together. This was our favourite bench; we would feed the ducks and one day noticed the female had little duckling with her. We would day dream and talk about the future, whispering about our wedding plans. Sixteen years' worth of memories…all reduced to rubble in a single evening.

And it was my fault.

Uncle Antonio was right. I couldn't charm my way out of this. Couldn't throw money or words or flowers at it and hope it would heal. Kelly wasn't the type to forgive betrayal, not when it was this deep. But I wasn't ready to let go either.

CHAPTER 13

Kelly

December 2024

It was finally the first week of December and there was a constant chill in the air, the kind that cut through coats and scarves, slipping straight into your bones. But even that winter cold couldn't compare to the icy ache that had lodged itself in my chest. Every breath I took felt heavier than the last, like my lungs were protesting against me.

I sighed and folded another jumper; one Dom had once bought for me on a random shopping trip. He'd held it up, grinning, saying it matched my eyes. I remembered laughing, teasing him that it was too expensive, but he'd bought it anyway. And now here I was, packing it into a cardboard box labelled with his name.

"I can't believe it's over," I whispered, my voice trembling. "It wasn't meant to be like this. We were meant to get married and start a family, but instead…"

"Kelly," Mia cut me off softly, reaching for my hand. Her voice was calm, warm, the way it always was when she tried to soothe me. "I know it's hard, but you deserve someone who will cherish you. Really cherish you."

"Yeah," Kennedy's sharper tone sliced through the room, making me flinch. She was pacing across the living room, arms folded. "Please stop crying over Dom. He's a liar and a cheater. You're better off without him."

I swallowed the lump in my throat and wiped at the tears that kept sliding down my face no matter how many times I told myself to stop. "Yes, I am. I just can't believe this. How could he do this to me? I trusted him so much."

"Honestly, he's not worth your tears," Mia said gently, helping me put some of Dom's books into the next box. She placed them carefully, almost too carefully, as though showing me that some things deserved care, even if the person didn't. "You have to be strong, Kel. You'll get through this."

Kennedy shook her head and let out an exasperated breath. "Honestly, I can't believe he would actually do this. He doesn't deserve you at all, you could do so much better."

I picked up a picture frame; we must have been Twenty at the time, Dom's arms wrapped around me as we laughed into the sun. The image blurred as fresh tears filled my eyes. "I just wish I could have seen the signs earlier. Maybe I could've even saved myself from this heartbreak."

"No." Mia was at my side in a second, wrapping her arms around me. "Don't you dare blame yourself. How could you have known? You trusted Dom, and that's not wrong. You loved him, Kelly, and that's okay. It's him who didn't value it."

Kennedy picked up one of Dom's hoodies from the sofa and threw it into the box with a crash. "Urgh, and now it's time for you to move on, Kelly. You deserve someone who will treat you with respect and love."

I forced a small smile, even though it felt weak and hollow. "Thank you both for being here. I'm really grateful. I don't know what I'd do without you two."

"Of course, sweetie. We'll always be here for you, no matter what," Mia said softly.

"That's right," Kennedy added, her voice fierce but steady. "We love you, Kelly. We've got your back."

They pulled me into an embrace, and for a moment I allowed myself to lean on them, to let their strength cover the cracks in mine. Dom had been part of my life for years, he wasn't just my boyfriend, he was my almost-husband, the man I thought I'd grow old with. But his betrayal had left not just me shattered but my friends too. Mia had adored him. Kennedy had tolerated him in her own fiery way. But his actions had left all of us broken.

A knock sounded at the door. Sharp. Heavy. Making my stomach lurch instantly.

"That's him," I whispered, my voice barely audible.

The thought of facing him twisted something inside me. I couldn't. Not when I was barely holding it together. I quickly retreated into my bedroom, closing the door softly behind me, leaving a gap just small enough to peek through.

Dom knocked again, louder this time. "Kel? It's me." His voice. That voice that once melted me now felt like sandpaper.

The door swung open, and Kennedy's low growl filled the air. "What the hell do you want?"

"Hi, Kennedy," Dom said cautiously. His voice had that nervous edge I knew too well.

Mia's softer voice followed quickly. "Dom, come in. You're here for your stuff, right?"

"Yeah. I thought Kelly would be here." He sounded uncertain, scanning the room, looking for me.

Kennedy crossed her arms, circling him like a lioness ready to pounce. "You've got some nerve showing up here."

Dom sighed heavily. "I…look, I just want to talk to her."

"Talk?" Kennedy scoffed. "You had months to talk. Now you're here to collect your junk, so do that and leave."

"Kennedy," Mia said softly, "maybe let him…"

But Kennedy wasn't having it. Her voice rose, anger spilling over. "You hurt my friend, Dominic. You're a selfish, cowardly jerk who doesn't care about anyone but himself!"

Dom was quiet. His head hung low, his hands fidgeting.

My heart twisted and I finally opened my bedroom door. His head shot up, and for a moment, our eyes met.

His were desperate, pleading, searching mine for something. Forgiveness, maybe. But all I felt was exhaustion.

He took a step forward. "Kelly, can I please have a word with you?" His voice cracked slightly.

I stayed silent. Instead, I handed him some of his old belongings, a stack of T-shirts, a watch he'd left behind. Finally, I picked up the stuffed bear. My throat tightened.

It was the bear he'd given me for my seventeenth birthday, the one he'd won at a fair after spending way too much money on tokens. He'd been so proud, handing it to me with that grin I used to adore.

He froze when I held it out. His voice shook. "I'm not taking that. I got that for you, Kel. At least keep it, it was special."

I stared at him, searching his eyes, but something was off. The words sounded tender, but his gaze flickered, restless, avoiding me. It felt rehearsed, hollow.

"I don't want anything to do with you," I said flatly, tossing the bear into the box.

He flinched like I'd slapped him. His jaw clenched as I sealed the box shut. Kennedy muttered something under her breath and stormed into the kitchen. Mia stood by the window, her chin trembling as if she might cry too.

I walked to the front door and pulled it open. "Here. Go."

Dom set down the boxes and turned to me, desperation spilling from him now. "Kelly, wait. Please. Just listen to me. I made a mistake, a huge mistake, but I still love…"

"Don't," I whispered, my hands trembling.

"Please, baby, we can fix this. We can carry on going to counselling, we can…whatever you want, tell me what you want. Just don't give up on us." He stepped closer, his voice breaking. "We were meant to get married, remember? Next summer, the vineyard, your dream dress, you want peonies, right? I'll make it happen, all of it. Just… don't throw this away."

Each word hit me like a hammer, but as I searched his eyes, I saw it again. That flicker. That emptiness. The way his mouth begged, but his eyes didn't follow.

"You're begging now because you lost control," I said, my voice trembling but steady. "Not because you love me."

"That's not true!" He tried to grab my hand, but I pulled back.

From the kitchen, Kennedy stormed back in. "Are you serious, Dom? You think you can cheat on her, lie to her face, and then show up with your crocodile tears talking about peonies and vineyards? Get out!"

"Shut up, Kennedy!" Dom snapped, his temper flaring. "This isn't about you."

"Oh, it's about me when you hurt my best friend," Kennedy shot back. "You don't get to stand here and play the victim."

"Victim?" Dom's voice cracked into a shout. "I'm not the victim! I'm just trying to make things right, but none of you will even let me explain!"

"There's nothing left to explain!" Kennedy yelled, her face flushed.

"Both of you, stop," Mia cried, stepping between them. "This isn't helping."

But the damage was done. My tears fell freely now. I gripped the door handle so hard my knuckles turned white.

"Kelly," Dom said again, softer now, almost whispering. "Please. Don't end us like this."

I looked at him one last time, and the weight of everything crushed me. "Get out, Dom."

His mouth opened like he wanted to argue, but when he saw my face…really saw it, he stopped. His shoulders sagged, and he picked up the boxes.

"I never want to see you again," I said, my voice breaking as I slammed the door shut.

The sound echoed through the flat. I slid down against the door, my body shaking with sobs. On the other side, I could hear Dom's footsteps retreating, heavy and uneven.

Mia rushed to my side, wrapping her arms around me. Kennedy crouched down too, her hand gripping mine.

I broke down completely then, the kind of sobbing that tore through me, raw and unstoppable. I wasn't just crying for what Dom had done, but for everything we'd planned, everything we'd dreamed that would never come true.

Dominic

All I wanted was to get home, kick my shoes off, pour a whiskey, and maybe let sleep take me before my thoughts dragged me under again. But when I exited the lift, I stopped dead. Amber was right there, leaning against my doorframe, arms folded, a smug little smile pulling at her lips. The hallway light caught her raven hair, casting a golden halo around her head that clashed with the devil in her eyes.

"Dom," she purred, straightening up, her voice silky and tempting. "Took you long enough."

My jaw tightened. "Amber. What the hell are you doing here?"

She pushed off the door, strutting towards me with that slow, deliberate sway of her hips, she knew got my attention. The belt of her long camel coat loosened with the movement, and I caught a flash of red satin beneath. My breath hitched, a warning pulse low in my gut.

"I couldn't just leave tomorrow without saying goodbye," she said, her gaze dragging over me. "Heading back home…but I figured you might want one last memory."

I shifted the boxes in my arm and sidestepped, unlocking the door, but I kept myself in the frame, blocking her way. "I don't think we have anything left to say. We're finished."

I put the boxes down inside the doorway.

Amber laughed softly, tilting her head, lashes fluttering. "Oh, Dom. Don't pretend you don't miss me. I know you."

Her fingers tugged the knot of her coat loose, and with a slow flick, the belt slipped free. The coat parted, revealing a red satin slip, the straps thin, the hem scandalously short. Stockings. Lace.

My throat went dry.

"Jesus Christ," I muttered, eyes snapping back to hers.

"You like it?" she teased, stepping closer. "I wore it for you. Thought you deserved a little send-off gift."

Her perfume hit me, oud and sweet vanilla, a scent that should have made my mind spin and fill me with desire. Now it clung heavy, almost suffocating.

"Amber…" I warned, my voice low.

She ignored me, closing the distance until her palms pressed against my chest. Her nails grazed lightly through the fabric of my shirt, and her mouth curved into a knowing smile. "Dom? Don't you miss me?"

I caught her wrists, pulling her hands away, but even that touch burned. "No," I said, forcing the word out. "I don't."

Her eyes widened slightly, then narrowed. She rose onto her toes, her lips brushing close to my jaw, her breath warm against my skin. "Don't lie. I can feel it, the way your heart's racing. The way you're looking at me."

And God help me, she wasn't wrong. My body betrayed me, my trousers tightened at the crotch, every instinct screaming to give in. The slip clung to her curves, the coat hanging open. Her nipples pressed through the thin fabric, silently begging to be bitten. Then the memories came unbidden, her legs wrapped around me, the taste of her mouth, the way she moaned my name.

But I forced myself to step back, creating space between us and shaking the image out of my head.

"You're wrong," I said, my voice harsher than I intended. "I don't want you, Amber. Not anymore."

"Come on, Dom," she whispered, letting her fingers trail slowly down my arm. "One night. Just one more night. No one has to know"

The heat coiled low in my stomach, my pulse thundering in my ears. For a heartbeat, I imagined it, dragging her inside, pinning her against the wall, and giving in. But then the image shattered, and the thought of Kelly crossed my mind.

"No." I spat out, forcing the word through clenched teeth.

Her eyes searched mine, and I could see her frustration rising, the desperation beneath the act. She pressed closer, her breasts brushing my chest, her lips so close I could almost taste the gloss shimmering on them. Her hand trailed down my body.

"You're hard," she whispered, a wicked grin spreading. "Don't tell me you don't want me."

I shut my eyes briefly, dragging in a sharp breath. She was right again, my body reacted, but it didn't matter. Wanting wasn't the same as choosing. And this time I was going to make the right choice.

I pushed her back gently but firmly until her shoulders hit the wall. "Amber, stop."

She blinked, stunned by the steel in my voice.

"You think this is who I am?" I continued, holding her gaze. "But you don't know me. I need you to leave."

Her lips trembled, her mask cracking. "You're lying to yourself. I know you, Dom. This is exactly who you are and when you finally admit it, you'll regret denying yourself this night of passion."

I shook my head, stepping back. "I won't regret it. The only thing I will ever regret is hurting Kelly."

The silence was thick between us.

Finally, she yanked the coat tight around her, tying the belt with jerky, angry hands. "Fine," she growled. "Enjoy being miserable, Dominic.

She gave me the middle finger, then turned sharply and stalked away.

I didn't move; I just stood there. Chest rising and falling, my hands clenched at my sides. My body still hummed with the heat she'd stirred. But I felt relief.

Now I needed a plan to win back the love of my life.

CHAPTER 14

Kelly

February 2025

The flat smelled strongly of hairspray, perfume, and the champagne Mia had popped open as soon as the two of them arrived. If I closed my eyes, it almost could've been a normal girls' night. Almost. But nothing about today felt normal. Not when it was Valentine's Day, not when it was Peter's wedding, and certainly not when I knew Dom would be there.

I stared at the black dress draped over my bed, smoothing the fabric with the flat of my palm. It was safe. Simple. Nothing flashy. I could blend in and avoid any extra attention, the way I wanted.

"You're not seriously wearing that, are you?" Kennedy's voice cut through the noise of the hairdryer, sharp as ever. She appeared behind me in the mirror; one eyebrow arched like a warning sign.

"It's fine," I said, shrugging. "I'm keeping it simple. I don't want to stand out."

Mia poked her head around the door, her curlers still clipped in. "Kelly, sweetie… you're gorgeous, but that dress is giving funeral vibes. And not in a chic way. You're going to a wedding, not a memorial service."

"It kind of feels like both," I muttered, the words slipping out before I could stop them.

The room went quiet for a beat.

Kennedy's eyes narrowed, though she tried to cover it up with a huff. "Alright, that was dramatic. But seriously, babe, you're not wearing black. Not tonight."

I frowned. "What's wrong with black? It's elegant, timeless…"

Mia disappeared back into the living room, and seconds later she returned, holding a sliver of scarlet fabric on a hanger. She dangled it like bait in front of me.

"No," I said immediately. "Absolutely not."

"Yes," Mia countered, eyes sparkling with mischief. "One hundred percent yes. This is the night for the red dress."

Kennedy let out a low whistle. "Oh, the revenge dress."

I blinked. "The What?"

"You know," Mia said, walking towards me with the dress as if I might bolt. "Princess Diana. She wore that black number after Charles cheated on her. It was bold, defiant, iconic. Your red dress is basically the same thing. This is your Diana moment."

"I can't believe you two are actually trying to turn this into a fashion statement." I groaned, burying my face in my hands.

Kennedy plopped herself down on the bed, smirking. "Fashion *is* revenge, babe. You think Dom's just gonna waltz into that reception hall with his smug little face and not notice you? Please. You in that red dress? He'll choke on his champagne."

I shot her a look. "That's not exactly the outcome I'm aiming for."

"Maybe not," Mia said gently, draping the dress across my lap. "But you deserve to feel good. Powerful. Like yourself again. He took enough from you…don't let him take your sparkle too."

My throat tightened, and I glanced down at the red satin pooling across my knees. It was beautiful. Dramatic without being over the top. And yet the thought of wearing it felt… risky. Like opening myself up to scrutiny when I already felt raw.

"I don't know if I can face him," I whispered. "I've avoided him for two months. Two whole months. What if… what if he tries to talk to me? What if I fall apart?"

"You won't," Kennedy said firmly. "Because we'll be right there with you. And if he tries to corner you, I'll pour my drink on him. Happily."

That almost made me laugh.

Mia sat beside me, looping her arm through mine. "Kelly, you don't have to prove anything to him. You're going for Peter, not Dom. And if it helps, pretend he's invisible. Tonight isn't about him, it's about celebrating love, even if it hurts right now."

I swallowed hard. "This could've been us in a few months. I should be planning my wedding; choosing flowers, cake tastings, fittings… not crying myself to sleep every night."

The words cracked halfway through, and the tears I'd been holding back all day threatened to spill over. Mia rubbed my arm, Kennedy shoved a tissue into my hand, before the tears ruined my eye makeup, and I let myself break for a moment.

"It's not fair," I whispered, voice shaking. "I loved him so much, I gave him everything. And he just… threw it all away. Like I was disposable."

Mia kissed the top of my head. "He's the disposable one, not you. Men like him are replaceable, Kelly. But you? You're one of a kind."

Kennedy nodded vigorously. "Exactly. He lost the best thing that ever happened to him. That's on him. You gave him your heart, and he stomped on it. That doesn't make you weak…it makes him an idiot."

Their words soothed and stung in equal measure. I dabbed at my eyes, trying to salvage what was left of my eyeliner.

"I'm terrified I'll see him with someone else," I admitted quietly. "Some woman hanging off his arm, laughing at his jokes. And it'll kill me."

Kennedy leaned forward, eyes blazing. "Then you kill him first…with that red dress. Figuratively, obviously. But make sure he knows exactly what he lost."

Mia grinned. "Revenge dress!"

"Stop calling it that," I muttered, though a reluctant smile tugged at my lips.

"Revenge. Dress!" Kennedy repeated, singsong, until I rolled my eyes.

"Fine," I said at last, throwing up my hands. "I'll wear the damn dress. Happy?"

"Ecstatic," Mia said, jumping up and clapping her hands. "Now, let's fix your makeup before the uber gets here."

Kennedy insisted on a bold red lipstick to match the dress, whilst Mia doused me with a spritz of her expensive perfume. The dress hugged my curves, the neckline daring but elegant. My hair was silk pressed and spilled past my shoulders in soft waves.

For the first time in months, I didn't look broken.

"You're a knockout," Mia said softly, almost reverently.

"Dom's going to faint," Kennedy said with satisfaction. "And if he so much as breathes in your direction, I'll unleash my inner pit bull."

I let out a shaky laugh. "You two are ridiculous. But thank you. For everything."

"That's what best friends are for," Mia said, squeezing my hand.

Dominic

The church smelled faintly of flowers and a mix of fragrances. I adjusted my tie for what felt like the hundredth time, my palms clammy even though it wasn't me getting married. Standing at Peter's side as his best man should've been an honour, but all I could think about was the fact that Kelly was somewhere out there in this very building.

Peter nudged me. "You alright, mate? You look like you're about to leg it down the aisle yourself."

I gave a half-hearted chuckle. "Nerves, I guess."

But it wasn't nerves. It was grief mixed with longing, a cruel cocktail. Two months of not seeing her, she was really good at avoiding me. And today—the very day of love itself, I'd have to watch her walk into this church, where *we* should have been getting married in the summer.

The church bells faded as the music began, and every head turned as the bride entered. She was breathtaking, her veil glinting under the lights, the train like a whisper of silk behind her. A collective murmur rippled through the pews.

Beside me, Peter's lips parted, and I saw his eyes glisten. He tried to hold it together, but a tear slipped free. Quietly, I slipped a handkerchief into his hand and pressed a reassuring arm to his shoulder.

"Go on, mate," I murmured. "It's ok to cry."

He gave me a watery laugh, dabbing his cheek.

I should've been smiling, caught up in my best friend's joy. But my eyes betrayed me, searching the crowd until I found her.

My heart stuttered in my chest. She was in a red dress, fitted, elegant, devastating. It hugged every curve I used to trace with my hands. Her friends flanked her, grinning and whispering in her ear, but I saw the flicker of nerves in her eyes. Her face now thinner than it had been, it made my heart sink. I was the cause of that.

Then she looked up. Our eyes locked across the room, and for one heartbeat, it was like the world had folded in half. God, she was magnificent. I wanted to look away but couldn't. My heart jolted. But then she blinked hard, looked away, and turned to her friends, as if the sight of me stung.

I forced myself to look away also, to stand tall, as Peter's bride made her way down the aisle. The ceremony passed in a blur. The vows, the laughter, the applause—all of it a sharp stab reminding me what I'd lost.

By the time we moved into the reception hall, my jaw ached from clenching it. Kelly had been moved across the room to sit with her friends; I was sat next to Aaron. We were no longer 'Dom and Kelly,' it was almost like the universe itself was determined to keep us apart..

Men hovered around her, leaning in too close, making her laugh and drinking in her smile like it was theirs to keep. This didn't surprise me; she was easily the most beautiful woman in any setting. And all I could do was sit, glass of whiskey in hand, pretending not to care. Finally, I couldn't take it anymore. I crossed the dance floor, weaving through the crowd until I found her swaying to the music, her friends cheering her on.

"Kelly," I said, my voice low.

She froze, turning slowly. Her smile fell the instant she saw me. "Dominic."

Can we talk? Please."

Her eyes narrowed. "Now? You pick *now*…at Peter's wedding?"

"Just for a minute."

She sighed, clearly torn, before muttering something to her friends and following me towards a quieter corner of the dance floor. The music thumped, but at least here we weren't drowned out completely.

"What do you want?" she demanded, crossing her arms over her chest.

"I just…" I ran a hand through my hair, searching for words. "You look… you look incredible tonight."

Her laugh was sharp, bitter. "Is that what you dragged me over here to say? Compliments don't erase what you did, Dom."

"I know they don't." My throat closed. "I just… I hate this. I hate seeing you smile like that and knowing it's not for me anymore."

Her eyes flashed. "Good. Maybe now you'll know how it feels to watch the man you planned a life with throw it away like it meant nothing."

I stepped closer, desperate. "I made a mistake, Kelly. The biggest mistake of my life. But I can fix this, if you just give me…"

She cut me off, her lips trembled before she set them firm. "You know I almost didn't come today; I Couldn't face *this*…a wedding. Knowing that ours will never happen. Do you know what it feels like, walking in here, feeling every pair of eyes on me? All our friends, all our family, knowing you slept with another woman?" Her voice cracked. "The humiliation of it. That's what you left me with."

Guilt hit me like a sledgehammer. I reached for her, but she stepped back. I tried to think of something to say to fix this but there were no words good enough.

My chest ached. "Tell me how to fix this. I can't imagine a life without you; paying for this damn mistake every day for the rest of my life."

"Get used to it," she spat, but her voice shook.

I had no answer. Only the hollow ache in my bones. Finally, I shook my head, defeated. "I can't watch you hate me anymore. I'll leave you alone, Enjoy your night, Kelly."

I stormed back to my table, heat burning behind my eyes.

Out on the floor, she lingered, her friends urging her to keep dancing. She swayed half-heartedly, her laughter gone. Then she just… stopped. Stood there in the middle of the floor, lost, hands falling limp to her sides as though the strength had drained out of her.

I watched, frozen, as she pressed trembling fingers over her mouth, trying to muffle the sob that escaped. The music played on, oblivious, couples spinning around her. Then she broke. Shoulders shaking, she turned and rushed off the floor, her friends instantly chasing after her, their eyes slicing into me like knives as they passed.

CHAPTER 15

Kelly

March 2025

It had been two weeks since the wedding. The wedding that left my heart feeling like it had been tossed into a blender and poured out again. I didn't want to admit it, but the image of Peter's face when the bride walked down the aisle, the way Dom had comforted him with a hand on his shoulder, still replayed in my head. The whole day was beautiful and heartbreaking all at once, it had…shaken me.

Now, as I sat squashed between Mia and Kennedy in the back of an Uber, I was determined to shake it off. We were headed to one of the best bars in town, and the girls were hyped, dressed to kill. Me? I was just… tired. But I wanted to let my hair down and at least try to have fun. I wasn't a big drinker, but I loved to dance, and a pretty fruity cocktail never failed to cheer me up.

When the Uber pulled up outside the bar, I plastered on a smile. The beat of the music thumped through the walls, and as soon as we hopped out, I could feel the buzz of excitement in the air. The place was already packed, people laughing, couples leaning into each other, groups of friends spilling onto the pavement.

Inside, the atmosphere was even louder, bass-heavy music, lights flashing across the crowded dance floor, and bartenders rushing around with trays of colourful drinks. The three of us made our way to a small table, laughing at nothing in particular, our voices raised to compete with the music.

I'd promised myself I would have a good time tonight. No thoughts of Dom. No thoughts of Amber. No thoughts of what had been and what would never be.

"Kelly, you're being a bit quiet," Kennedy said, giving me a look that told me she wasn't buying my act. "I think it's time we order some drinks." She led us towards the bar before I could argue.

I wasn't fooling them. I was never good at hiding how I felt, especially not from Mia and Kennedy. They could read me like an open book.

"No, I'm fine. We're going to have a good time tonight," I said, forcing a smile that felt as stiff as my too-tight heels.

They exchanged one of their knowing glances, the kind that made me want to roll my eyes. They wanted to fix me, patch me up with laughter and dancing, but I wasn't sure I was ready.

Kennedy reached across and squeezed my hand. "I know it still hurts, Kel, but don't let him ruin your night. Not tonight. Please. Let's have some fun."

I nodded, pretending her words had landed, and picked up the mojito that had just been placed in front of me. We clinked glasses, and I took a long sip, the mint and lime stinging my tongue…the rum immediately making my head swirl.

The bar grew busier by the minute. The dance floor pulsed with bodies, the DJ spinning tracks that had the crowd shouting along. I tried to focus on the energy around me, but Dom kept sneaking into my thoughts. The last time I'd seen him; his face had looked so tired. And still—so handsome it hurt. I had been cold, because I had to be. He deserved it, but that didn't mean I didn't care. How could I not? We'd built years together. Memories. We comforted each other during the lowest moments of our lives. You don't just erase that in a couple of months.

"Kel, there are so many hot guys in here tonight," Mia said, nudging me with a grin. "Should we hit the dance floor?"

I almost told them I was ready to head home, to curl up in bed and wallow quietly. But the look on their faces stopped me. They weren't letting me off easy.

"Yes," I said, pushing myself up before I could change my mind. "Let's dance."

Mia and Kennedy whooped and dragged me to the floor. And maybe it was the music, maybe it was their laughter or just sheer exhaustion from feeling sad all the time, but I gave in. I let myself go. My hips swayed, my arms moved freely, and soon I was laughing, and dancing like I hadn't in ages. For a little while, I wasn't the girl who'd been cheated on. I was just Kelly, out with her friends.

After half an hour, I was sweating, my curls sticking to my face, and my shoes had finally declared war on my toes. I waved to the girls, pointing towards the bar, and slipped away to find a seat.

Collapsing onto a stool, I ordered another mojito and closed my eyes, letting the rhythm of the music thump through me while I caught my breath.

"Wow," a familiar accented voice said from behind me, making me nearly topple off the stool. "I'm impressed by your dance moves."

My eyes flew open. "Oh my God, Erik!"

Before I could fall, his strong hands caught me by the waist, steadying me.

"Woah don't worry. I've got you," He said, smiling that easy, confident smile that made my stomach do a flip.

I jumped up and hugged him. "It's so good to see you! I thought you weren't coming until next weekend?"

"Hello, beautiful," he said, still holding onto me a little longer than necessary. His cologne hit me, sharp and masculine, and I had to force myself to step back. "I wasn't meant to, but I've got a meeting on Monday that I can't miss. And you… you look amazing. How have you been?"

I shifted in my seat, suddenly self-conscious under his gaze. "I've been… okay. Lots of changes since we last spoke, but… I'm ok."

"Really?" He sat down beside me, his knee brushing mine. "What's happened?"

My chest tightened. Of course, I couldn't hide it.. "Dom and I broke up," I admitted, my voice quieter than I intended.

His expression softened. "I'm so sorry, Kelly." His thumb began circling the back of my hand, and my stomach fluttered at the contact.

I cleared my throat. "It's okay. I'm… getting through it. What about you? Here for business right?"

"Yes," he said with a teasing grin. "Although you didn't reply to my last four emails, so I wasn't sure if I'd get to see you."

Heat rushed to my cheeks. "Sorry. I've just… been swamped."

"That's okay. I'll be around for a couple of months. We'll have time. And I remember you mentioned another fundraiser before the end of the year. Maybe we can talk about that?"

I smiled despite myself. "I'd love that. I've got a few new ideas you might like."

He studied me, eyes twinkling. Then, without warning, he stood and held out his hand. "Dance with me?"

My stomach dropped. "What?"

"Dance with me," He repeated, his accent curling around the words.

I hesitated, glancing at the dance floor. Mia and Kennedy had spotted us and were already mouthing, *Thor! Say yes!* like giddy schoolgirls.

I laughed nervously. "Sure. Why not?"

Erik's grip was warm and sure as he led me onto the floor. He was a surprisingly good dancer, moving with confidence, never once making me feel out of step. His hands rested at my waist, his eyes locked onto mine, and my breath quickened.

"Kelly," he said softly, leaning closer. "I haven't been able to get you out of my mind. I didn't push before because of your relationship. But now… now I'm wondering if I have a chance." His voice was steady, his gaze unwavering. "I know you're still healing, but would you give me that chance?"

My heart raced. My legs almost gave way. The word slipped out of me in a whisper. "Okay."

His smile spread slow and certain, and he lifted my hand to kiss it. The butterflies in my stomach turned into a full-on storm.

We danced for what felt like forever, his hands strong and steady, his presence calming and electrifying all at once. Eventually, I rested my head against his chest, listening to the solid beat of his heart. He was bold, direct and unafraid to show emotion. A man who didn't shrink from what he wanted. That was new to me. That was—exactly what I needed.

Suddenly, Erik tilted my chin up. He leaned in, and I let him, closing my eyes as his lips pressed against mine. The kiss was firm, yet tender. Gentle enough to not frighten me, passionate enough to make my pulse race. It was my first kiss with anyone other than Dom. And it was different, exciting and bloody liberating.

When the lights flicked on suddenly, we pulled apart and laughed breathlessly.

"I've been dreaming of that since I first met you," Erik murmured, pressing a kiss to my cheek.

I stared into his deep ocean-blue eyes, speechless. For the first time in months, Dom wasn't hovering in my head. There was only this moment, with this man, and the possibilities that lay ahead.

We said our goodbyes, and I met Kennedy and Mia outside, buzzing with questions and practically bouncing around me. I couldn't stop smiling, letting their laughter wash over me as I soaked up some of their energy.

I leaned back, exhaling softly. "Do you two want to stay over? We can order pizza and talk about Erik," I said with a grin.

"Oh my gosh, yes!" they squealed in unison.

Their laughter filled the car as we sped home.

Dominic

The meeting with my uncle had just wrapped, and my head was still buzzing. I sat in the driver's seat of my car, hands on the wheel but not turning the ignition yet; I stared at the dash as though it could give me answers.

Uncle Antonio hadn't just praised me—he'd handed me the most important contract we could have.

"Domenico," he'd said, voice as steady as his cufflinks were gleaming, "I think it's time you stopped hiding behind smaller projects. I want you to lead the Knightsbridge contract. A multi-million-pound account, our biggest in years. You've got the skill for it. Now prove it. Secure that contract for us"

It had been like someone set a fire under my chest. Terrifying and thrilling all at once.

And yet, the first thought I'd had was *I can't wait to tell Kelly*.

Then reality had settled in. I didn't tell Kelly things anymore. She wasn't at the other end of the sofa, sipping tea and waiting to hear how it went. I wasn't in her life like that anymore.

I rubbed my jaw, exhaling hard through my nose. The leather of the steering wheel creaked under my grip. I had to figure out ideas, a strategy to blow this jewellery house away, but the space in my head that should've been brimming with creative pitches was still clogged with thoughts of her. All I think about is her.

I finally started the car, pulling into traffic. I was halfway through mentally drafting a pitch about "heritage meets innovation" when a flash of movement outside caught my eye.

There she was. Walking into the local supermarket with her shopping bag looped casually at her wrist, her hair a glorious crown of coils around her face, wearing her simple beige coat—the one she used to throw on for quick errands. Just seeing her, knocked the air out of my lungs.

Without thinking, I slowed, swinging the car into the car park and switching the engine out. My pulse banged in my ears.

Don't be pathetic, Dom. You're not some teenager lurking around to bump into a crush.

But I was already climbing out, already grabbing a basket at the door like I actually planned to do some shopping. The sliding doors hissed shut behind me, and I was in the harsh white supermarket lights, heart pounding like I was about to commit a crime.

I found her in the produce aisle, inspecting a punnet of strawberries. I pretended to compare two cucumbers like my life depended on it. Out of the corner of my eye, I watched her tuck her hair behind her ear. That familiar gesture nearly broke me.

Finally, I cleared my throat. "Didn't expect to see you here."

She glanced up, startled, then composed in an instant. "Dom…Dominic." Her tone was polite. Civil. Distant.

I managed a smile. "Doing the weekly shop?"

"Something like that." She dropped the strawberries into her basket and moved down the aisle. I followed at a safe distance, pretending I needed carrots.

We ended up side-by-side again near the peppers. She gave me a thin smile, clearly weighing whether small talk was worth the effort. "How's work?" she asked at last, the words careful, almost reluctant.

For a second I wanted to scream *everything is shit without you,* but instead I straightened, and clung to being polite. "Good. Busy. I actually just had a big meeting with my uncle this morning."

Her brows rose slightly. "Oh?"

"Yeah. He's… he's giving me the Knightsbridge jewellery house contract. The multi-million-pound deal." I let out a dry laugh, scratching the back of my neck. "Biggest responsibility I've had so far. Honestly, I'm nervous as hell, but he trusts me with it."

Something softened in her expression, just for a flicker. She shifted the weight of her basket, looking at me properly for the first time. "That's huge, Dom. Really. I'm glad he's finally letting you show what you can do."

Her voice had that warm steadiness I used to lean on. For a second, it felt like old times.

"You think I can handle it?" I asked, too quickly. Too desperate.

Her lips pressed together, then she nodded. "You always figure things out. You're stubborn that way."

That nearly undid me. I forced a laugh, tried to play it casual. "Stubborn's one word for it."

There was a pause. The hum of chatter from other shoppers filled it. I wanted to keep her there, keep her talking, anything to stretch the moment.

"So…" I gestured at her basket lamely. "Stocking up on essentials?"

"Yeah," She lifted it slightly. Milk, bread, fruit. Comfort things. "Nothing exciting."

I grinned weakly. "Still avoiding crisps? Or do you sneak them in now?"

Her eyes flicked to me, cool again. "No, I don't."

Right. She wasn't mine to tease anymore.

We drifted into the bread section. She reached for a seeded loaf, and I was slammed with memories. Sunday mornings, her toasting that exact bread, butter melting, and her laughing because I always stole the first slice.

I clenched my jaw. "This place… it feels weird running into you here."

Kelly didn't look up. "It's a supermarket. Not exactly destiny."

Her dismissal stung, but I couldn't walk away. Not yet.

"Do you ever…" I stopped myself. Too much. I swallowed. "Never mind."

"What?" she asked cautiously.

"Do you ever miss how simple it used to be? Just… us arguing over what brand of tea bags to buy?"

For a heartbeat, her mask slipped. Then she shook her head, straightened her shoulders. "That was another lifetime."

I forced a nod, though my chest felt crushed.

We ended up queuing together, her a step ahead of me. I watched her unload her basket onto the belt: bananas, milk, that loaf of bread. Mundane items, but each one a trigger of something we'd shared. She glanced back once, caught me staring, and looked away quickly.

When it was her turn, she paid swiftly, packed neatly, and then she turned to me. "Well. Congratulations again on the contract. I hope it works out."

That polite distance again. I hated it.

"Thanks," I managed. "Really, Kelly. That means more than you know."

She gave the faintest nod. "Goodbye, Dominic."

And then she was gone. I abandoned my basket. I didn't even know why I'd picked up half that stuff. Standing there, I watched her retreating figure through the glass, the bounce of her hair.

The ache in my chest spread like fire. We were strangers now. And every polite exchange was another nail in the coffin of what we used to be.

I stepped outside, the damp air hitting my face, and saw her car pulling away. I stood there like an idiot, watching the taillights until they vanished. Inside my head, a drumbeat: *She's slipping away. She's slipping away. Do something before it's too late.*

I gripped my car keys so hard the metal edges dug into my palm. I knew I needed a plan. Something bigger than chance encounters in supermarkets. Something bold enough to show her I wasn't the same man who'd let her down. Because if I didn't, I was going to lose her forever.

CHAPTER 16

Kelly

With a towel wrapped around my head, I stepped out of the shower, padding softly across my bedroom carpet. My coils were still damp, thick and heavy, and I rummaged around my vanity for my wide-tooth comb.

"This is going to take forever," I muttered under my breath when I finally found it. I tugged it gently through a section that desperately needed detangling, hissing as it snagged, then relaxing again when the curls gave way.

My phone lit up, and my heart skipped. Erik.

I snatched it up so quickly the second towel around my chest nearly slipped.

"Hello?" My voice came out lighter, higher, a note of excitement escaping before I could reel it back.

"Hey Kelly," Erik's voice rolled through the speaker, deep and warm, like velvet dipped in honey. I closed my eyes, letting it wash over me. "How are you?"

I swallowed, trying not to sound too eager. "Hey Erik. I'm great, thanks for asking. What about you?"

"I'm great too. Just… been thinking about you a lot." His tone softened into a whisper, like he was sharing a secret with me. "Sorry it's taken me this long to call. I've been swamped with work."

"That's okay. I know how it is with these super important meetings," I teased, but my pulse betrayed me, fluttering like I'd just run up the stairs. "So, what have you been thinking about?"

He chuckled low. "That kiss. Couldn't get it out of my head. It was… amazing."

I pressed my free hand to my chest as if that would calm my racing heartbeat. "It was quite a kiss," I admitted, a nervous giggle slipping free.

"Are you still up for a date?" he asked, confidence threading through his words.

"Yes, I am," I replied, perching on the ottoman at the foot of my bed. "What did you have in mind?"

"Well, what's your favourite restaurant?"

I blinked in surprise. Dom never asked questions like that; he always picked places that suited him. "La Belle Époque," I said, smiling despite myself. "I haven't been in ages. I hope you like it."

"Oh, French? I'm open to trying new things. Tell me more."

"It's quaint, romantic, with food that's to die for. The escargots, the coq au vin…" I trailed off dreamily, already imagining the ambience.

"Perfect. When are you free?"

I flipped through my diary, though my mind was already racing to outfits. "Friday night, around eight?"

"Friday at eight it is," he said warmly. "Can I pick you up?"

"Yes, please. That would be wonderful." I couldn't keep the smile off my face, heat rushing to my cheeks.

We said our goodbyes, and I all but threw myself onto the bed, burying my face in the pillow with a squeal I hadn't made in years. Butterflies, actual butterflies, were stirring in my stomach. I hadn't felt this giddy since I was a teenager sneaking late-night calls.

Friday night arrived in a blur. I'd slipped into my new black dress, the one that hugged my figure without being too much, pairing it with red heels for just the right pop of colour. My makeup was soft but defined, a touch of shimmer at my eyes, and gloss on my lips. Still, in the car beside Erik, I found myself fiddling nervously with the ends of my hair.

"You look sensational, Kelly," he said, glancing at me while guiding us through Friday night traffic. His voice carried no hesitation.

"Thank you," I murmured, heat creeping up my neck. "You look very handsome too."

His smile broadened, and my nerves eased, replaced by warmth.

La Belle Époque was exactly as I remembered, golden chandeliers casting a soft glow, plush velvet seating, ornate wallpaper in deep crimson tones, and a grand piano in the corner playing something low and romantic. The air smelled faintly of butter and garlic, and I couldn't stop the wave of nostalgia.

Dom had always squirmed in places like this, as though the luxury spotlighted insecurities he couldn't shake. But Erik? He walked in like he belonged. It made me feel lighter, like I could just enjoy the evening without worrying about whether my date was comfortable.

We slipped into a candlelit booth, the waiter already on hand with a bottle of mineral water and some menus.

"So," I asked, once our waiter drifted away with our orders. "Do you have siblings?"

"Yes. A younger brother, he's twenty-two and graduating university this year." Erik's expression softened, and he reached across the table to take my hand, his thumb brushing lightly against my knuckles.

"That's wonderful. You must be proud." My mind drifted towards the point of contact.

"More than proud. He's my best friend," he said simply. "One day you'll have to meet him." His eyes caught mine, steady and warm. "What about you? Any siblings?"

I smiled faintly. "Two sisters. The youngest, Alexis, is twenty-three; she's sweet as sugar. And then Zara, the eldest. She's thirty-five, and we butt heads constantly. But under it all, we love each other."

"That's how it goes, huh? Arguments and love in equal measure." He replied chuckling.

We lingered there, swapping family stories, laughing about childhood pranks and awkward teenage years. He told me about how we and his brother would into lots of trouble with the locals, and I confessed to cutting Zara's Barbie's hair when I was seven. With every laugh, every small story, I felt the threads of connection weaving tighter.

Dessert arrived, a glossy crème brûlée with the perfect sugar crack, and I found myself staring at him over my spoon, surprised by how easy it felt.

"Kelly," he said softly, pushing at the melting ice cream in his dish, "I've had an amazing evening with you. Thank you for saying yes to this date."

"Thank you, Erik. It's been wonderful," I said honestly, warmth blossoming in my chest.

Back at my flat, we stood close, the night air cool against my skin. I tilted my face up towards him, my pulse drumming, my body caught in the stillness before something inevitable. His hands slid around my waist, steady but gentle, pulling me closer. My arms looped around his neck instinctively, my red heels giving me just enough lift to narrow the space between us.

"You make me nervous," I whispered, embarrassed but unwilling to lie.

He smiled, lowering his forehead to mine. "Good nervous, I hope?"

"Very good nervous."

His lips brushed mine lightly, like a question. The first kiss was soft, tentative, then another, slower, firmer, sending sparks down my spine. I melted into him, my fingers tightening against the back of his neck.

He deepened the kiss, and for a breathless moment, the world shrank down to only the rhythm of his mouth against mine. My chest rose and fell quickly, my thoughts blurring into sensation, the press of his body, the heat radiating between us, the way his hand traced small circles at the small of my back.

When he finally pulled back, it was slow, reluctant. My lips tingled, my breath caught in shallow bursts.

"Wow," I whispered, grinning helplessly.

"Yeah. Wow." He rested his forehead against mine, both of us laughing softly at nothing.

I wasn't ready for anything more, not yet, and thankfully he didn't push. He simply kissed my cheek, wished me goodnight, and let me slip inside.

I leaned against the door for a long moment after Erik left, still tasting him on my lips. My fingers brushed over them absentmindedly, and I smiled like a fool. That kiss, gentle, careful, but electric, had lit something in me I thought had burned out a long time ago.

But as soon as I let myself exhale, another thought crept in, uninvited. Dom. The weight of all our history pressing in. I hated that he could still intrude like this, like some ghost who refused to stay buried. I pressed my head back against the door and shut my eyes. Was I really ready for this? For Erik? For… someone new?

Because that's what this was, wasn't it? More than just a date. Erik wasn't playing around. I could feel it in the way he looked at me, the way he listened, the way his hand lingered on mine. He liked me. Really liked me. And if I kept seeing him, I couldn't pretend it was casual forever. That wouldn't be fair to him…or to me.

I sighed, running a hand through my hair. Did I still love Dom? God, I didn't even know anymore. What if Erik was just a distraction I was using to numb the ache Dom left behind? The thought made my stomach twist. I couldn't do that. Not to Erik. He didn't deserve to be someone's rebound or safety net.

But tonight, had felt… different. Easy. Natural. Erik made me laugh until my stomach hurt, he made me feel seen in ways I hadn't in years. And that kiss, it was sweet but full of promise. It left me tingling head to toe. Maybe I owed it to myself to stop overthinking, to stop living half in the past and half in the future, and just… be.

I guess it's okay for me to see how far this goes without fear or guilt dragging me down.

I smiled again, as I turned away from the door. Erik was good for me. And if I was brave enough to let him in, maybe…just maybe, he could be the start of something real.

Dominic

Traffic on the way home had been horrendous, the kind of rush hour that made your shoulders ache just from sitting still. My tie felt like it was strangling me, my head pounded from back-to-back meetings, and all I wanted was to get home, kick off my shoes, and drown the day with silence.

But something else had caught my eye and at first, I thought my brain was short-circuiting, replaying an old memory. But it hadn't been in my head, she was really there, just across the road.

Even now as I paced my kitchen floor, I couldn't get the sight of her out of my mind; Kelly stood under the golden glow of the awning at "La Belle Époque." The same restaurant she'd begged me to take her to once. And she wasn't alone. A man hovered close beside her, tall and sharp in a tailored navy suit. His hand rested on the small of her back, easy and confident, like he'd known her for years.

My breath hitched and my head spun just thinking about it. I ripped the fridge door open and grabbed a can of beer.

Of all places… *that* place.

The memory was vivid. I remember her begging me for months. Apparently we'd been going to the same old places, the casual pubs, the pizza joints, the cosy spots by the canal. She wanted something "special," her word. Somewhere people booked weeks in advance and dressed up for.

I'd hated every second. The décor was sleek to the point of being soulless—white tablecloths so crisp I was afraid to put my elbows down, chandeliers like props from a period drama. The menu might as well have been written in code. "Pan-seared pigeon with foraged nettle reduction." "Velouté of something-or-other." When I asked for a medium-well steak, the waiter's eyebrow nearly left his forehead.

It wasn't food, it was theatre. Ninety quid for a plate that looked like garnish. I'd left hungrier than when I arrived.

I made good money…more than good. I could afford a life of luxury; my uncle and I had done well for ourselves over the years. But I felt like an intruder, a boy…an orphan from humble beginnings pretending to belong.

But Kelly had glowed. She'd fit right in. I'd watched her sip wine, red lips against crystal glass, her laughter tinkling into the room like she'd been born in that world. She'd shone in her dress that day, her eyes bright, her voice alive with stories. And I'd sat there with my jaw clenched, hating it…hating the pretension, and the price tag.

But today, watching her stood outside that same door, she looked even more at home. And the man beside her? He matched the setting perfectly. Crisp suit, confident stance, the kind of effortless polish I could never fake.

Together, they looked like they belonged on a glossy magazine spread: *Couple of the Year, dine in fancy French restaurant.*

I sunk into the couch, draining the can before I was even comfortable. Jealousy burned hot and ugly in me; It wasn't rational, I knew that. Kelly didn't owe me anything. I was the one who'd blown it, the one who'd thrown it all away with a single mistake. And yet, seeing her smile at someone else, hearing her laugh float across the road, I wanted to slam my fist into the steering wheel. Or better yet, into *his* face.

I missed her. God, I missed her. But the hardest part wasn't the missing. It was knowing she'd moved on. Already.

Pride sat like a stone in my throat. What else could I have done? Maybe I should have parked up, stormed across the road and dragged her away from her date? I'd have looked like a lunatic.

Besides, I had no right. She wasn't mine to claim anymore.

I had to get my head into gear for work.

I had a meeting with my uncle that afternoon and it kept played in my head like a drumbeat. Recently, he'd been giving me lots of extra responsibilities; Not just stock checks or supplier calls. If I could just impress him, it would cement me not just as the nephew playing shopkeeper, but as someone who could lead. It was pressure and hope rolled into one, and it consumed every thought when I wasn't thinking about her.

I could secure my future…my family's legacy. I needed every ounce of discipline, every idea; The meeting with the jewellery house in Knightsbridge had to be perfect.

I stared at the black screen of the TV, hungry but not bothering to feed myself. Seeing Kelly today had really shaken me, she looked radiant—happy. That guy held the door open for her, and she slipped inside, giving him one of her smiles that used to belong to me. My stomach twisted and I noticed a pain in my jaw from clenching. I was jealous…no, terrified. She was slipping further away from me and if I didn't do something soon, I'd lose her forever. Maybe I already had.

CHAPTER 17

Kelly

Evening light slanted through my curtains, painting the living room a warm gold. I had my legs curled under me on the sofa, a half-finished novel in one hand and a glass of merlot in the other. It had been almost a week since my first date with Erik, and even though both of us had been busy, he'd managed to plan something small for later this week.

I found myself smiling into my wine glass as I thought of him. It was still early days, but the anticipation of seeing him again made the quiet of my flat feel lighter, less lonely.

The intercom buzzed suddenly, startling me. I wasn't expecting anyone. Setting my book aside, I padded barefoot to the receiver.

"Who is it?"

"Kelly? It's Uncle Antonio."

My heart gave a small jolt. Uncle Antonio? I hadn't seen him in months.

I quickly buzzed him in, barely giving myself time to smooth my hair before the knock came at the door. When I opened it, and there he was, impeccably dressed as always, his grey suit pressed sharp, a silk tie knotted with care. His presence filled the doorway with that effortless authority he carried.

"Uncle Antonio," I said, both surprised and a little guilty. "What are you doing here? It's so good to see you."

He smiled, but there was something tired in his eyes. "Passing through the neighbourhood after a late meeting. Thought I'd take a chance. You don't mind, do you?"

"Of course not, come in."

He stepped inside, taking a measured glance around. I realised with a pang that I hadn't seen him properly since everything with Dom unravelled. I'd ignored his calls at first, partly out of shame, partly because I hadn't wanted to be dragged back into old wounds.

I gestured towards the sofa. "Can I get you a drink? Wine? Tea?"

"Wine would be nice, thank you."

I poured him a glass and handed it over. He sat opposite me, crossing his legs neatly, and for a moment he simply studied me. His eyes lingering on my face, making me feel self-conscious knowing I had lost a lot of weight, and my eyes had now become a little hollow.

"How are you, Kelly?" he said finally asked.

"I'm fine, Uncle… I'm getting better." I tried for a reassuring smile, though it wavered under his gaze.

He sighed, swirling the wine in his glass. "I didn't know, you know. About Domenico and.... about the entire story."

My stomach tightened. I sat down, folding my hands in my lap. "I should've called. I'm sorry. I didn't mean to ignore you. It was just… hard, back then. I couldn't face explaining it all."

He shook his head gently. "You don't owe me an apology, my dear. I just wish you hadn't shut me out. I rang you because I worried…not just for you, but for him as well. And I couldn't understand why it all went so wrong."

I took a slow breath. "He made his choices, Uncle. There wasn't room for me in them."

His face hardened, a flash of disappointment crossing his features. "A foolish boy," he muttered. "I thought better of him. I truly did. You were good for him, Kelly. Steadying. And he…well, I hoped he might grow into the man I know he could be. Instead…"

He trailed off, shaking his head again.

"Instead, he threw it away," I finished quietly.

His eyes met mine, full of a sorrow that stung deeper than I expected. "Do you know, I've always seen you as family? As the daughter I never had. I pictured you both at the head of our table one day, carrying forward not just the business, but the spirit of family we've fought to preserve. When Domenico let you go, he didn't just lose you, he robbed us all of that future."

Tears prickled at the corners of my eyes. I blinked them back, setting down my glass before my hands betrayed me. "Uncle, please don't say that. I don't want you to feel as though you've lost me. You haven't. You'll always be family to me, whatever happens between Dom and me."

He reached across, covering my hand with his large, warm palm. "You've such grace, Kelly. Even after all that pain. I only wish Domenico had half your strength."

A silence hung between us, heavy but not hostile. I thought back to the nights I'd lain awake, wondering if I'd been too harsh, if I should have fought harder for us.

"I'm seeing someone new," I said softly, almost afraid of his reaction. "His name is Erik. It's still early, but… I'm happy."

Antonio leaned back, studying me for a long moment. Then he nodded. "Good. You deserve happiness. Don't let my nephew's mistakes cast a shadow over it."

We sat for a while after that, sipping wine, the silence companionable now. He asked about my work, my family, even laughed when I told him about the disastrous pasta I'd tried cooking last week.

When he finally stood to leave, he kissed my cheek, taking me in with a sadness just for a moment. "Take care of yourself, Kelly. And don't be a stranger again."

"I won't. Promise."

As the door closed behind him, I leaned against it, exhaling deeply. My chest ached with the weight of his words, but there was relief too. Relief that the bond hadn't been broken. That I still had family in him, even if Dom was gone from my life.

Dominic

I wore a path in the carpet outside Peter's office, pacing back and forth like a man waiting for judgment. My chest thudded against my ribs, heavy and uneven, every beat a reminder of the choices I'd made and the wreckage that trailed behind me. My palms were clammy, my throat tight, but still I kept pacing.

I trusted Peter. Out of everyone left in my circle, he was the one who wouldn't sugar-coat the truth. That thought alone gave me just enough courage to finally stop in front of his door, drag in a deep breath, and rap my knuckles against the wood.

Without even glancing up from his computer screen, Peter's voice cut through the air. "I was wondering how long it would take before you decided to come in." He clicked something on his keyboard, calm as ever. "What have you done now, Dom?"

I pushed the door open with a weak laugh, rubbing the back of my neck. "Wow. Am I really that predictable?"

"You're not bad," he said, removing his glasses with a dry smile. "But you're always up to something. Sit down before you wear a hole in my carpet."

I obeyed, though I sat on the edge of the chair like a man perched on a cliff. "I need to talk to you about something serious," I began. My voice cracked in the middle, and I leaned across his desk, desperate for him to understand. "It's been eating me alive, Pete. I can't sleep; I can't eat. My mind just… it won't stop."

That got his attention. He set his glasses down and leaned back. "Alright. Tell me."

"It's Kelly." Her name left my mouth like a prayer I wasn't worthy to say. "I can't stop thinking about her. Since the breakup, it's been nothing but her. Every day. Every night. I close my eyes and she's there."

He sighed heavily, the kind of sigh that comes with years of friendship.

"And the worst part?" I added bitterly. "She's with someone else now. Some…guy." I spat it out like a bad taste. "I saw them on a date the other day, he had his hands all over her. I hate it, Pete and I hate knowing I lost her to someone like…him."

"Are you kidding me?" He pushed back from the desk so hard his chair squeaked. He stood, glaring at me as though he could physically knock sense into my skull. "You had Kelly. You were engaged to her. You had everything most men dream of. And you threw it away… for Amber."

"I know!" I jumped to my feet, unable to stay still. My hands raked through my hair as I paced again, Peter's employees went silent outside the office, I tried to lower my voice. "I know, okay? This was the worst mistake…"

"You keep calling it a mistake," He scoffed, folding his arms. "Don't do that. Don't dress it up as a mistake. That wasn't some slip of judgment; it was a choice. You made a deliberate decision, Dom. And now you want to act shocked at the consequences?"

I stopped in my tracks, wide-eyed and frantic. "Don't say that. Don't make it sound final. There has to be a way back to her. Right? Tell me there's a way."

Peter's jaw clenched. "Do you trust me?"

"Yes," I said without hesitation. "You know I do."

"Then listen carefully, because I'm only going to say this once." He sat back down and gestured for me to do the same. Reluctantly, I followed, my knee bouncing under the desk.

"You need to let Kelly go."

The words landed like a punch to the gut. My heart nearly stopped, my mind reeling. "What?"

"You can't keep chasing her. You can't hold on to the past and expect her to stay frozen in it. If she chooses to let you back in one day, that's different. But right now? You have to leave her alone. She's been through enough heartbreak because of your decisions. She deserves peace. Space."

I shook my head, numb and raw all at once. "But I love her." My voice cracked on the word. Love…it sounded too small to contain what I felt.

"I know you do," he said gently, though his eyes stayed firm. "But love doesn't erase betrayal. You chose to sleep with someone else. That wound doesn't heal because you're sorry now. If it's meant to be, maybe the universe will find a way. But not because you forced it."

His words clanged around in my skull, unwelcome yet undeniable. I tried to swallow them, but they burned like fire.

"You can't rush back into this," he went on, his tone sharpening. "This isn't like when we were nineteen and you shut yourself away for two weeks after a fight. This isn't some teenage stunt. This is real. This is heartbreak—the kind that scars. You can't bulldoze your way through it."

I lifted my head, eyes narrowing. "So, what then? What do you want me to do?"

He hesitated, then leaned forward, his voice dropping low. "…Work on yourself."

My laugh came out bitter. "What the hell does that even mean?"

"You've been running from your demons for years," he said, his tone thick with sadness. He walked around the desk and sat next to me, lowering his voice further. "When your parents died, you didn't grieve. You didn't even cry at the funeral. You just shouldered the weight of everything and kept marching. But burying your pain doesn't mean it isn't there. It leaks out in the worst ways, like this. Like sabotaging the one good thing you had."

His words cut me open. I stared at him, stunned, because a part of me knew he was right.

"You're my best friend," he said softly. "You're like a brother to me, Dom. And I'm saying this because I want the best for you. Stop punishing yourself. Stop punishing everyone else. Face what's inside."

I exhaled slowly, feeling defeated. "I hear you," I murmured. "You're right."

He gave a short nod, then stood and returned to his desk. "So, what's the plan?"

I slumped back in the chair. "I don't know," I admitted, my voice hollow.

"You need to figure it out, bro." He slid his glasses back on, already logging into his computer as if the matter was closed.

I rose to my feet, heavy with confusion but forcing a polite tone. "Yeah. You're right. Thanks for your help, man. I really do appreciate it."

I reached for the door handle, but Peter's voice stopped me.

"Dom?"

I turned.

"Promise me you won't chase Kelly down. Leave her alone for now." His eyes searched mine, full of worry.

I chuckled, partly to ease the tension, partly to mask the storm inside me. "No, I won't. I promise."

"Good."

I smiled, nodded, and walked out. The door clicked shut behind me, sealing the room…and his advice inside.

But the truth? I didn't care how right Peter was. Kelly was the love of my life. She was the one, and I couldn't just let her slip away. I would do anything…anything to win her back.

As I strode down the hallway, a smirk tugged at my lips. *After all, promises were made to be broken. Maybe that's why I'm in this mess.*

Pulling out my phone, I opened my notes app: *Contact Dr. Grady this week!* I typed, searching my memory for where I'd stashed her business card. If Peter was right about anything, it was that I needed to face my past. To dig into the wounds I'd hidden and finally confront them.

I refused to keep destroying the people I loved. But Kelly? She wasn't gone. Not yet. And God help me; I wasn't done fighting for her.

CHAPTER 18

Kelly

Numbers swam, merged, and blurred on my computer screen until they looked more like raindrops on a window than data I was supposed to care about. I realised I had been staring blankly at the spreadsheet in front of me and my head had begun to pound. Today had been busy, back-to-back meetings, presentations, a barrage of emails, and a tense call with some investors who had apparently forgotten how to use polite words. My head throbbed and my shoulders ached. I was ready to shut the whole thing down and go home.

I reached for the power button when a soft knock landed on my office door. Probably a surprise visit from Mia and Kennedy, I could do with the distraction but really I felt drained from the day. I sighed, forcing cheer into my voice. "Come in!"

When the door swung open, it wasn't Mia or Kennedy. It was Erik, standing there in a perfectly cut shirt, holding two steaming cups of coffee. He leaned against the doorframe, smiling in that way that always looked a little dangerous and a little boyish all at once.

"Hey," he said, lifting the cups. "Thought you might need a break after work today."

I laughed, instantly lighter. "You are amazing. Thank you. Honestly, I definitely need a break."

"Perfect," he said, stepping inside and setting one of the cups in front of me. "Because I was thinking we could go for a walk. There's still some light out, and the park's looking good today. Fresh air, a bit of sunshine…grass. You know, things we office people forget exists."

I raised an eyebrow but turned to glance out the window. Sure enough, the late afternoon sun was beaming down, golden and inviting. A warm breeze carried leaves across the pavement. The sight tugged at me.

"That…" I smiled. "That actually sounds like a great idea. Give me two minutes to freshen up."

He nodded, as though he already knew I'd say yes.

I hurried into the small bathroom down the hall. My reflection looked as tired as I felt, but I dabbed on a bit more powder, a touch of mascara, and sprayed my favourite perfume on my neck. I pulled my curls out of the scrunchie, spritzed them with water, and shook them free until they framed my face again. I looked and felt good today; better than I had in a long time.

When I returned, Erik was standing near my cabinet, absently holding a framed photo that had been lying face down. It was of me and Dom from two years ago, before everything had crumbled. His expression was unreadable.

I cleared my throat, forcing brightness. "I'm ready!"

He set the photo back down quickly, almost respectfully, and gave me a smile. "Then let's go."

We walked side by side through the park, sipping our coffees. For the first few minutes, silence stretched between us, but it wasn't heavy. It was that relaxed kind of quiet, where you didn't feel the need to fill it. The late sun painted everything gold: the pond shimmered, children's laughter carried across the grass, and a couple of joggers passed us by.

I inhaled deeply. "It feels so nice to be out of the office. Sometimes it feels like I'm trapped in those four walls, like the air itself goes stale."

Erik chuckled. "Like you're living in a bubble."

"Exactly!" I laughed. "Like you forget there's a whole world outside."

"And when you finally step out, it's like…"

"…you can breathe again," I finished for him.

We looked at each other and grinned. That easy synchronicity always startled me, like we'd been in rehearsal all along without realising.

We kept walking, talking about work in vague terms and about nothing at all. He teased me about how seriously I frowned at my screen. I teased him back about how smug he got after finishing a proposal. Eventually, we came across an old wooden bench half in shade, half in sun, and sat down. My legs welcomed the break.

I leaned back with a sigh. "Thanks for rescuing me from death by spreadsheets. I really appreciate this."

"You are my number one priority," he said simply, brushing a coil away from my face. The gesture made my breath catch. "Always on my mind, Kelly. I figure it's my job to look after you."

My heart stumbled. My knees went jelly-soft, and I was grateful I was already sitting. For a moment, I couldn't trust my voice, so I just leaned against him instead. His chest was warm, steady, solid beneath the soft cotton of his T-shirt. The rhythm of his breathing calmed me.

We sat like that, his fingers eventually lacing with mine. He lifted my hand and pressed a gentle kiss to the back. The world narrowed to the touch of his lips against my skin, the sound of birds overhead, the late sun wrapping us in warmth.

Time passed quietly, until his voice pulled me back.

"Kelly…" He shifted slightly, turning so he could see my face. "Do you think you're ready for something serious?"

The question startled me. My eyes snapped open, scanning his expression. But his face wasn't demanding, or worried, it was curious, open, careful.

"I don't know," I admitted slowly. "I mean, I'm really enjoying us. I like what we're building. But my breakup with Dom was…" I hesitated. "It was horrendous. I don't want to rush into something and repeat the same mistakes. I just want to… take things as they come."

Erik nodded, brow furrowed but kind. "You never really told me what happened. I mean, it's none of my business, but… you seemed happy with him."

"He cheated on me," I said bluntly, twirling a coil of hair around my finger like a nervous tic. "With his assistant. Then he lied about it. I didn't hear it from him; I heard it from my friends. That's what broke me most. Not the cheating, the lying."

"Oh, wow." His lips pressed together in disapproval. "That's… horrible. I'm so sorry, Kelly. You didn't deserve that."

I gave a small, nervous laugh. "I'll be okay. I'm still healing. But I'll get there."

"Hey," he said softly, squeezing my hand. "We can go slow. As slow as you need. No pressure."

The relief that washed over me was almost dizzying. It was scary opening up again, letting someone close, but Erik made it feel possible. More than possible. Safe.

"I'd like that," I whispered. "Because I do trust you. More than I expected to."

Something flickered in his eyes at that. He rubbed his thumb gently along the back of my hand. "For what it's worth, I've got healing to do too."

"Really? Do you want to tell me?" I asked, leaning in, curious.

He hesitated, then smiled wryly. "I've had my fair share of heartbreaks. Been single for about four years now. So, you know… just quietly trying to figure out how to date again. How am I doing so far?"

I laughed, the tension easing. "You're doing great."

"Good. Because I don't want to mess this up."

"And what do you actually want?" I asked softly. "From all of this?"

He paused, thoughtful. "I want someone kind. Honest. Adventurous. Someone I can laugh with, and trust. Eventually, yeah…settle down, marriage, kids. That's the dream."

My lips parted in surprise. It mirrored my own.

"Funny," I said quietly. "That's exactly what I want. A man who makes me feel safe, who I can trust completely. A man who shares my dreams so we can build a life together."

We stared at each other.

"Like we're reading off the same page," he said.

"The exact same paragraph," I murmured.

He leaned forward, cupping my face in his hands, and kissed me. It was sudden, passionate, and it startled me, but only for a second. Then I melted, the world dropping away. His lips were warm, certain. And the electricity that shot through me left me dizzy.

He pulled away and I smiled, heart hammering, and rested my head back on his chest.

Dominic

I'd been walking down the High Street, no real destination in mind, just a head full of noise I couldn't switch off. Then out of the corner of my eye I saw Mia emerging from one of those boutique shops with a bag in hand. My heart leapt into my throat.

This was my chance.

"Mia!" I called; my voice cracking more than I wanted.

She froze mid-step, her shoulders tightening, before she turned slightly. The look on her face when she saw me said everything—annoyance, maybe even disgust. Without a word, she pivoted and started walking, fast, the opposite way.

Panic surged in my chest. "Wait…Mia, please!" I jogged to catch up with her, weaving between pedestrians. "Just stop for a second. I need to talk to you."

She didn't even glance back. Her strides were purposeful; I don't think I'd ever seen her move so fast. It was like I was invisible, like I hadn't once been welcomed into her home, laughed with her over dinner, called her a friend.

"Mia!" My voice was desperate now, passer-by gave me a funny look, and others got out of my way. "We've known each other for years! You can't just pretend I don't exist. Please. Just five minutes."

That did it. She halted abruptly, spinning on her heel to face me. The glare she fixed on me nearly knocked me backward.

"You've got five minutes," she snapped. "Use them wisely."

I swallowed hard, nerves rattling my chest. Mia was usually so soft spoken and gentle, I don't think I had even seen her angry, until today.

I hadn't planned the words, but they tumbled out anyway. "I miss her. Kelly. God, I miss Kelly so much. I can't eat, I can't sleep, I can't think straight. I know I screwed up, Mia, but I want her back. I need her back. Please help me. What should I do?"

Her arms crossed tightly, her chin tilting as if she was putting up a shield. "You don't get to want her back, Dom. You had her. You had everything, her love, her loyalty, her trust, and you threw it away. And now she's happy."

The word cut deeper than I expected. Happy. Happy without me.

"Happy? No, I know her, Mia. I know her heart. We had something real. Please, just tell her I reached out. Tell her I…"

"No." Her refusal was sharp, absolute.

I stared at her, stunned. "What do you mean no?"

"I mean," she said, her voice steady as a blade, "I won't be telling Kelly anything. She doesn't need to know you cornered me in the street with this little sob story. Because

Kelly is my best friend, and my loyalty is with her…not you."

I felt like she'd just slapped me. "But Mia… we were friends too. Doesn't that count for something?"

"It counted," she said coldly. "Until you betrayed her. Until you betrayed us. Do you have any idea what it was like watching her break? Picking up the pieces after you shattered her? You don't get to cry friendship now, Dom. You forfeited that when you made your choices."

Her words hit me like stones. I staggered back, grasping for something, anything, that might sway her. "I was stupid. I know I was. But I've changed. I'm not that man anymore."

"Maybe you're not," she said, her eyes narrowing. "But that doesn't matter. Kelly doesn't owe you another chance. And I'm not going to be the one to open the door for you to hurt her again."

I dropped my gaze to the pavement, shame and frustration boiling in my stomach. "You really believe I'd hurt her again?"

Mia's voice softened, but it wasn't kindness, it was finality. "You already did. And once was enough."

I opened my mouth, but nothing came out. The excuses, the promises, the pleas, they all felt hollow under the weight of her unwavering stare.

"Kelly is moving on. She's healing. She's found someone who makes her smile again. If you care about her at all, even a fraction of what you say you do, you'll leave her alone. Don't text her. Don't show up at her door.

Don't involve me, or Kennedy, or anyone else. She deserves peace. And you're not part of that picture anymore."

The finality in her words drained the fight out of me. My chest caved, the air heavy and thin all at once.

Mia glanced at her watch. "Your five minutes are up."

And just like that, she turned on her heel, walking away with the same brisk determination as before. This time, I didn't chase her.

CHAPTER 19

Kelly

April 2025

I had been buzzing all afternoon, making sure tonight's dinner party would be flawless. Erik and I had been dating for about a month, and I was so excited for Mia and Kennedy to finally meet him. The thought of them all in the same room made my stomach flutter with anticipation. I moved around the kitchen, double-checking everything, humming along to the soft classical music I'd put on earlier. The summer sun spilled through the windows, lighting up my flat like it knew tonight was going to be special.

I wore my favourite knee-length dress, the deep blue and white floral pattern catching the light, paired with nude sandals that somehow made me feel effortlessly elegant. My makeup was light, just a touch of mascara and lipstick to enhance what I already had, though I couldn't stop glancing at my reflection. Once satisfied, I marched into the dining room to make sure the table looked perfect.

Every piece of cutlery and glassware was laid out just right; perfection mattered tonight. Bottles of wine and prosecco chilled on ice, a platter of hors d'oeuvres beckoning my friends to grab a bite. I lit a few candles to add warmth and atmosphere. Stepping back, I took a deep breath, ready to welcome my girls.

A knock at the door jolted me out of my thoughts. My heart did a little flip. I ran a hand over my hair and did a last check in the mirror.

"Coming!" I called, trying to sound casual.

The door swung open to reveal Mia and Kennedy bouncing in excitement. They both grabbed me at once in a bear hug.

"Oh my gosh, I'm so excited! Is he here?!" Kennedy practically squealed, dragging herself inside, searching for our special guest.

I rolled my eyes at the chaos, "Hi ladies! Come in, grab a drink," I said, laughing as Mia joking pushed past me. "No, he's not here yet, but he's on his way."

"Good, then we have time to catch up," Mia said, her eyes twinkling with mischief.

They made a beeline for the dining room, drinks in hand, eyeballing the spread.

"Kelly, this is stunning. You've outdone yourself," Kennedy said, popping a grape in her mouth like she was on a cooking show.

"The décor, the music, the food… everything is just perfect," Mia added, leaning on the table dramatically, as if I had created a five-star restaurant.

I grinned, feeling that warm flush of pride. "Thank you, only the best for my favs," I said, winking.

Mia's gaze lingered on me a moment longer than necessary. "Speaking of favs…" she said slowly, swirling her glass. "You look so happy, glowing even. Does Erik have something to do with that?"

Kennedy nodded vigorously. "Doesn't she? I didn't know happiness could be contagious, but here we are."

I couldn't stop the smile from spreading. "You have no idea. He's like… the missing piece of the puzzle. Everything's brighter when he's around. Gentle, kind… honestly, he's great."

"We know it hasn't been long since Dom," Kennedy said, pouring herself another glass. "How do you feel now? Completely over him, right?"

I fiddled with the napkins, trying not to get emotional. "I'm taking it one step at a time. I really like Erik, but I don't want to rush. My heart's still tender, but I'm letting him in."

Mia and Kennedy shared a look; their smiles tinged with worry. Kennedy waved her hand in the air dramatically. "No sadness tonight, ladies, no tears. Kelly, take your time. Protect your heart."

Mia nodded emphatically. "Just… don't string him along, okay?"

"I promise I won't. He knows how I feel," I reassured them.

The conversation turned lighter as I shared stories of our dates. My friends were relentless with questions about his kisses, and I had to dodge their teasing cries of boos. They grilled me on every detail about him, including my plans to introduce him to my parents, both of them nodding sagely at the mention of my dad.

About an hour and a half later, there was another knock. I nearly jumped, spilling my drink. "He's here!" I whispered, excitement bubbling over.

I turned to my friends with mock severity. "Behave!" I wagged a finger, then swung open the door.

Erik stood there, looking effortlessly perfect in a leather jacket, collared shirt, and jeans. His hair was in a bun, which only highlighted his sculpted features. Flowers peeked out from behind him, a cheeky surprise.

I leaned in for a kiss, feeling his warmth wrap around me as he lifted me slightly before gently setting me back down.

"Sorry I'm a little late," he said, offering me a bouquet of peonies he knew I would love.

"Oh, these are beautiful. Thank you, I love them. And no worries, we were just catching up," I said, turning to find Mia and Kennedy practically frozen, jaws dropped, eyes wide.

"Ladies, this is Erik," I said, rolling my eyes at their dramatics. "Erik, meet my best friends, Mia and Kennedy."

"Hey ladies," Erik said warmly, starting to remove his jacket.

Kennedy nearly tripped over the table leg in her rush to greet him. Mia stretched her arm like she was about to take a selfie with him.

"Hi! I'm Mia… but call me Mimi. My friends call me Mimi," she said, in a tone I hadn't heard before, pure over-the-top charm. No one had ever called her Mimi.

I laughed, already seeing the chaos unfold. Kennedy, on the other hand, was circling him like he was a prize animal.

"Wow, so tall! You must be strong too, right?" she said, stopping in front of him to inspect him.

"You must be Kennedy," Erik said, clutching his jacket like a shield.

I couldn't hold back a loud laugh. Poor guy looked like he'd just walked into a lion's den. "Leave him alone! Erik, sorry—they do this to everyone new." I led him to the table. "Sit, sit, before they scare you off."

He smiled, easing into the chair. "Lovely to meet you ladies. Kelly has told me so many wonderful things about you."

Mia leaned in, grinning. "Nice to officially meet you… even if we *are* terrifying."

I placed the flowers in a vase and poured fresh glasses of wine. Hors d'oeuvres were sampled, and conversation flowed easily, Erik bantering effortlessly with my friends.

"Kelly said you were an investor," Kennedy asked. "What do you invest in?"

"All sorts really, mainly property and land," he said, glancing at me. "Lately, I've been into charity work too."

"That's amazing," Mia said. "And you're helping with Wings of Hope."

He smiled at her, nodding in agreement.

Kennedy leaned forward, whispering dramatically, "So… what's it like dating Kelly?" and winked at me.

"She's amazing! I'm so lucky," he said, eyes twinkling.

"Flattery will get you everywhere, sir," I said, nudging him with a giggle.

"He's smooth, huh?" Mia said, laughing.

"No, I'm honest," Erik said, taking my hand and kissing it. "She's incredible. I just want her to be comfortable with me. Excited to see where this goes."

A short silence fell as Mia and Kennedy exchanged smiles.

"He's amazing…"

"We love him…"

"Welcome to the group…"

"I'm so happy for you both…"

We all burst into laughter, and I bent down to peck him on the lips. "Welcome to the group," I whispered, stepping back.

Glasses clinked, and conversation resumed.

Dinner was served, and Erik proved engaging, charming, genuinely interested in everything we talked about.

By the end of the evening, Mia and Kennedy were helping me clear the table, Erik pitching in to tidy up the remaining dishes and drinks.

Eventually, my friends left, giving hugs and compliments, their energy still buzzing in the flat.

"This was so much fun, Kelly. Thanks for inviting us," Kennedy said, pulling on her jacket.

"Mia nodded vigorously. Erik is amazing, well done taking a chance," she added.

"Thanks girls," I said, grinning. "I appreciate all your advice."

"When is he meeting your parents?" Kennedy whispered to me as she walked out.

"Later this week. Pray for me… you know my dad," I said, scrunching my face.

Erik shook hands with them both, hugging them tightly. "Lovely to meet you both. Let's do this again soon."

As the door closed, he turned to me with his cheesy grin and two thumbs up.

"I think that went well," he said.

"Yes! They love you. Now you just have to charm my parents… especially my dad."

"Oh!" he said, scrunching up his face in mock horror.

I laughed, pulling him close. Tonight, had been perfect.

Dominic

Sat in the waiting room of Dr. Gradys clinic, my palms were damp, and I tried desperately to stop grinding my teeth. I finally made it to therapy. That was a word I'd avoided for years because men like me didn't need it—we carried on, drank strong coffee, buried things under work, and hoped the ground didn't split open. Yet here I was, ten minutes early, my heart rate going a hundred miles an hour.

The door clicked open, and a calm voice called my name.

"Dominic?" Her tone was professional but not cold. She gave me a small, steady smile. I followed her into the room, softer lighting than I expected, two chairs angled towards each other, and that small table with a box of tissues perched right there like some sort of warning.

"Take whichever seat feels comfortable," she said.

Comfortable. That word barely existed in my body these days. Still, I sat, leaning back like I didn't care, though my knee started bouncing almost immediately. She noticed, of course she did, but didn't say anything. Just clicked her pen and asked, "So, what brings you here today?"

The question was simple, but my mouth went dry. What do I even say? That my head was a mess? That I couldn't sleep? That every time I thought of Kelly my stomach twisted because I imagined her with someone else, laughing, glowing in a world I no longer had access to?

I cleared my throat. "Work stress." My voice sounded hoarse. "I've been under pressure with a big contract. Thought it'd help to… you know, talk to someone."

Dr. Grady nodded, jotting something down. "Work stress is a common reason people come in. Can you tell me more about what that feels like for you?"

My jaw tightened. I hated this…being dissected. But I forced the words out. "Long hours. My mind never shuts off. Even when I'm home, I'm replaying emails, pitches, numbers. Sometimes I wake up at 3 a.m. and can't get back to sleep."

"Insomnia?"

"Yeah. That, and…" I hesitated, picking at the seam of my suit trousers. "Nightmares, I guess. Not every night. But most."

Her pen paused. "Do you remember what you dream about?"

My chest prickled. I wanted to lie, say they were about nothing, just random static. But the images were too sharp. I looked away. "Sometimes it's… past stuff. Arguments. Mistakes. People I let down." My throat thickened, and I swallowed. "Other times it's things I can't even explain. Just this… feeling like I'm trapped. Like the walls are closing in."

She let the silence hang, not rushing me. That was worse, somehow, it gave space for my thoughts to echo louder.

"Do you notice anything that triggers those dreams?" she asked gently.

Kelly's face flashed in my mind, clear as day. Her laugh, her eyes when she caught me lying. The moment I knew I'd lost her. My chest burned, and I shifted in my chair.

"Stress," I muttered. "Mostly the pressure from work, I guess."

She nodded again, eyes narrowing, like she knew I was skimming the surface. Maybe she did.

"Dominic, you mentioned mistakes. People you let down. Is that something you'd like to unpack here...could it have something to do with Kelly maybe?"

The question was too precise, like a hand pressing on a bruise. I clenched my jaw. "Not right now."

"That's okay," she said, her voice calm, almost disarming. "We'll go at your pace. This is your time, your space. I want you to feel safe enough to open up when you're ready."

Safe. The word nearly made me laugh. I hadn't felt safe in years. I crossed my arms, trying to look unaffected, though my leg kept bouncing. "I'm not great at this talking thing," I admitted, surprising myself.

"You're doing fine," she replied softly. "It's normal to feel guarded in the beginning."

I let out a breath I didn't realise I'd been holding. My eyes drifted to the tissues, then back to her. "Do people actually… get better from this? From talking?"

She tilted her head. "It's not about 'better' in the sense of flipping a switch. It's about learning to manage, to heal at your own pace. Sometimes it's about finding clarity.

Other times, it's about finding the strength to forgive yourself."

Her words lodged somewhere deep, where I didn't want them. Forgive myself. Was that even possible?

I shifted again, the air in the room suddenly heavy. "I guess I've been carrying a lot. More than I realised."

The silence stretched again, but this time it didn't feel hostile. Just… there. Like she was holding it for me.

I rubbed my face with both hands. "Look, I don't want to waste your time. Half of me doesn't even know why I came here."

"Maybe the part of you that showed up today is the part that knows you deserve help," she said, her voice steady.

I looked at her then, properly. She wasn't judging. She wasn't rushing me. For the first time in months, maybe years, I felt something shift in my chest, a small crack in the armour.

Then she flipped her notepad back a few pages, "Dominic…can we talk about the past?" she asked gently.

That word, past, landed like a brick. My jaw clenched. "Okay."

"What does that word 'past,' bring up for you?"

Images hit me like shards, not just Kelly's face crumpled in disappointment, but my parents too. The last time I saw them. No, I don't think I'm ready to talk about all that yet.

"They bring up… guilt," I muttered finally. "Like I failed."

"Failed who?"

"Everyone." My voice cracked, and I hated how it sounded.

Dr. Grady leaned forward slightly, not pushing, just present. "Go on."

I laughed bitterly. "Where do I start? I had something good with Kelly. Solid. Real. And I… I ruined it. Every argument, every lie, every moment I chose pride over honesty, it stacked up until there was nothing left."

Her pen paused. "So, all this about your relationship with Kelly…do you think maybe your parents death plays a part in this?"

My throat felt dry. I rubbed my jaw. "Yeah…maybe." Admitting that felt like swallowing glass.

"Ok, we are getting somewhere. Today lets focus on Kelly," she said softly.

I tried to keep my voice steady. "She was… everything. Sharp, funny, stubborn as hell. She challenged me, called me out when I was being an ass. But she also… she had this way of making the world feel less heavy. Like I wasn't just carrying bricks all the time." My chest ached, and I let out a long breath. "And I lost her. Because of me."

"What happened?"

I stared at the floor. "Pride. Anger. I hated being wrong, hated being vulnerable. She wanted openness and I gave her walls. She wanted warmth, but I was cold to her. And when she begged for any kind of connection I couldn't or wouldn't give it to her. Instead, I pushed her away."

"And now?" Dr. Grady's voice was barely above a whisper.

"Now she's gone. And worse…" My throat burned. "She's happy with someone else. I saw her, smiling and laughing with him. In her world, I don't even exist anymore."

The room went quiet, except for my uneven breathing.

"That must be painful," she said.

"Painful doesn't cover it," I snapped, then caught myself. "Sorry. I just…yeah, it hurts. More than I thought it could."

She nodded slowly. "It sounds like you're grieving. Not just the relationship, but the version of yourself you thought you'd be in it."

Grieving. The word lodged deep, and I shifted uncomfortably. "Maybe. Or maybe I'm just pathetic…jealous of something I ruined."

"Jealousy is human," she said. "But underneath it, I hear guilt. You carry it like armour, but it's also a weight that's crushing you."

My eyes stung, and I blinked hard. "I don't know how to put it down. It's been part of me for…well since the first time I came to see you at sixteen years old."

"Hmm," she said carefully, "This just means that you are human. Grief can be freeing if you allow it to be. But if you decide to keep it locked up, you can end up becoming a prisoner in its cage.

That hit something raw. I sat there, tossing around her words trying to make sense of it, my fists clenched involuntarily.

"I just… I don't think I can let go," I admitted, my voice low.

"That sounds like trauma," she said gently. "Have you considered that part of why you're here—why you walked into this room, is because you want to stop bleeding from the same wound?"

Bleeding. That's exactly what it felt like, slow, relentless.

"I don't even know who I am without all this weight," I whispered.

"Then maybe," she said softly, "that's the work we do together. To help you find out."

I stared at her, the silence thick. Something in me cracked further, it was enough to make my shoulders slumped and my hands loosen. For the first time in months, maybe years, I felt the faintest flicker of relief? Like maybe I didn't have to carry this alone anymore.

"Maybe it's time for your healing Dominic," she replied, looking at me earnestly. Her notepad and pen lay on the table. It had been seventeen years since our first meeting, and truly I felt tired of this burden.

The word, healing, lingered in the air. I didn't know exactly what that looked like. But for the first time, I was willing to try.

CHAPTER 20

Kelly

We arrived at my parents, and I felt both excited and jittery, leading Erik up the familiar driveway, the pebbles crunching under our shoes. My childhood home hadn't changed much over the years; the white roses Mum loved were still blooming on either side of the path, and the old brass knocker glinted in the sunlight. But my heart thumped as if I were sixteen again sneaking in past curfew.

Erik's hand was warm in mine, and when I glanced at him, I caught the slight lift of his shoulders as he drew in a deep breath. Calm on the outside, sure, his expression was cool, collected, but I could feel the nerves in the way he squeezed my fingers just a touch too tightly.

"Relax," I whispered, flashing him an encouraging smile. "They don't bite."

"Your dad might," he muttered, low enough for only me to hear.

I chuckled, though my stomach was tying itself into knots. Erik was only the second boyfriend I'd ever introduced to my parents. Mum was usually sunshine wrapped in human form, but Dad... Dad was militant when it came to boyfriends, sharp as a blade, and never one for small talk, he didn't mess with his girls. I desperately hoped Erik wouldn't be intimidated.

Before I could overthink it any further, the front door swung open. Mum's face lit up like the sun itself.

"Oh, my goodness! Look who it is! Ray...they're here!" She wrapped me in her arms and peppered my cheeks with kisses before I could even say hello.

"Mum!" I laughed, wriggling slightly. "You're crushing me."

"Nonsense, you love it," she said, finally pulling back to look me over. "You look stunning. Radiant! Oh, my heart!"

"Hi, Mum," I said, hugging her again. "I love your hair, the new cut suits you." Then, stepping aside, I introduced, "Mum, this is Erik."

Erik handed her the champagne he'd been carrying. "It's lovely to finally meet you, Mrs. Bamford. Kelly's told me so much about you."

"And aren't you a charmer," Mum beamed, taking the bottle. "And handsome too. Come in, come in." Without hesitation, she gave him a hug, and Erik looked briefly startled before recovering, hugging her back politely.

She ushered us inside. "Your father's in the garden. He insisted on grilling today of course, you know how he is with that barbecue." She rolled her eyes affectionately and bustled off toward the kitchen. "I'll grab some drinks."

My pulse quickened again as I led Erik towards the back doors. The familiar scent of charcoal hit me before we even stepped outside. There was Dad, sleeves rolled up, tongs in one hand, flipping steaks while the old radio blasted a Marvin Gaye classic.

He looked up as we approached. "There's my baby girl," he said, setting the tongs aside and wiping his hands on a cloth. He hugged me with one arm, firm and protective.

"Hi Daddy," I murmured, giving him a kiss on the cheek.

"This is Erik… my boyfriend," I added, my throat dry.

Erik extended a hand. "It's a privilege to meet you, Mr. Bamford. Thank you for having me."

Dad eyed him for a beat longer than was comfortable, then took his hand in a grip that made Erik's knuckles whiten. "Welcome," he said curtly, before turning back to the steaks.

I shot Erik a quick smile and squeezed his back, whispering, "See? No biting."

He whispered back, "I think he's sharpening his teeth."

I smothered a laugh.

Mum soon reappeared, carrying a tray of drinks and crisps. "Right, settle yourselves, the food's nearly ready."

We sat at the garden table, Erik complimenting the garden's layout. "It's magnificent. Feels like something from a magazine spread."

Mum waved off the praise. "Oh, thank you, dear. Please call me Andrea. None of this 'Mrs. Bamford' business."

"You may continue to call me Mr. Bamford," Dad interjected without turning from the grill. "Or General."

"Dad!" I groaned, heat rushing to my cheeks.

He finally turned, the corners of his mouth twitching. "Fine. Mr. Bamford will do."

Erik grinned politely. "Of course, Mr. Bamford."

Mum rolled her eyes dramatically. "Ignore him. Tell us about yourself, Erik. Kelly doesn't share nearly enough details."

Erik sat straighter, and for the next few minutes he told them about his childhood, his job, his family. He was articulate, honest, and charming, I could see Mum soaking up every word. Dad, meanwhile, scrutinised him as though assessing a new car he was about to purchase.

Finally, Dad leaned forward. "What about your past relationships? What were they like?" His voice carried just a shade too loud, too deliberate.

Erik hesitated. "Well, my last…"

"Ray," Mum cut in smoothly, pointing at the grill. "I think your steaks are smoking."

Dad whipped around, muttering under his breath as he checked the meat. I caught Mum's eye and mouthed, "Thank you."

She winked at me.

Erik let out a tiny sigh of relief, massaging the back of his neck.

When the food was served, the tension eased. Mum sang along to the music, Dad grumbled about overcooked steaks, and Erik gamely joined in when "Ain't No Mountain High Enough" came on. Before long, even Dad cracked a grin.

By dessert, Erik and Dad were in a mock-serious debate about football teams. "That's not a real team," Dad scoffed. "Supporting them is like backing a donkey in a horse race."

"Better a loyal donkey than a fickle stallion," Erik countered, and everyone burst out laughing.

For the first time that day, Dad actually laughed too.

When it came time to leave, we lingered at the door. Mum hugged us both fiercely. "Don't stay away too long, Kelly. We're only twenty minutes down the road, you know."

"I know, Mum. I'll come by more often, I promise."

Then, to my shock, Dad shook Erik's hand firmly and clapped him on the shoulder. "It was good to meet you. Next time, maybe I'll convince you to support a real football team."

"I'll look forward to it, Mr. Bamford," Erik said warmly.

Walking back to the car, Erik laced his fingers through mine.

"You did brilliantly," I whispered, still buzzing. "He's usually impossible, so it's a good start."

Erik smirked, confidence fully restored. "I told you; I wasn't worried."

I laughed, tiptoeing up to kiss him. "You're amazing. I knew they'd love you."

Dominic

Today's workout session with my personal trainer was amazing. Muscles loose, sweat cooling on my skin, and that steady rush of endorphins making me feel…stress free, for the first time in months. Between the gym and Dr. Grady's sessions, I'd been building a routine that felt good. Clean. Balanced. My flat had become a sanctuary lately; it still felt too quiet, but it was finally uncluttered and peaceful. Exactly what I needed.

I headed towards my car, stretching out my shoulders as I walked, when a familiar scent caught my attention…and then she came into my line of view.

She was leaving the yoga studio, mat tucked under her arm, water bottle swinging by her side. She looked as gorgeous as ever. Even with her hair slightly mussed from class, she managed to pull off effortless grace. A small smile played on her lips and, for a second, my heart skipped a few beats.

I thought about changing direction, saying a quick hello. Surely, it would be harmless. It wasn't like I'd be chasing her down. And if I didn't say anything at all, wouldn't that be even weirder? Pretending she didn't exist?

But before I could move, her smile widened, except not for me.

A familiar tall, broad-shouldered man strode towards her with the kind of confidence you couldn't fake. Blond, sharp-jawed, that too-handsome-to-be-real type. He wrapped his arms around her waist like it was the most natural thing in the world, and she tilted her face up to him with that same smile…brighter now. Then he kissed her—so this is Erik.

And she kissed him back. Fingers sliding through his hair.

It felt like someone had swung a sledgehammer into my ribs. I froze; breath caught in my throat. What the hell was I expecting? I guess their date had gone well that night. Kelly was the kind of woman men dreamed about, and this guy? He looked like he'd stepped straight out of a Calvin Klein billboard.

I slowed my pace, ready to slip past unnoticed, but then I heard her voice.

"Dom?"

I turned, pasting a puzzled look on my face, praying she couldn't see the storm inside me.

"Hey, Kelly," I managed, waving like it was casual. My throat felt tight. "How have you been?"

"I've been good, thanks." Her eyes softened. Then she turned slightly towards him. "This is Erik, my boyfriend. Erik, this is Dominic."

Boyfriend. The word landed like a punch.

The man extended his hand, smiling like he owned the room even though we were just standing on the pavement.

"So, you're the infamous Dom," he said.

"It's Dominic," I corrected automatically, tightening my grip in the handshake.

His smile didn't falter. If anything, it widened. "Dominic it is. Pleasure."

I forced my own polite smile, but inside, I was taking inventory, chiselled chin sharp enough to cut glass, broad shoulders that probably filled out a suit perfectly, ocean-blue eyes that seemed annoyingly genuine. I straightened, trying to match his height, but he still had a couple of inches on me.

"Nice to meet you," I said flatly, before glancing back at Kelly. "Good to see you, Kelly. Enjoy your session?"

"I did," she said brightly. Her voice—it always did something to me. Familiar and grounding, like home. And God, I missed it. I missed her. "The classes here are really good."

"How's work?"

That jolted me. Work. Always the safe topic.

"Busy… but fine," I said, shifting from one foot to the other. My tongue felt clumsy. Vulnerable wasn't a look I liked.

"Work is always time-consuming, isn't it?" Erik chimed in, his arm around her waist, relaxed as ever. "I wish we all had more hours for leisure. Balance is important."

His tone was easy, friendly even, like we were two guys at the pub rather than competitors circling each other. And to my surprise, there was no edge in his words. Just… sincerity. The confidence of someone who didn't need to prove anything.

"How are you liking the gym, Erik?" I asked, though the words tasted bitter. "It's one of the best in London. Kelly and I have had a joint membership since it opened."

"Yes, it's been excellent," he said, still smiling. "Actually, I'm one of the main investors for the London branches. It's nice to hear good feedback from regulars."

Investor. Of course he was. The guy probably had a portfolio the size of a small country.

I caught a flicker of something on Kelly's face, her smile dimming just for a second. Had she noticed the tension running through me? The subtle flare of my nostrils, the pulse thudding at my temple? I tried to mask it, but I wasn't sure if I pulled it off.

"Anyway," I said quickly, desperate to retreat before I lost whatever composure I had left. "Lovely seeing you, Kelly. And you too, Erik. I should get going…I've got calls to make."

I shook their hands, hers soft and achingly familiar, his firm and warm. Then I walked to my car, fighting not to look back.

Once inside, the silence pressed in. My reflection stared back at me in the rear-view mirror, eyes darker than I remembered. I closed them and focused on my breathing, slow inhale through my nose, long exhale out my mouth, just like Dr. Grady taught me.

But it didn't stop the ache. Didn't stop the reel of images in my head, Kelly's smile, the way she fit so easily in someone else's arms, and how alive she looked there.

I leaned back, exhaling through clenched teeth. The grief cut deeper than I'd expected. Not just for the love I'd thrown away, but for everything else: her friendship, her support, her touch.

Her heart.

CHAPTER 21

Kelly

June 2025

Today was our three-month anniversary, and somehow that fact alone made my stomach knot. Three months shouldn't feel like such a milestone, but with Erik, everything always felt heightened, like he had a way of turning even ordinary moments into events worth remembering.

The car he'd sent to pick me up was parked neatly outside my building when I came down, a sleek black Bentley Flying Spur that looked like it belonged to a movie set rather than my reality. The driver, in his sharp suit and polished shoes, opened the door for me like I was someone important. I murmured a "thank you" as I slid into the buttery leather seat, inhaling the faint scent of new car mixed with sandalwood.

It was ridiculous how quiet the ride was. The windows must have been soundproofed, because the chaos of London—the horns, the chatter, the constant rush, faded into a low hum. My building was behind me, and I suddenly felt like I was being ferried into a world that wasn't mine.

I fiddled with my clutch in my lap, glancing out the tinted windows. The city lights danced in streaks, reflecting back at me, and I found myself thinking: why am I nervous? Erik wasn't new to me. He'd been in my space, at my flat, on my sofa with takeout containers and Netflix. He'd laughed with me in baggy hoodies, kissed me in the messy warmth of my kitchen.

But tonight was different. Tonight, I was stepping into *his* world. And something in me worried that his world was too far from mine.

When the car pulled up, I had to crane my neck back just to take in the building. Glass, steel, lights glittering like a crown at the top. The kind of place I'd passed on the Tube and thought, *I wonder who lives up there?* Now I knew: Erik.

The concierge greeted me the moment I stepped inside, as if he'd been waiting. "You must be Miss Bamford. Good evening. Mr Andersson is expecting you." He didn't even need me to say Erik's name. My cheeks warmed.

He used a sleek black key card in the elevator, pressing a button that simply read "PH." I clutched my bag tighter, trying to look casual, but inside I felt like a schoolgirl being allowed backstage for the first time.

When the doors slid open, Erik was already there, grinning, holding a bouquet of pink peonies, my favourite. He remembered. He always remembered everything. I melted a little as he swept me up into his arms, strong and effortless, and I laughed into his chest.

"You're unbelievable," I said, inhaling the flowers. "Only for you," he replied, with that warm confidence that made everything sound like a promise.

Inside, the apartment was exactly what I expected and nothing like I expected all at once. Cream marble floors stretched across an open plan space, polished so well the lights shimmered in them. Floor-to-ceiling windows wrapped around the living room, giving a view of the whole city, a twinkling sprawl that made me feel both small and special at the same time. The furniture looked like it belonged in a magazine—sleek Italian leather sofas, low glass tables, a fireplace that looked far too beautiful to ever be used.

My heels clicked softly as I followed him through the space. The kitchen gleamed with chrome fittings, spotless and professional, like he had a chef tucked away somewhere.

The dining table had been set like we were at a five-star restaurant. Candles flickered between elegant place settings, and I tried to keep my jaw from dropping. Had he done this himself? Or had staff swirled in here earlier, perfecting everything down to the last napkin fold?

We ate, we laughed, we drank champagne that never seemed to run dry. He made me feel like I belonged, even though every detail around me whispered that I didn't. Servers appeared like ghosts to clear plates when we moved to the sofa, and I realised, with a guilty pang, that of course he hadn't done this alone.

Still, he'd thought of everything. He'd wanted tonight to be perfect for me.

The problem was me.

When he leaned in later, his lips brushing mine with a tenderness that quickly deepened into hunger, my chest clenched. It wasn't that I didn't want him. I did…God, I did. But want wasn't the same as *ready*. My mind buzzed with warning bells, my heart racing like prey.

"Wait…Erik, hold on." My voice came out shaky. I stood, desperate for space. I slipped into the bathroom, locking the door behind me.

The mirror didn't lie. My cheeks were flushed, my eyes wide, and I looked like someone about to run. I gripped the sink, trying to reason with myself. But my body didn't care. The idea of crossing that line made my stomach twist…what did this mean?

After what felt like forever, I re-emerged. He was waiting, calm, his smile unfaltering. "Shall I take you home?" he asked gently.

Relief and shame tangled in me. "Yes, please."

The car ride back was thick with silence. The kind where you think of a thousand things to say but can't push a single one out. I stared at the city lights as they blurred past, guilt gnawing at me.

When we reached my flat, Erik's voice broke the quiet. "Can I come up for a few minutes?" His expression was unreadable.

I hesitated. Why? What did he want to say that couldn't be said in the car? But I nodded, and we went upstairs.

Inside, I busied myself making coffee just to fill the silence. By the time I sat beside him, I could feel his nerves vibrating in the air.

"Kelly," he began, his hand finding mine. His eyes were bright, almost fierce. "I know it's only been three months. But these three months…they've been the best of my life. When you're around, everything feels lighter. I don't want to pressure you; I know your last relationship ended badly. I just want you to trust me and know that you're not just any woman to me. I think I'm falling for you, no—I know I'm falling for you. And I don't want anyone else. I'm ready to move forward, but…I don't know if you are. I don't know where I stand."

His chest rose and fell as if he'd sprinted.

I stared at him, heart hammering. *Falling for you.* The words hung in the air, heavy, shimmering, terrifying.

"I…" My throat closed up. Tears burned behind my eyes. "Erik, I care about you. I really do. But I'm not ready for that. Not ready to say those words, and not yet ready to be intimate. I'm still figuring out how I feel, I'm sorry. I just don't know what to…"

My voice cracked. The tears slipped before I could stop them.

A shadow flickered across his face, hurt, maybe disappointment—but then he forced a smile, squeezing my shoulders. "Hey. It's okay. No pressure. I just wanted you to know how I feel. Maybe one day you'll feel the same. Please don't cry."

He pushed a tissue box towards me. His voice was calm, but I caught the flicker of something beneath it, a bruise forming where my words had landed.

I wiped at my cheeks, ashamed. "I don't know what's wrong with me."

"There's nothing wrong with you," he whispered, pulling me into his arms. His warmth enveloped me, his hand rubbing circles on my back as my sobs shook through me.

But even as I clung to him, I couldn't escape the gnawing thought: I was holding back. And no amount of luxury, no breathtaking views, no whispered confessions could change the fact that my heart wasn't quite ready to leap.

Dominic

Peter's 34th birthday was going amazing, it felt great to forget about work and hang out with friends—the music was loud, drinks flowing, jokes flying around like we were all back at school again. But I 'm not all there, not properly.

I laughed in the right places, remained as charming as ever and even give a speech. But my heart wasn't in it, my head isn't either. It's elsewhere, with her. It's always with her. I stepped out of the bar for some fresh air, hoping the breeze might clear my head. It doesn't, if anything, it just blows memories of her back into my face.

Leaning against the wall, I pulled out my phone. Her name is already at the top of my chats under *favourites.* So many unread and unopened messages. All blue ticks and no replies. *Maybe I'm blocked, I deserve to be blocked.* My thumbs hover over the screen like they had everyday this past week.

Hey. Just checking in, you up?

Sent. I watched the screen like an idiot, hoping the little typing bubbles would pop up. They don't. *Yeah, she's definitely blocked me.* I let out a sigh and slipped the phone back into my jacket pocket. I really should leave it here and leave her alone. But I can't, not tonight, and definitely not ever. Thoughts of her plague my waking and my sleeping moments. It's almost like I can't function; I can't truly be me without her.

I felt like a shadow or an intangible entity, formless and void. She was—is my light, my anchor… my lighthouse. And I destroyed it all. But in my heart I feel like tonight might be different, like I'm at a crossroad and whatever happens tonight will shape everything. I just know it. I need to see her, to look into her eyes. I need to fix this, tonight.

Muscle memory taking over my body, and I began to walk. Hopefully, I could use the time to gather my thoughts, run through every possible version of how tonight could play out. I know I have to brace myself for the worst-case scenario, but I refused to dwell on that. The alternative—saying nothing or walking away and letting silence choke out every hope we might have, that scared me more.

I passed the café on the corner, the one she used to drag me to every chance she got.

"Dom, try something new for once," she'd say, eyes wide with fake innocence as she ordered me an oat milk matcha. It tasted like grass, and I spent the entire time there brooding and grumpy. She was just so happy to be spending time with me. *I'm such a fool.*

The tree just outside the park still had out initials carved into its side. *D + K, 4eva*, I smiled as I passed it. I had carved it on a drunk summer night with my pocketknife. I remember the squeal of excitement she let out when I agreed to her suggestion. That was the summer before she went off to university, we were so nervous about the distance. But we survived it, and it only made us stronger.

She was colour and chaos and warmth, I craved her presence, and she craved mine. And just like that, I ruined it. I keep trying to convince myself that I made just one mistake. That it was a meaningless stupid slip. But the truth? I'd felt her pulling away. No…I pushed her away, maybe years before this.

Maybe as far back as when my parents passed. I should have tried harder, maybe listened more, and taken therapy seriously, anything. I should've been the man she needed and deserved, not some ego driven idiot with a point to prove. But I allowed myself to drown in my emotional constipation and instead of being vulnerable with the woman I love, I wanted to feel…I don't know. Something, anything. And I did—for one night and I lost everything that mattered. I had arrived outside her apartment building and braced myself.

Everything looked the same, the potted plant in the foyer, the same flickering lights on the lift buttons, but it also felt foreign, cold. Like the warmth and familiarity, I once felt in this space had packed its bags and gone with her smile and possibly her heart.

Her front door also looked the same. I knock. No answer, maybe *I should leave.* I hear footsteps, heavy ones. Then the door swings open.

"Oh? Hey Dom?"

My mood instantly shifts; her new Swedish guy is stood in front of me. I stepped back a bit, he's tall, taller than me. And still as handsome as the last time I saw him. My jaw and my fists instantly clench.

"It's Dominic. What are you doing here?" annoyance drips from my voice.

"Evening to you too," He chuckled and ran his fingers through his luscious blonde locks. *I could seriously punch him right now.*

"Where's Kelly?"

"She's really not in the mood to chat right now, Dom. Go home."

"I'll ask her myself."

"You've already done enough mate. Don't make this worse."

"Erik, who is it?" I heard Kelly's voice, somewhat muffled.

My chest flipped and I instinctively stepped forward, but Erik broadened his shoulders and blocked my path. She appeared behind him a few moments later, wearing a hoodie…my hoodie and grey joggers. Her hair was piled high in a messy bun, her eyes were red and puffy, and I noticed the remnants of her liner. She had been crying, my heart cracked open.

"Kelly," I breathed.

She blinked when she saw me. Just stood there, no smile, no "hi." Nothing.

"What's going on? Are you okay?" I glanced at Erik and then back at her.

"I'm Fine."

"You don't look fine."

"What do you want Dominic?"

Ouch. But I barely notice her use my full name, a flip switches, and I turn to Erik.

"What the hell did you do to her?"

"Hey, calm down Dom, she…"

"Don't flipping call me Dom. Why is she crying? What did you do?" I squared up to him, my voice rising.

"You're projecting," He replied, stepping closer and lowering his voice. "You hurt her. You. Not me. So don't come here acting like some protector."

"No, she looks like she's been crying for hours."

"Guys, please stop this."

"Yeah it's called healing. But somehow you keep making it harder." He snapped now standing in the hallway with me. Kelly pulled unsuccessfully on his arm to get him to go back into her flat. The sight made my blood run cold and Erik's words stopped me in my tracks.

"Seriously, is everything okay?" I turned to Kelly and tried to catch her eyes.

"I told you, I'm fine. Please just go," she sighed, obviously fed up all the way to her bones.

"No not until we talk. I need to—I *have* to talk to you," I blurted out desperately, realising this isn't going the way I had imagined.

"You can't just show up here in the middle of the night, this isn't going to fix anything." Arms crossed and finally letting go of Erik, but she still hadn't looked me in the eye.

Erik finally decided to give us some privacy, but he bent down, giving Kelly a kiss on her cheek before he does. A final punch in the gut for me before he retreated into the flat. *What an ass!*

"I'm sorry." I said breathlessly, grabbing her left wrist. "I know I said it already, and I've sent so many texts and voice notes…but that's not enough. I need you to see it. To feel my apology."

I knew I was rambling, but I didn't care. This was make or break, so I had to give it everything.

"You cheated on me, Dom."

"I know."

"I don't think you do. It wasn't just a silly kiss; you made everything we shared a lie. Our entire life…existence together."

A lump lodged in my throat, and I felt myself retreating, I had to face this and own what I've done. I let go of her wrist.

"Do you have any idea what that did to me? Sixteen years, you wasted sixteen years of my life. And I will never get that back."

She swallowed hard and I realised it's my turn to speak but I have nothing, so I froze.

"It meant nothing…" I replied weakly.

"It meant *everything*," she cut in. "Because it broke *everything*."

"I miss.."

"STOP!" she finally looked at me, but these aren't the same loving, warm eyes I'm used to. They are cold and distance, like I was a stranger. And I guess to her that is exactly what I am now.

I swallowed hard, trying to keep it together.

"Even now you don't get it. It's goes back way before your cheating. I bet you can't even pinpoint the exact moment you changed. But I can and this isn't the Dom I fell in love with. I refuse to accept a counterfeit, and I refuse to keep doubting and losing myself whilst I search and plead for the real you."

Tears slip down her cheeks now, but her voice remains steady. The silence is deafening. Erik slowly approached the door, wrapping his arm around her shoulders.

"You need to leave, Dom," she said, backing away and shutting the door. "Goodnight."

I stare at the closed door for a moment before I take a deep breath and turn around. My feet carried my regret as I slowly walked down the stairs and into the cool night air. Every step was a new emotion, bitterness, rage, but mostly shame. Kelly Bamford was gone. I shoved my hands into my jacket pocket and head back to the bar.

CHAPTER 22

Kelly

The lingering heat from Dom's grip on my wrist still buzzed in my veins, like a dull ache. Still facing the door, I tried to compose myself and catch my breath. The sudden jolt of his presence had stolen the air from the room, leaving everything cold and heavy in its wake. He used to be so familiar to me, he used to be all that mattered, and my heart hammered a frantic rhythm as I realised that now he was *just a guy I dated.*

Trying to steady myself, I turned and faced Erik. Sweet, kind Erik, his eyes, quiet and searching were fixed on me. I swallowed hard, struggling to find words that wouldn't make this day any worse. Our three-month anniversary had well and truly gone down the drain.

"Erik," my voice was low and tentative as I walked towards him. "I'm so sorry about today, Dom, everything. Our entire night has been ruined; I didn't expect Dom to just pop up unannounced…so random."

He let out a small awkward chuckle but didn't say a word. The weight of the silence settled on my shoulders, heavier than I'd expected. I knew I didn't have the correct words to save the evening, and my eyes flickered to the floor, arms now wrapped around my body as his gaze undressed me, exposing some secret I was too scared to admit.

"Kelly, he still loves you." His statement was said as a matter of fact, it was gentle like a caress, but his eyes and body language were filled with pain and disappointment.

"I know but…" my voice barely a whisper as I tried to keep the trembling away. "..but that doesn't matter anymore."

His eyes narrowed, searching mine like he was trying to find the hidden truth behind my hesitation.

"And what about you? Do you still love him?"

The question hit me like a splash of cold water to the face. I blinked at him, trying to hold back the flood of memories that surged in uninvited. I looked away, my hands fidgeting nervously. I never would have thought this question would feel so big or so dangerous to answer. I knew exactly how I felt about Dom, but I couldn't allow myself to admit that.

"No, I don't." I shook my head and trained my voice to be stable; it took almost all of my willpower. "But I still care for him, and I think I always will."

"I get it, he was a big part of your life." Taking a cautious step towards me, he held my hands in his and lowered his voice. "I just want us to be honest—really honest. No pretending, no hiding. If this is going to work, we need to set clear boundaries, lay out what we expect of each other."

"I agree, I want that too." I looked up into his eyes and felt nothing but comfort and relief. He was someone who understood this mess, the fear, the confusion and my need to figure it out in my own time.

"If anything changes, we say it. We don't keep secrets or lie to each other." I felt a little bit deceptive but I'm not entirely sure why. I'm definitely still pissed off and I guess a part of me even hates Dom. But I'm not hundred percent certain if I love him or not, maybe I should have said that instead of saying *No, I don't.*

But now I looked at Erik and he's stood smiling at me, the corners of his eyes crinkled, making my heart flutter. I know I don't love him, but I could. He was perfect, and he ticked all the boxes. The only thing missing is that he isn't Dom. I really need to figure this out.

"Good, because I'm really enjoying what we have. Even if it is messy."

"Messy, that's definitely the right word," I laughed weakly and snuggled into his chest.

"It's getting really late; I should give you some space. Tonight, has been a lot." He gave me a polite smile, but I don't miss the uncertainty that flashed briefly across his face.

"Ok," I whispered, feeling almost completely drained after the events that took place. "Thank you for always looking after me. It means so much."

"It's my job and my honour." He gently lifted my chin with his fingertips, his touch feather-light but steady. My breath hitched the moment his lips met mine, the kiss is soft, warm and tentative; like he was trying to tell me something without uttering a single word. I felt the subtle tremble of his breath as it mingled with mine. I placed my palm on his chest and felt the faintest pulse of his racing heart underneath his skin. It's like a quiet promise of something good, something safe. But my heart felt twisted, I want to lean into him, to get lost and surrender to this moment, to feel connected.

Yet a shadow lingers—memories of Dom, flashes of our love still tangled in my mind. I decided to shut that door as Eriks hands caress my back and cradle my nape. His lips part mine and I remained there, captured, breathless and lost in the moment. He pulled away suddenly, turning and walking out the front door.

I stood, frozen in the middle of my flat wondering what the heck had happened today. Trying to catch my breath, I looked around the empty room like it was about to swallow me whole. Then I'm overtaken by a whirlwind of emotions as I walked towards the door to lock up for the night.

Dom's voice replayed in my mind; sharp and desperate. Why does he still have this hold over me? He's destroyed me in every way imaginable. But the way he looked at me—like I was the answer to something he couldn't find anywhere else. Our love had been perfect, it was once a blessing, a dream or a wish come true. But now it was a waking nightmare. I felt cursed to suffer this heartbreak forever; was there no way I can ever recover from this?

I should have known better, Dom had always been charming. He was very good at making anyone seem like they were the only person in the room. I know that holding on to him was like clutching at smoke, he had always been his own man. He was stubborn, making his own mind up and hating change. At one time I actually believed he would change for me…but now I know that was a deception I fed myself. I can't continue to be so stupid.

And then there was Erik; he stood there with his open heart and hope dripping from every word he spoke. He doesn't deserve this; to be waiting for me to figure out if I could ever love him or not. Tears started to burn the back of my eyes but this time they didn't fall. The weight of this indecision was crushing me, and I felt suffocated in its heaviness.

For now, I can wait and let it all play out, that's the easiest option. But if there was any hope of figuring this out without causing any more pain, I know I had to remove myself from this completely—from both of them and unravel my feelings alone. The thought frightened me, because in the end when all was said and done, I knew I would have to let Dom go—once and for all.

But tonight, I couldn't do anything else, it was now past midnight. Thankfully, I had no plans for Sunday. I curled up on my side of the bed…no, no longer "my side" just…in bed, and I wrapped my blanket around myself like a shield. Outside, the quiet hum of Saturday night poured through the windows, a soft reminder that life kept moving, even when it felt like I was in limbo.

Dominic

The bar was still alive with laughter at nearly one in the morning. Music pumped through the speakers and people swarmed around, drinks in hand. Everyone was buzzing, soaking up the atmosphere. But me? I felt enveloped by the heavy feeling in my chest, detached from the noise and trying not to completely sink into my own personal pit of despair. Trapped in a loop, replaying the entire evening, mulling over my thoughts, my anger and frustration twisted up in my gut.

I was supposed to be here partying with my best friend, but instead I was hidden away in a dark corner sulking. Finding it hard to believe that this really was the…

…*what the heck is he doing here?*

Sitting at the bar was Erik, looking calm and collected like he owned the damn place. I liked to pride myself on being a confident man, poker faced and almost *emotionless*—but lately I was nothing but an emotional wreck, a volcano waiting to erupt. This guy oozed confidence. A part of me was glad he hadn't spent the night with Kelly, and I chuckled secretly to myself as I imagine her kicking him out of her flat.

He scanned the room and noticed me sitting in the corner booth. I could swear he threw a smug little grin my way and maybe even tipped his drink in my direction. My blood began to boil. I know I've had probably a little too much to drink and maybe it caused my decision making to be a little bit warped, but I know that look. He looked too relaxed, like this is all too easy for him and I'm not a worthy opponent. Like Kelly was already his and I had lost; and that stung me in a way I couldn't ignore.

I pushed myself up from my seat, the bar tilting slightly, but that didn't stop me. My legs carried me without hesitation; every step was heavy but necessary and I was fuelled with determination…and booze. I had to show him that I was still in this fight and would never give up. Kelly wasn't his prize to claim. Not yet anyway.

He noticed me making my way to him and put his glass down, his head tilting and that infuriating smirk curled up at the corners of his mouth.

"Dom," his voice casual as if we were meeting for a friendly chat, his use of my nickname made me see red.

I sneered, letting the venom show.

"What do you want? I'm just trying to have a drink." His eyes flicked up narrowing.

"I want to know what your intentions are towards Kelly. You show up like some sort of prince charming, an answer to all her problems. But you don't know her, not like I do."

He leaned back against the bar; arms crossed; he let out a deep exhale.

"So, tell me, do you believe she belongs to you? She's not a prize to be won."

His words felt like a punch in the face, and I clenched my jaw so tight my teeth ache.

"I know her inside out; I know all her dreams and desires." My voice was low and thick. "I am her knight in shining…"

"You broke her heart." He cut me off. "I think she deserves better than whatever you have for her."

I noticed his fists clench as he got off the bar stool and faced me. That doesn't scare me, but that line—what he just said; that was the real pain I had been trying to ignore. Before I could stop myself, my arm shot out and connected to his chin.

But it wasn't the satisfying punch I had imagined all evening. Instead, I felt a searing sharp pain shoot through my hand. Like a snap. My wrist jolted, my fingers burned and an angry, burning ache spread up my arm. I'm sure I had broken my hand. Erik however, barely reacted; he shook his head slowly and wiped the spot of blood from his lip.

"Dumb move, Dom."

The volume in the bar seemed too quiet now and the chatter had turned into murmurs. The atmosphere had shifted and was thick with tension, I waited for him to make his move.

"Oi!, Chill, both of you! Dom, not here mate." Peter was suddenly there, trying to pull me away, one hand in the air like a referee calling a timeout.

I barely noticed him; anger blurred any sense I had left. My vision was narrowed in on Erik and I knew I wasn't done with him just yet.

Peter stepped closer, his voice steady but firm.

"Dom, mate think about what you're doing. You're only making this worse than it already is."

I shrugged him off, barely hearing and I swung again. My fists flying out raw and wild, propelled by years of bottled-up frustration and heartbreak. Some hit their mark, but most were dodged or blocked by Erik.

"Enough, both of you." A voice called as a burly man—maybe the bouncer, pushed his way through the crowd that had formed.

I'm now being held back by a group of men while Peter tried to calm Erik down. Then they shook hands and something in me comes lose.

"Fucking dickhead." I growled as I shook them off and lunged at him, eyes wild and desperate.

But he didn't hesitate this time. He stepped forward and threw a punch that caught me right on the temple. The world tilted, colours and shapes swirled behind my eyelids. My legs wobbled and I tried to steady myself, but the ground fast approached my face. Eriks voice was the last thing I hear, low and cold as it cut through the haze.

"You should have stayed in your booth."

Then darkness claimed me.

CHAPTER 23

Kelly

The shrill ring of my phone tore through the silence of the early morning like a warning siren. I flung my eyes wide open, and my arms shot out, sending the glass of water on my bedside table flying across the room. The darkness in my room felt heavier than usual, my heart instantly pounding, *who the heck could be calling me at 4am.*

I reached for my phone, dread curling cold in my stomach as I see the unknown number flashing on my screen.

"Hello, am I speaking to Miss Kelly Bamford?" the voice was urgent, clipped. A woman from a hospital at the edge of town—St. Catherine's Medical Centre.

"..Yes?" I reply, fear creating its own reality in my mind. *Could it be my mum…dad? Oh my gosh, maybe it was Zara? She's so far from home and we barely see her…*

"Dominic Moretti has just been admitted. He's had an incident, and you're listed as his emergency contact." Her voice interrupted my thoughts, and I stumbled when I heard Dom's name.

"Dom? OH MY GOD, is he ok? What happened?"

"Please can you come in immediately? We will explain everything when we you arrive."

My breath felt too shallow, and I felt a little lightheaded. I threw on some clothes without thinking and raced to my car. The streets were empty and I'm grateful because every second felt like an hour. I tried not to imagine the worst, but my mind was a storm—memories of Dom were like a broken glass, and I began to regret our last encounter.

I arrived at St. Catherine's, the harsh white lights of the emergency entrance were alien, cold and unforgiving. I nearly collapsed, both with relief and sadness when they gave me an update of his injuries, concussion, sprained hand, black eye and multiple bruises. A nurse led me to a small room where Dom lay; he looked so broken. Laying in the bed unconscious from the alcohol and the blow to his head, his face reminded me of that innocent sixteen-year-old I fell in love with. Gone were the furrowed brows and untrusting eyes that a life of grief, pressure and responsibility had bestowed on him.

His beautiful face, now swollen and bruised, the black eye nearly completely shut. His hand, wrapped in bandages, fingers twitching now and then like he's trying to fight whatever pain consumed him. But the most devastating thing was the pallor of his skin, the slow uneven rise and fall of his chest beneath the thin hospital gown.

With a deep sigh I sank into the chair beside him, my hands trembled as I reached out, brushing a loose strand of hair from his forehead. My fingers felt cold against his warm skin and the tears I'd been holding back spilled freely.

"Dom," I whispered, my voice barely audible. "What the heck happened to you Dominic?"

I paused, sending up a silent prayer as I swallowed the lump that had formed in my throat.

"I hate seeing you like this. I'm here…I'm here with you. You're not alone."

A rush of memories flooded my mind—seventeen-year-old Dom sneaking in through my bedroom window to wish me happy birthday, all the promises we made laying in the park under the stars, the laughter that used to fill any room we were in, our first time making love…my chest tightened with the weight of everything left unsaid. Most especially, this love that refused to die quietly inside me.

I held his limp hand in mine and wept in silence with my head laying on his chest. I felt at home, the sound of his heartbeat, though faint, was home. So familiar, safe and I grieve knowing that it may never be like this for us ever again. Once he wakes up, I will have to retain my boundaries, and I may never have this moment again. So, I leaned over him and kissed him lightly on the lips.

"I love you Dom," I whispered, willing him to hear me even in his unconscious state. "No matter what happens between us, I will always love you. You surround my every being, all my senses are full of you, and I may never love another man…"

"Ahem."

I swung around in my chair, startled to find Erik staring at me. His eyes tired but fixed on me, the pain evident in them.

"I knocked but I don't think you heard me. I thought he was alone."

"Erik, what are you doing here?" I wiped my tears but felt the warmth of embarrassment creeping up my neck as I wondered if he heard anything I said.

"We had a fight at the bar.."

"What the hell…"

"…he started it. The ambulance brought us both in," he continued and showed me his bruised face and the plaster on his brow. "I never wanted it to end like this."

For a moment, I couldn't speak. my emotions felt out of control like a mix of disbelief and frustration.

"Why didn't you just walk away. Both of you, all you did today was try to one-up each other and now look."

"I called you, multiple times." He studied my face. "After we arrived, but you didn't pick up."

"I was…"

"Here…you were here," he said, nodding slowly, as if now understanding how the scales of my affection tipped. "I get it now, I don't know how I didn't see it before."

"Erik, no its not that…"

"No Kelly, I heard everything you said to him," He chuckled, like it was a joke and the punchline was him.

"You don't have to defend or explain yourself. It was always clear that you still love him, but I thought I had a chance, no matter how miniscule. Now I know that I will never have a chance."

I froze, I had nothing to say, no rebuttal, no argument. Nothing. The pain and exhaustion in his voice is too much to bear. I felt exposed with nowhere to hide.

"I'm sorry."

"Don't be, but if you want some advice; I think you should forgive him and try again. A love this strong has to be worth another chance surely."

I shook my head slowly, holding back tears as they filled my eyes. Erik doesn't know the whole story; this betrayal runs deeper than just Dom's cheating. The road to my forgiveness is long and narrow and Dom keeps missing the mark.

"I have decided to go back to Sweden," he continued gently. "This won't change our business arrangement; I'm still with you on your Tawenga project. But I think it's best if we put some distance between us and remain… just business acquaintances."

"I understand."

"My secretary will send you an email in a week's time, with details on my investment. I hope you can figure all this out and I wish you all the best, Kelly. I really do."

"Thank you Erik, for everything."

He gave me a sad smile and then quietly left the room, shutting the door behind him.

I sat back into the chair beside Dom, my hands now trembling, from the sharp sting of loss. Even though I didn't love him, he was never *just a guy*, he was good. Too good, patient, kind, steady and supportive. He didn't deserve this mess, didn't deserve for me to play with his heart. And truly, I didn't mean to, but I had no business dating anyone when my last relationship still remained unresolved in my heart…and in reality.

My eyes drifted back to Dom's still form, his hands pale and fragile in mine. Part of me ached with love for him, raw and stubborn. Another part screamed that I needed to let go, I knew giving in to our love again could break me for good. I was caught somewhere between holding on and letting go, between heartbreak and hope.

"Why does this have to hurt so much?"

I gripped his hand tightly, as if my strength could pull him back to consciousness.

Minutes passed like hours, and the sterile hum and beep of the machines filled the silence. Then slowly, his eyelids fluttered, and he groaned. But when he saw me, a flicker of recognition passed through his eyes, and I could swear they welled up.

"Kelly?" he croaked, voice hoarse and slurred. He reached out weakly, and I took his hand in mine, holding on like he was *my* lifeline.

"Thank you for coming," he croaked.

I squeezed gently, heart breaking once again. *Back to reality I guess.*

"Don't mention it," I replied.

Dominic

The hospital doors slid closed behind us and I breathe a breath of fresh air for the first time in twenty-four hours. Kelly opened the passenger side door and helped me in, steadying me as I lowered myself into the seat. I felt a bit useless and very embarrassed to be in this situation. The bandage around my hand made it throb painfully; likely because I was due another set of painkillers, but it was nothing compared to the anguish in my heart.

I was shocked but also relieved to see her sitting there when I woke up. She looked like she had been crying and a part of me felt happy to know that she potentially still cared. We spent time in silence at the hospital, but it was a familiar silence. She helped me sit up and spoke with the doctors on my behalf. She tried feeding me, but I decided to do that on my own, I needed to prove I wasn't totally incapable.

The drive home was also silent, this time strained and uncomfortable. It filled every crack and corner, making the space between us vast and hollow. Her hands gripped the steering wheel so tight, like it physically held her together. I stared out the window, not wanting to meet her eyes but aching to do so at the same time. I shut my eyes and willed the journey to be over so I can rest at home, my ego felt battered, my heart raw and my pride wounded.

We finally pulled up outside my flat, and I limped pathetically behind her, feeling like a shadow of the man she once knew. She settled me on the couch, handing me water, my pills and a cold compress for my eye. I looked at her then—her face cold, distant, reserved and my heart clenched. I swallowed hard, pain twisting my gut in knots.

"Kelly," I began, my voice hoarse and filled with gravel. "Have you spoken to Erik…um…I attacked him at the bar, I wasn't thinking… I'm so sor…"

"I know, he was at the hospital." She turned away and began gathering her things. "He told me everything. We broke up."

"Oh, I'm so sorry."

"Don't worry about it. Just get better."

"I'm so sorry, not just for things with...Erik. But everything. For cheating, for lying…for everything else."

"You still can't say exactly what 'everything else' is. Even now." She looked at me with eyes full of disappointment. "Even now that it matters the most, you stand behind your wall. You keep hiding from me and I can't do this anymore."

Then she stepped closer. Slowly and deliberately, she placed her hand on mine. Her fingers trembled a bit and I felt a rush. The way her skin felt against mine reignited a desperate hope I didn't know I had left.

"You don't know how it felt to get that call from the hospital," her eyes held my gaze as they welled up. "I thought I lost you, Dom. And then seeing you lying there unconscious in the hospital…"

She brushed a strand of hair from my forehead, like she had done countless times in the past and that was enough of an invitation for me. I leaned forward and gave her a quick kiss on the lips, she jumped back slightly with a soft gasp, her eyes wide with shock—hesitation and then conflict. Then they softened and she leaned in, just a little and without delay my lips found hers.

Her lips were softer than I could remember, and I claimed her hungrily with mine. We were two ravenous beings that were starved of each other for too long. My heart hammered against her chest, and every nerve came alive with longing.

I wanted to pour everything I had into this moment, I yearned for every part of her, I craved her entirely. Her soft gasps became my undoing, and I pulled her closer to me, ignoring every physical ache—my only wish was to repair the aches in both our hearts. I traced my tongue from her neck down to her chest, as she threw her head back. Her breathing mixed with soft moans as I fumbled with the buttons on her blouse.

But then I felt her hand on my chest, pushing me away as she scooted away from me. For a fleeting second, I had started to believe that maybe this could be it, maybe I had finally been forgiven, and I could have my woman back.

"I think we should stop Dom."

"Kelly what is it going to take for you to forgive me?" I asked, feeling defeated, tired and in pain. I had given everything and nothing seemed to be working. This can't be it; I can't lose the love of my life forever.

"I can't do this," she said, voice low but firm. "I need more than your apologies, your kiss or even sex. This isn't just about the cheating. And if you can't understand that, then I guess we can't move forward."

"Help me understand."

"Dom, I spent sixteen years carrying this relationship, I'm done. You're going to have to figure this out for yourself…or…or maybe its best if we just go our separate ways."

Her lips trembled as she said this, and I tried reaching for her again, but she shook her head and stepped further away.

"Do you still love me?"

"What? This isn't about…"

"Kelly, tell me…tell me you don't love me, and I'll leave you alone." What I saw in her eyes felt like knives in my chest.

This time she didn't hesitate.

"I don't love you…not anymore."

It was a lie; I could see it in her eyes. But it was her shield, her way to keep herself safe and protect her heart…from me.

"Kelly…"

"I have to go."

Before I could stop her, she was gone, slamming the door behind her. I sank back onto the couch, my heart battered and bleeding, my body aching, and my mind spinning with the echo of her final words.

CHAPTER 24

Kelly

It had been three days since I last saw Dom, three days since he asked me that ridiculous questions and three days since…I refused to even think about it. Work this week has been a blur of emails, meetings and polite small talk, that I neither processed nor appreciated. Everything felt muted, like I was moving underwater. I kept telling myself it was for the best, that I needed the distance and to keep focused on the plans with Wings of Hope. But the truth was, I missed him…*us*. Desperately.

Instead of heading to back to my flat, I drove out to my parent's house. Home. I always feel so grounded and secure when I'm there. It reminds me of how simple and carefree life was before everything got so complicated. I could really do with dad's silly jokes and maybe being around my parents would numb this ache in my chest.

The familiar scent of mums cooking wrapped around me as I walked through the front door, garlic, tomatoes and a hint of thyme. The house buzzed with warmth and…pop music? And then I heard a familiar voice.

"Kelly!"

I barely had time to set down my bag before Alexis came bouncing out of the living room. She threw her arms around me in a tight hug, almost knocking the air out of me.

"You didn't tell me you were coming!" I laughed softly, hugging her back.

"It's just meant to be a quick weekend break." she shot back, digging her fingers into my side and grinning. "Mum said, you'd been working so much. Look at us, both sneaking home like we're teenagers."

I took her in properly. At twenty-three, Alexis had the same spark she'd always had, the same bright eyes and easy smile. She looked grown up though, more confident, carrying herself with a maturity that hadn't been there when she first left for uni.

"Have you heard from Zara?" I asked as we make our way to the living room.

"We had a very brief phone call last week. I barely get a chance to speak to her anymore."

"Hmm…same here."

"So…" she said, tucking her legs under her and giving me that mischievous younger-sibling smirk. "…how's Dom?"

She points at her ring finger and motions for me to show her my engagement ring. Even hearing his name felt like pressing on a bruise. I tried to steel my face, keep it casual, but I knew this was going to be painful. She had always had a soft spot for Dom, he was like a big brother to her, and I knew she was about to be as heartbroken as I was.

"What?" she sat up, grin fading. "Don't tell me somethings wrong."

I stared down at my empty ring finger and stretched it out for her to see. "We…we broke up."

Her gasp was so sharp it made me wince. "What? Kelly, no. You and Dom?"

She moved to sit beside me, clutching my hands and looking at my finger in disbelief.

"I can't believe this. You guys were…God, you were *The Couple*. Everyone knew you two were solid. You've been together forever."

"I know," I whispered. My throat tightened.

"But your love was…it was different. I looked up to you guys. I thought, 'if I can have half of what they have, I'll be lucky.' And now you're telling me it's over?"

Hearing that made something shatter inside me. I relay the events of the past six months to her and watch as her entire demeanour shifted. Her eyes welled up, then her sadness turned to anger and then… her eyes softened, and I wasn't sure exactly what that meant.

"Things aren't always as simple as they look from the outside." I rubbed my palms over my knees whilst staring straight at the TV screen.

"This doesn't even sound like Dom." Her voice wobbled as she placed a hand on my knee. "So, what now? Is that it for you guys?"

I swallowed hard and turned to face her, trying to find the words and scared of repeating it.

"Well, it wasn't just the cheating and arguments, it was everything else over the years. You wouldn't understand." I hesitated but the words came tumbling out before I could stop them. "I told him I didn't love him anymore."

The room went completely still. Alexis blinked at me, stunned into silence for a moment. Her mouth opened, then closed again, like she couldn't quite process what I'd said. Then her voice burst out, sharp and disbelieving.

"YOU TOLD HIM YOU DON'T LOVE HIM???"

Her words cut through the air like shattering glass. I flinched because hearing it said aloud like that—loud, raw, incredulous, made me feel the weight of it all over again. And in that moment I remembered Dom's face, the way his brows furrowed, and his eyes desperately searched mine. The way my own voice trembled and broke, betraying the truth even as I spoke the lie. I was unable to meet Alexis's eyes, riddled with guilt, I looked down at my hands and struggled to control my breathing and the tears that burned my eyes.

"What all the shouting about?" Mum walked in with a tray loaded with cups of teas and a plate of biscuits. I didn't text to let her know I was coming but somehow she knew I was here. Maybe this is that mother's instinct she always talked about. Dad was not far behind her; he had a floral apron around his waist, but I knew he wasn't doing any cooking. Most likely just keeping mum company in the kitchen, the thought made me smile.

"Hello, my darling, it's so good to see you," Mum said warmly, giving me a kiss on each cheek. Her eyes warming as she looked at me and Alexis sat together on the sofa "Such a blessing to have two of our daughters visit unannounced."

"Yeah…I thought I'd come by after work." I forced a smile, my voice thinner than I wanted it to be.

"Good to see you petal." Dad placed his mug down and leaned over to kiss the top of my head. "Is everything alright? Have you been…crying?"

That was it. Just a simple question, and a weight pressed against my chest. I thought my heart was about to crack in half. My throat already closed, tears threatening and I hated how quickly the mask slipped. The way my family looked at me made this so difficult, and Alexis still curled beside me gave me a knowing glance. Mum must have noticed the wobble in my lip because she set the tray down quickly and came to sit on the other side of me. She wrapped an arm around my shoulder, her familiar scent of lavender wrapping around me.

"Darling," she whispered, "What's happened?"

"Is it Erik? I knew…?"

"Erik? Who's Erik?" Alexis looked at me in confusion. I had left Erik out of the conversation strategically; I didn't think I would be here having a major breakdown and have to spill everything.

I broke. The tears came fast and heavy, soaking into mums blouse before I could even form words. My body shook against hers as the sobs ripped out of me. I felt Alexis shift, and she hugged me, soft sniffles escaping from her.

"Erik and I broke up…its...this whole thing is such a mess," I managed, my voice hoarse. "I've made it all so complicated, I still love Dom, but I told him I didn't. Erik told me he loves me, but I couldn't love him back…because of Dom. Now he's left because I broke his heart. And now…now I don't know what to do."

The silence that fell across the room was not awkward but weighted with shock as everyone tried to digest the word vomit that I just spewed out. Dad lowered himself into the armchair across from us, his brow pulling together.

"Oh, Kelly," mum murmured, pressing a kiss into my hair as she rocked me like I was a child again. "I'm so sorry, sweetheart."

"I didn't mean it—what I said to Dom, but…I just wanted to be free from it, from him. But the second I said it, I saw the look on his face, and I knew I'd broken him." My voice cracked on the last words, and I wiped my tears, but the tears just kept spilling.

Dad leaned forward, resting his elbows on his knees. His voice was calm and steady, the same tone he always used when he wanted me to know I was safe.

"Love isn't always neat, darling. Sometimes its messy and painful." He reached across and squeezed my hand, grounding me.

"Your mum and I…well, we've had our share of fights too."

"…And break ups."

"She's right. There were times we nearly gave up."

"That's true. Thirty-seven years together, and it hasn't all been easy. Mum nodded, giving him a rueful smile.

"But the thing that got us through was honesty, forgiveness…and remembering why we fell in love in the first place," he said, winking playfully at Mum.

"But what if I can't forgive him? …or even trust him again?"

Mum gathered me tighter against her chest.

"It's alright to still love him," she whispered into my hair. "Love doesn't vanish just because someone makes a mistake. But it doesn't mean you have to accept everything either. You have the right to protect your heart."

"You will know when you have given everything." Dad's voice was steady, filled with quiet wisdom. "That's all any of us can do. Give it our all. You can't live in fear of being hurt. But you also can't force yourself to stay away, if your heart refuses to let them go."

"And when there's nothing left to give, and there's no change…," Mum cupped my face then, wiping my tears with her thumbs. Her eyes shone with love and empathy. "…then you know that it's time to let it all go. And begin your healing."

"You don't have to decide right now, just let yourself feel, sweetheart." Dad joined in with our cuddle, enveloping all of us in his arms. "Don't ever punish yourself for loving someone, it's the bravest thing in the world."

I nodded and let out a big sigh, my voice too shaky for words but I let their words sink in. Mum and Dad were right, I *had* given it everything I had, maybe it was time for me to let go and finally start to heal.

Dominic

July 2025

The air was thick and humid that afternoon, making my shirt cling to my back and forcing me to shrug off my jacket, though I didn't really want to. Somehow, it felt like an emotional support blanket and today I knew I would need all the support I could get. Sadly, I'd managed to push away everyone I knew, so here I was. Alone.

I sat on the bench on the path in the graveyard, staring at the stone that bore their names. It had been years, but every time their anniversary came around, it felt like I was sixteen again. My emotions felt raw and hollow just like that day, as I stood there and watched the earth swallow the only anchors I'd ever had. But yet, my feet stayed still. Planted where I sat and refused to move towards them. Not yet.

My arms stayed crossed and my body rigid, I already knew my face was blank. I had mastered that expression over the years. Grief had long ago become something I filed away in a locked box inside my heart. I didn't let it spill; didn't let it show. That was the only way I'd learned how to survive it.

Beside me was a bouquet of white Lillies, Mum's favourite. I made sure to get a bouquet each year when I visited them…their grave. I couldn't bring myself to visit on any random day, but I made sure I was here every year. Today I felt heavier than I usually did on their anniversary, and sitting here alone, with no one to witness me fall apart, I wanted to cry, scream.

There were questions I needed answered. Why my parents? Both of them? I didn't even get to say goodbye; but those feelings lived behind a door that I refused to open. I knew if I opened it, it was possible I wouldn't be able to control the flood and I knew I would never get it closed again.

And then I saw Kelly. She moved quietly through the rows of headstones, the hem of her skirt blowing in the wind, her hair pulled back in that simple way she always wore it when she didn't want to be seen. But that was impossible, she was breathtaking, and time stopped whenever she was around.

It had been a month since she told me she didn't love me anymore. Ouch!, that was painful. I shocked I didn't die from the heartbreak. I'd never see her look so cold or distant, it cut straight through me and left me gutted. And now, here she was, walking towards the one place I couldn't bear to see her. I'm not sure why it shocked me to see her. She came every year without fail; subconsciously I knew she would be here.

We used to do this together, we would sometimes have a picnic right there, beside my parents. Other times we would sit on this bench and have a chat…but this year was different. I stayed still, almost frozen, watching as she reached the grave. In her hands, she held white lilies…she was always so good at remembering the important things.

God, she's an incredible woman. I watched as she crouched down, laying them gently on the ground, her fingers brushed the carved stone, like they were flesh and blood. And then, as if her body couldn't hold it in any longer, she began to cry. Her shoulders trembled, and she wiped at her face. Sat on the patch of grass, she tidied up the plot, removing the dead flowers from the silver vase—that I was sure she had bought, to make way for the new ones.

The sight of her doing that broke something in me. Not just because she was crying, not just because she remembered my mother's favourite flower, but because she was here, still carrying pieces of me, even when she claimed she didn't love me. For a second I felt the urge to run to her, instead, I stood slowly, tucked the flowers under my arms and shoved my hands deep into my pockets.

My steps were slow, measured, almost mechanical, until I was beside her.

"Kelly," I said quietly, my voice low and even.

She straightened, swiping at her eyes, and turned to me. for a moment, her face softened, then tightened again into something polite, guarded.

"Dom," she said, her voice small, like she wasn't sure if she had the right to say my name anymore.

We stood there in silence for a beat; two strangers bound by a history neither of us knew how to hold anymore.

I crouched down, grabbing hold of my lilies and I just stared at them, remembering the afternoons when my mum used to keep fresh vases of them…a lump formed in my throat, but I pushed it down. Pressing it deep until it was buried beneath everything else. I placed the lilies carefully on the ground beside the vase, my movements robotic, not really sure how to act. She picked them up and mixed them with hers in the vase. I'm grateful.

No words came from either of us, no prayers or whispered memories. Just the silence I had perfected over the years of pretending I wasn't broken. I felt weird to be on the receiving end of that.

"They would have liked these," she said softly, shifting beside me, her eyes on the flowers.

"Yeah," I gave a short nod, my jaw clenching.

"Your…"

"They…"

We chuckled awkwardly, and for the first time that day, we actually looked into each other's eyes.

"You go first," I say motioning towards her.

"Your parents were amazing." She replied, her voice crackling slightly.

"Yeah, they were." I swallowed hard, keeping my face blank and my tone clipped. "They…would have loved you still."

Once side of her mouth lifted in a shy smile and then she looked away, focusing once again on the headstone. The silence stretched once more, charged with things neither of us would say. I wish I could lay my heart down and tell her how I felt, how much I missed my parents, how I still grieved, how the weight of it all was killing me. But the words stayed locked inside, and I refused to give her that small part of me.

She shifted again, cleaning the dirt from her skirt and then she wrapped her arms around herself.

"Well," she murmured, her eyes flicking towards me, then away, "I should…I should go."

I wanted to beg her to stay, to not leave me standing here with nothing but stones and silence but something…my pride, my fear maybe, kept me rooted. I nodded forcing the muscles in my jaw to unclench.

"Yeah, Take care, Kelly."

She hesitated, her lips parting like she might say more, but then she just gave me a small, sad smile…the kind that felt like a goodbye. Then she turned away and walked down the narrow gravel path. I watched her until she disappeared around the corner and then I was alone again.

I stared once more at the lilies; hers and mine mixed together. Yeah, my parents would have definitely loved her, even now with us broken up. I know they would have encouraged me to fight for her. I shoved my hands back in my pockets, standing stiff, a chill now ran down my spine. Even in this heat and my heart screaming inside my chest, my face remained as emotionless as ever. Well trained. I wouldn't cry; I wouldn't fall apart. Not here and not ever.

CHAPTER 25

Kelly

The gravel crunched beneath my shoes as I made my way towards the cemetery gates, each step heavier than the last. My mind was still reeling from that awkward encounter with Dom. He was worse than usual, his voice flat and distant, made me feel like I was a stranger to him, like I meant nothing. It should have been easier, I think. We had been broken up for nearly a year now and I was nearly at peace with my decision. But somehow I still carried him around like a bruise. Press too hard, and the pain was right there, raw and fresh.

As I neared the iron gates, I spotted someone leaning against the wall just outside, arms folded, a cap pulled low over his forehead. Uncle Antonio. He noticed me almost instantly and straightened up with that wide grin he was known for. His energy was always so addictive, warm, a little cheeky and impossible to ignore. He always made me smile, even on crappy days like this one.

"Well, well, Kelly. Buonasera," he called out, stretching his arms as though I was a long-lost daughter finally coming for a visit. "Didn't expect to see you here today."

"Hello Uncle. I was just paying my respects." I scrunched up my face sadly and gestured behind me. "I would not have missed it even though…Dom and I are…you know."

"To my big brother and sister-in-law? Of course, my dear. I understand."

I nodded in agreement but stayed silent as I watched his eyes glaze over, he wiped them roughly and let out a deep sigh.

"It still feels so surreal, doesn't it? Almost like it all happened yesterday."

"It does," I replied quietly.

There was always something so boyish about him, even with lines around his eyes and his salt and pepper stubble. Like life hadn't managed to knock the mischief out of him. He shoved his hands into his jacket pockets; a stance I had seen Dom mimic many times. He reminded me of Dom in many ways; they could have easily passed for father and son.

"You know, sometimes I still expect him to call me. It's a hollow kind of disappointment each time I remember he's not here."

I nodded, not trusting myself with words at that moment.

He gave a short chuckle, but it was tinged with sadness.

"Yeah. They were both so amazing. Your Dom? He's a lot like his mother you know. Soft-hearted, though he hides it well. His dad was the stubborn one."

I bit down on my lip at the mention of Dom, soft-hearted? Sure! He's currently the cause of ninety six percent of my tears.

He must have noticed the change in my demeanour because his tone shifted and became gentler.

"I know things between you two…well, went a bit sideways. Don't worry, I'm not here to pry."

"It's so complicated," I replied, wrapping my arms around myself.

"Complicated," he echoed, nodding. "That's code for 'bloody painful,' isn't it? He chuckled when I let out a shaky laugh.

"Look, I'll say one thing, and then ill shut up. Your choice what you do with it."

"Oh…ok, go ahead." I braced myself.

"He's made mistakes. Big ones. I won't defend him because you don't deserve excuses. But…" he gestured vaguely towards the graves behind me, his face sobering.

"If his mum and dad were here, they'd be proud of the man he's trying to be. Nowhere near perfect. But trying. And I'll tell you this, Kelly, I partially blame myself for who he is, I think a few of my issues and inner demons sifted into him, and it saddens me to see that I could have been a better guardian…father figure to him. But you; you've always brought out the best in him. Always."

My eyes stung, but I refused to let the tears fall this time.

"Now, I could stand here all day and tell you forgiveness heals the soul, blah, blah, blah. But you know what? Forgiveness doesn't always mean reunion. Sometimes it just means you put the bag of rocks down so your back stops aching."

I nodded slowly. His words struck something deep inside me. I exhaled shakily, my lips trembling.

"That's just it. I don't know if my heart can take much more. I've forgiven and forgiven and…it's like I've been patching up cracks on a wall that's already crumbling. At some point, I have to stop pretending the foundation isn't broken."

"That right there, sweetheart, is wisdom." He reached out for my hands and gave them a squeeze. "And let me tell you, wisdom costs more than diamonds. You've earned it the hard way."

The tears finally spilled over, and I angrily wiped at my cheeks. All I seem to do these days is cry and it was getting tedious.

"I just…hate that it has to hurt this much."

"Course it hurts," he said kindly, pulling a Kleenex out of the pack and handing it to me. "You loved him. Hell, maybe you still do. That doesn't disappear overnight. But don't mistake love for obligation. You don't owe him your future just because he had your past."

I stared at him speechless.

"See, I'm not just a pretty face," he winked and grinned at me. "I've got the odd nugget of wisdom tucked away."

"You are ridiculous." Despite myself, I laughed through the tears.

"Ridiculously charming, maybe," he said with mock offense, patting his chest. "And hey, for the record? Whatever you decide, you're family. Always have been. You don't stop being part of our clan just because you and Domenico aren't…" he made a vague hand gesture.

"…Engaged…dating…in a relationship." I tried to help complete his sentence.

"…whatever label you used to slap on it."

"I should go," I whispered after a long silence.

He nodded, but not before pulling me into a hug. He had always felt like a second father to me, and I felt comforted in his arms. As usual, he smelled of tobacco and bourbon…of home, Dom's childhood home. And I took a deep breath.

"Take care of yourself my dear. And don't let anyone; especially my daft nephew, make you forget how much you're worth.

When he pulled back, his grin returned, lightening the mood.

"Now, go on. Before I start crying too and ruin my reputation."

Dominic

The drive to Kellys parents' house felt longer than it should've been. Every streetlamp I passed illuminated pieces of my regret like a spotlight. I gripped the steering wheel until my knuckles ached and turned white. I was half expecting the car to veer off course just to punish me for daring to show up here. To be honest, I'm not entirely sure what possessed me to even make this trip, but there was something niggling in me; telling me this was the right thing to do. I owed it to them, and to Kelly. But I knew this conversation was not going to be pretty.

I knew visiting her parents wasn't going to twist her arm into forgiving me. but I had recently decided to go to therapy; this time by myself and for myself. I had to face the people I had hurt, whose trust I had shattered alongside hers. It was about swallowing every ounce of pride I had left and fighting past the fears I had. I can't continue to run from myself—I had to start being accountable and I guess this was the firsts step.

When I pulled up outside their house, I sat in the car for what felt like forever. Shame overcame me and I went over my dialogue in my mind, whilst silently encouraging myself to get out the car and not turn around. My right hand gripped the door handle, and I stared at the glowing porch light, the warm welcome it gave was undeserved. I caught my reflection in the rearview mirror and noted how tired I looked. Older than my thirty-four years of age, it was obvious from my hollow cheeks that I had lost weight, and my eyes looked puffy and red from a lack of sleep.

Opening the car door, I got out and made my way to the front door. It was now or never. The door opened before I even knocked and Kelly's mum, Andrea, stood there in her apron, a watering can in her hand. The moment she saw me, she gasped and then her face softened, but then the warmth fell away and what was left was caution. She had every right to be tentative, I deserved that.

"Dominic," she said softly, her voice a mixture of surprise and something else I couldn't name. "Come in."

I stepped inside, the familiar scent of her cooking and lavender. For a split second, my eyes closed as I took it all in—my home away from home. The atmosphere filled my sense, it felt like stepping into a memory, of our childhood, those fun summer night playing games or watching movies with her family. Memories that I didn't quite belong to anymore.

Her dad, Ray…Raymond…Mr Bamford was in the living room, seated in his armchair like a king on his throne, arms crossed, his expression stony. The weight under his gaze pressed down hard, suffocating me. I had always been intimidated by Mr Bamford, even now as an adult, he still towered over me at six foot four—against my six feet. And he was a burly man with a booming voice; I always felt like a little snot nosed kid when he was around.

"Good evening, Mr. and Mrs. Bamford," I managed, my voice tighter than I wanted.

"Oh Dominic, dear there's no need for…"

"…there is need for it. Let him speak Andrea. What are you doing here son?"

She smiled faintly but stayed quiet, sitting in the armchair beside her husband and letting him take the lead. He didn't rise, didn't even offer me a seat. Just stared like he was measuring every mistake against his daughter I had ever made.

"I came to apologise."

"You have some nerve showing up here, young man."

The words hit their mark; I simply nodded and took it.

"I know."

"You wasted my daughter's time," he continued, voice growing louder.

"You wasted her youth. You made her believe in a future, made her believe in *you*, and then you treated her like shit. You proposed to her, Dominic. Promised her forever, and then you cheated on her like she was nothing."

I stay silent, Mrs Bamford silent beside her husband as he rants. Her arm threaded through his, I'm sure only as a way to keep him from flying at me and raining down well deserved punches.

"And now you want to *apologise*? This must be a sick joke."

I swallowed hard. The urge to try and explain or come up with some sort of excuse flickered but I killed it. Today was about accountability not justifications.

"You are right," I said quietly. "I did all of that."

His eyes narrowed, as if he was waiting for me to break, to fight back or to lie. But I stood there, hands by my sides, forcing myself to meet his gaze.

"She's better than this," He went on, fury burning through every syllable. "She's always been too good for you. I knew that from the very first moment you stepped through that door."

Those words hurt almost as much as losing Kelly did. But maybe that was what I needed, to hear the truth from someone who loved her. No sugarcoating.

"I know," I said again, voice shaking. "And I don't deserve her forgiveness. Or even yours. But I'm here because I owe it to you all, to bare myself and take whatever you throw at me. I can't change what I did, nor can I take it back. But I'm trying to fix myself, so that maybe one day, I can once again be the man she deserves. Even if she never wants me again, but I hope…I'm hopeful for a second chance."

Her dad leaned forward, eyes blazing.

"So that's it? You're here to convince us to soften her heart? To beg us to speak on your behalf and give you another chance?"

"No," I said quickly. "I'm not asking you to change her mind. That's her choice. I came here because I've been running from myself and my emotions. I've been ignoring the truth for too long. I've locked all my emotions up, refusing to face everything I've lost, and…I…I don't know."

The room went silent. My desperation leaking like an open wound, with raw honesty. For a moment, no one moved. Then he let out a sigh and rubbed his palm over his face in frustration or maybe exasperation.

"This change in you didn't just happen, we all watched you change before our very eyes."

"What do you mean?" I asked, blinking at him stupidly.

"When did this change happen? How did you go from the boy who adored her to the man who destroyed her? Do you really not know?"

"I…I don't." I hesitated, throat dry. "I just know somewhere along the line, I lost myself. I became someone I don't even recognise,"

He leaned back, exhaling, and then fixed me with a stare that pinned me to the spot.

"I know when it happened, we both do." He gestured towards his wife and then pointed at the chair, finally inviting me to take a seat.

"We watched it happen, Dominic. We saw a young boy lose his family and then lose his identity. You got lost in your grief. And you've been wandering ever since."

The words hit me like a punch to the gut, not because they were cruel, but because they were true. My mouth went dry and the memories I had tried to avoid all these years slammed into me. The walls I built to keep it all out, worked so well that it kept everything out, including the people I loved.

"I…" my voice faltered, breaking in the middle. "You're, right."

Admitting it out loud in front of them, felt like peeling off my skin. Vulnerable, exposed for the first time in years. But it also felt good to let the burden I had been carrying go, finally.

The sound of the clock ticking on the wall was the only thing breaking the silence. Then Mrs. Bamford stepped closer, her hand brushing my arm gently. Her eyes were kind and full of sorrow.

"We understand you are hurting," she said softly. "It doesn't excuse the hurt you caused her."

"I know," I whispered.

"But we understand, I'm glad you were brave enough to come and see us today."

"You want some advice? Stop trying to win her heart back like it's a prize." Mr Bamford said, his voice softer than I had ever heard it in all the years of knowing him. "Fix yourself first. Find out who you are without her. Because the boy we know…the one who loved her fiercely, he's buried under all that pain. Until you face that, until you heal that, you'll just keep destroying everything that has meaning to you."

He was right, everything he said was correct. It was painful to hear but I needed to hear the truth. I turned to both of them, feeling the weight of the past seventeen years.

"I'm sorry, for everything. For breaking her heart, for letting you down, for not being the man you thought I'd be."

Mrs. Bamford's eyes glistened, and her dad gave a small nod, not approval but acknowledgement. And maybe that was enough for now.

CHAPTER 26

Kelly

The smell of roasted coffee beans and warm pastries hung in the air like a hug—not one I wanted, but one I needed. "Café Macchiato" was bustling with the usual mid-afternoon crowd; students hunched over laptops and mothers balancing toddlers on their laps. The low hum of conversation weaving around the clink of cutlery and steaming milk.

I sat at a corner table with Kennedy and Mia; they had offered to volunteer and had been helping me with some of my plans for the charity. I really appreciated their help; they pushed me to keep going with this project even when I thought I couldn't. The barista arrived with our drinks, and I smiled inwardly; our drinks told a short story of our personalities.

Kennedy, ever the minimalist, had a black Americano; no fuss, no sugar, "I'm sweet enough." She would always say like it was some kind of mantra. Mia, loud and unapologetically indulgent, had a large caramel latte topped with whipped cream and sprinkles. She stirred it absentmindedly, letting the cream melt into the coffee. And me? I had my usual—a chai latte. Warm, spiced and sweet enough to take the edge off. Comfort in a cup.

Our table was crowded with papers, budget sheets, donor lists, proposals, expenses. The bright folder in the centre held our plans for the new school in Tawenga, the planning of this project had taken nearly the entire year, and I still couldn't see the finish line. Kennedy, my own personal accountant, tapped her pen against a spreadsheet.

"We're still short. Significantly short. If we want to break ground in the next 3 months, we need at least another fifty grand."

The number landed like a weight on my shoulder.

"And with the accommodation for the children, plus separate housing for teachers?" I swallowed, staring down at the figures until they blurred together.

"Well, that will be…one hundred and fifty grand in total," She replied, quickly crunching the numbers on her calculator.

"I've emailed every contact I have, sent out newsletters, blasted social media," Mia rambled, swiping through her emails. As a journalist she had a contact list worth more than money could buy. "They're all complaining about this cost-of-living crisis, yet their bank accounts are filled with millions…billions even. It makes no sense."

"We have the fundraiser in three months, that usually brings in a good amount of money." I looked back on the numbers from last year, they were fantastic, I just hoped would be able to raise double the amount this time around.

"Yes, last year was a success. People love an excuse to dress up and write checks," Mia replied as she leaned forward to look at the statement, her long brunette curls bouncing around her face.

"Last year could have been better, don't forget we also had to pay for the premises, servers, entertainment." Kennedy huffed, rolling her eyes at the both of us.

Their voices blended as they bickered gently, and I tried to focus. But then the door opened and the tiny bell above it chimed, drawing my attention. I let out a short gasp.

I knew it was him before my mind even registered it, like we were tied to each other by some invisible string. He walked in with that air of self-possession he always carried, only, this time, something was different. He wasn't in his usual crisp black suit or polished shoes. He was wearing jeans. Actual jeans—and trainers, with a cream button-down shirt, the sleeves rolled up casually, revealing his muscular forearms. The jeans hugged the curve of his firm butt perfectly. I had almost forgotten how sexy this man was.

"Hmmm."

I blinked, momentarily forgetting how to breathe and realising the noise I made was audible and not in my head like I imagined.

"Kelly?" Kennedy nudged me. "You Okay?"

I forced my eyes back to the papers.

"Yeah…yes I'm fine just tired."

But my gaze betrayed me almost instantly, darting back to him as he stood at the counter. He ordered something—I couldn't hear what, but I saw the way he smiled politely; almost cheerfully, at the barista. My stomach flipped.

He turned then, scanning the café, and his eyes landed on me. Just for a moment but long enough to pull me into that familiar gravitational field I hated and craved in equal measure.

"Kelly…Good to see you," he said, his voice warm and polite. Then he nodded at Mia and Kennedy. "Ladies."

They both murmured greetings, their eyes darting between us like they were witnessing an exotic animal sighting. But Dom's attention stayed on me. Soft and deliberate, and for the briefest second I forgot every reason I'd had for walking away.

"Hi Dom," I managed to keep my voice even and calm, as though my sudden uneven breathing was starting to make me feel dizzy.

He held my gaze for another second before moving on, choosing a table across the café, far enough to give us space, but in my direct line of sight. Of course. He set down his book, a battered paperback that looked oddly familiar. Pride and prejudice—that's mine. It's shocking enough to see him reading fiction, but a classic regency novel? What's happening here?

"Since when does Dom come here?" Kennedy whispered, raising her brow.

"Never," I reply too quickly. "He doesn't like this place."

Mia smirked knowingly but mercifully said nothing.

Our meeting resumed, or at least it did for them. Kennedy outlined numbers and Mia pitched more fundraising ideas for the future, but all I could see was Dom. When his order arrived, I nearly fell out of my seat. A coffee and…a caprese sandwich? My mouth fell open slightly in disbelief. I'd spent years trying to convince him to try that exact sandwich whenever we ate here. He'd always scoffed, dismissing it as overpriced tomatoes and mozzarella. And now, here he was, eating it like it was the most natural thing in the world.

I giggled out loud.

"Kelly." Mia's hand waved in front of my face. "Hello? Earth to Kelly."

"Sorry," I muttered, picking up my pen again, and began to scribble something meaningless on the edge of the budget sheet.

By the time we wrapped up, my brain was fried. Mia had convinced Kenndey to at least agree to some new ideas and had decided on new deadlines. And I…well, I'd barely absorbed half of it. How could I, when Dom sat so unnervingly at ease, sipping coffee like he belonged here.

"Okay Ladies, lets finalise these plans next week," Mia said, glancing between us as she packed her things. "And Kelly…I'll see you bright and early tomorrow?"

"Yeah," I replied forcing a smile.

"Get some rest tonight please, don't stay too late at the office." Kennedy squeezed my shoulder and gave me a hug.

"I won't, I promise. Thank you both for all your help and input."

They left together, chatting as they walked out the door, leaving me alone with my stack of papers and a heart that felt entirely too heavy.

I packed my things away slowly, on purpose. My hands weren't steady, and I needed them to be. Each folder slipped neatly into my bag; each sheet stacked with care. I was nearly done when my pen rolled off the table and clattered to the floor. I bent down to grab it, heat rushing to my face as I realised how close Dom was in my peripheral vision.

I stood, clutching the pen, ready to leave. But as I slung my bag over my shoulder, the neat pile of paperwork I'd so carefully stacked slipped from my grasp. Papers fluttered everywhere, scattering across the floor like confetti.

"Damn it," I whispered, dropping to my knees to gather them. My cheeks burned as I scrambled, praying no one was watching—especially not him.

Dominic

My session with Dr. Grady was painful today, I'm glad I decided to take the day off. Her questions dug up a lot of old wounds I'd plastered over years ago. By the time I left, I'd felt raw. Stripped down to nothing. Completely bare.

So here I was, having a pick me up or… *me time*, as they called it. Ridiculous phrase. But I was doing it and in jeans of all things, trying to see what life looked like when I wasn't suffocating inside my armour. The book in my hand was also helping; I hadn't been able to throw it out— or give it back when Kelly and I broke up. I picked it up a few days ago, mostly out of boredom, but it had hooked me in immediately. Rich layered storytelling, just like her, I thought. Always more beneath the surface.

Her friends had just left, and she was busy packing away her papers into a neat pile. I tried not to stare, but my eyes betrayed me. And then…she dropped everything. Sheets scattered across the floor like leaves in the wind. Before I even thought about it, I was on my feet.

"Here," I said, as I crouched down, reaching for the papers closest to me.

She glanced up, startled, flushed.

"Oh…thanks."

We both reached for the same page at the same time, and her hand brushed over mine. Warmth and familiarity flooded as I sucked in some air sharply.

"Sorry," she whispered, laughing nervously.

"Don't be, It's fine." I shook my head. It was more than fine; I missed the way she touched me. I handed her the stack I'd gathered, and together we corralled the last of the wayward pages. When she stood, juggling her folder and bag, I straightened also. The words were out before I could stop them.

"Let me walk you back. Are you going home or back to the office?"

She hesitated, her lips parting as though she might refuse.

"Alright. The office."

We left, and it felt normal to be walking side-by-side again. Instinctively, I slowed down, so she didn't have to increase her steps to keep up with me. But also, because I didn't want the short walk to come to an end. I just wanted— no, needed to be beside her. That was enough for me.

"You've been busy," I said, eventually, nodding towards the folder tucked under her arm.

She gave me a small smile, though it didn't quite reach her eyes.

"Yeah. The charity. We're still trying to raise funds for the school in Tawenga. The deadline's coming up and well…we're short."

Her voice shifted then, warming with that familiar passion I hadn't heard in so long.

"These kids; they don't just need classrooms Dom," she said, her eyes sparking as she tucked a loose coil behind her ear.

"Some of them have lost everything. Parents, homes, safety. They deserve more than the scraps life's handed them."

I nodded, keeping my gaze steady on her.

"So, you want to give them shelter, a place they can finally call home?"

"Yes," she exhaled, almost frustrated, like the weight of it was pressing down on her.

"I wanted to build accommodations alongside the school, dorms for the homeless kids. A safe haven for them, somewhere they can make memories and feel…protected." Her voice broke slightly, and she gave a small shake of her head. "Maybe even apartments for the teachers, but we haven't raised enough, and I don't know if we will. I might have to scrap that part of the plan."

Something tugged at me then, an ache: seeing her look so defeated.

"You can't let that go," I said, quietly studying her face.

"I won't. But sometimes good intentions aren't enough. Dreams don't pay for labour and cement," She replied, her lips pressed into a thing line.

I listened. Really listened for the first time. To the fire in her words, the conviction that burned through her exhaustion. She was extraordinary. I'd always known it but seeing her like this; determined and absolutely unyielding, reminded me of everything I had taken for granted. For the first time in a long time, I was finally seeing her.

Most people would have just moved on when things got difficult, but not her. She carried this burden in her bones; the same way she carried everyone she loved. Including me, once. We reached her office building sooner than I wanted and she stopped at the door, turning to face me.

"So…caprese sandwich?

"Uh…so you noticed?" I chuckled, nervously rubbing the back of my neck.

"Yup, I did. Impossible to miss."

"It was good. Not cheap tasting at all."

"I know…and what about the book?" she eyed me up with a smirk, crossing her arms as if to say *I told you so*. "I've been looking for that."

"Oh, yeah, that's good too. I'm really enjoying it. I hope you don't mind if I keep it for a bit longer?"

"Not at all, keep it. I have some others you may enjoy when you are done with that one." She turned around and gestured towards the door. "Thanks for walking me back."

"Thanks for letting me," I nodded, handing her bag and folders back to her. It was a struggle not to reach for her.

There was a pause as though she wanted to say more, but instead she gave a polite smile and walked into the building.

CHAPTER 27

Kelly

August 2025

Saturdays were usually my chill out day; I got to the office in the late afternoon; I enjoyed the quietness as I went through emails and any work left over from the week. No rush of phone calls, no one bothering me with questions. Just me, my coffee, a few precious hours to breathe, and on days like today, Mia joined me. But today the second I pushed the office door open; late for a meeting with her and breathless, my hair pulled back in a wonky bun, I knew it would be anything but relaxed.

Mia was bouncing up and down in the middle of the room like a teenager at a concert.

"Oh my gosh, put your bags down! Sit down! Something's happened!"

My stomach dropped.

"What? Don't tell me…is it bad news?"

"No, nothing bad," she rushed out grinning from ear to ear and returned with the business laptop. "Something amazing."

"Spit it out, Mia."

"It's a miracle…we got the donation, Kelly."

"What do you mean, *the* donation?" my bag slid off my shoulder with a thud.

"No, you don't get it," she said, shaking her head like she could barely believe it herself. "We've got the donation. All of it…more even. Two hundred thousand. It's in the account., it came in after hours and I only saw it when I logged in about thirty minutes ago."

"Shut up!" I gasped, covering my mouth.

"Look!"

I stepped forward, grabbing the laptop, my pulse racing as my eyes scanned the statement on the screen. There it was, as clear as daylight:: *Tawenga Project- £200,000*

"Who's it from? Erik?"

"Let's check," She urged, practically snatching the laptop from my hands.

She scrolled, squinting until the line appeared: *Bella Gioielli.*

I froze; my voice dropped to a whisper.

"Dom?"

"What? What?!" Mia was now jumping up and down like a bunny rabbit. The excitement was obviously too much for her.

"That's Dom's company, Mia. What's he playing at…"

"…Do you think it was a mistake?" she cut me off and stared me down. "Hold on, what exactly did you have to give him for him to send all this money."

"Mia! I didn't give him anything." I spun around to face her. "Plus, Dominic Moretti doesn't make mistakes. Not with his business and definitely not with money."

"Well, people don't just wake up and decide to hand over two hundred grand." she folded her arms and smirked at me.

Heat rushed to my cheeks, and I looked at the clock; 4pm. I grabbed my coat and bag.

"Kelly, you just got here. Where are you going now?"

"Lock the door when you leave, babe. I'm going to find out what the hell Dom's playing at."

The drive to his flat felt endless. My mind was a storm of gratitude, suspicion and a drop of irritation that I couldn't quite shake. If this was some kind of power play, some way of making me owe him—would he do that?

My fist pounded against the sleek door. It opened after a pause, and I took in the sight of him; dressed down in grey joggers and a plain white t-shirt. His hair was slightly mussed, and for once he looked…relaxed.

"Kelly? Is everything…"

"Don't 'Kelly' me. Did you just donate two hundred thousand pounds to my charity? My heart pounded against my chest.

"Straight to the point." His brow lifted and he gave me a playful smirk.

"Answer me."

"Yes." no hesitation, just a simple truth laid bare.

I blinked at him, stunned by his bluntness.

"Why?"

He exhaled, leaning against the doorframe like he wasn't about to back down.

"Because I wanted to."

"That's not an answer."

A faint smile tugged at his mouth, but it wasn't mocking. It was soft, and he looked straight at me them, his eyes unguarded.

"It was you. You inspired me."

"Me?"

"Yes, speaking with you a few weeks ago. Talking about Tawenga, about those kids, about your plans and how determined you were to make it all happen. Do you even realise what you sounded like?" his voice dropped lower, more intent.

"It was like watching someone burn alive…in the best way possible. You were fierce Kelly. Alive. And for the first time, I actually heard you clearly."

"Dom…" I swallowed hard.

"I knew I had to do something. To help you get there and to make it all real."

His words left me spinning. The sincerity in them, the vulnerability he showed. This was nothing like the Dom I'm used to, but it was everything like the Dom I fell for.

"That's it?" I whispered, searching his face for a catch. "That's your reason?"

"Yeah. That's it," he said simply. "No strings attached or conditions. I'm not asking for a plaque on the wall or a thank you speech. I just …wanted to help."

I pressed a hand to my temple, my thoughts tumbling over one another.

"God sometimes you infuriate me," I laughed shakily, though it wasn't completely from amusement. "You could have just told me you were planning on doing this."

Then his eyes roamed slowly over my body and his tongue glazed his lips. And that was my undoing.

"Kelly, I…" he started, but the rest of his words were lost when I pressed my mouth to his.

The kiss was everything, fire, release and a quenched thirst all at the same time. It was anything but gentle, it was desperate and urgent, the kind of kiss that said everything that had been unsaid for too long. My hands fisted the fabric of his shirt, pulling him closer, needing to feel him inside my veins.

For half a second, he froze, shocked, and then he gave into the kiss. One strong hand cupping the back of my neck, the other gripping my waist. Anchoring me like I might fly away. I stumbled forward, pushing him back into the flat. The door clicked shut behind us, trapping us in the moment.

"Kelly…" he murmured against my lips, but it wasn't protest. It was surrender.

"Don't talk," I whispered back, not wanting to break the atmosphere with unnecessary words.

Every unspoken word, every suppressed feeling, every ounce of confusion spilled out between us as our mouths clashed again and again. My skin tingled where his hands roamed and my heart hammered against my blouse, I was sure he could feel it.

My lips parted under his, and the kiss deepened, slower now, but hungrier. His tongue teased against mine in soft unhurried strokes, like he was memorising the taste of me. It sent sparks shooting between my legs. I angled myself and then pushed him hard against the door, he let out a groan and then laughed, his hands gripping tighter against my waist.

"God, Kelly…" he whispered, like it was a prayer, or a curse.

His fingers slid beneath the hem of my blouse, underneath my bra and grazed over my bare skin. I shivered, arching into his touch, every nerve set alight. I don't understand how I managed to hold myself back from this man.

I tugged at his shirt, impatient, and he broke the kiss just long enough to pull it over his head. My eyes drank him in—lean muscle, toned abs and that trail of fine hair that formed a path. Our clothes became a blur, buttons slipping open, zippers undone, fabric tugged aside. Every brush of his skin against mine sent another shockwave through me. The air hit my bare chest but then the warmth of his hands were there, caressing before his mouth followed claiming with a reverence that made me dizzy.

"Dom…" I gasped; my voice unsteady.

"Say it again," he murmured, his breathe hot against my skin, and my knees wobbled.

"Dom," I breathed, and he groaned like he had been starving for the sound.

My head tipped back, a whimper spilled from my lips.

"Should we do this?

"Tell me to stop and I will," his voice heavy.

I couldn't. In one swift motion, he lifted me, his strong arms hooking under my thighs and I wrapped myself around him instinctively. He carried me through the flat, our mouths still fused, barely pausing as he kicked open the bedroom door and laid me down on the bed.

His lips trailed from my neck, to in-between my cleavage and then lower, unhurried enough to drive me wild, until the warmth of his breath hovered exactly where I ached for him most. My body clenched, every nerve straining, before he pressed a lingering kiss that tore a gasp from my lips.

The first sweep of his tongue had my back arching off the bed. He moved with a maddening balance of patience and hunger, savouring me like he had been starving and was finally allowed to taste the one thing he craved the most. He gripped me, holding me steady when the intensity made me twist away. My hands clawed at the sheets, thighs trembling as control slipped through my fingers.

When I finally dared to look down, the sight of him between me, and stole what breath I had left. His eyes were dark, his jaw tense with focus, and the raw intimacy of it broke me open. The pleasure hit so fiercely that I cried out his name, undone entirely by his mouth.

His hands skimmed every inch of me like he was discovering me for the first time. And when he finally slid inside me, it was slow. My goodness, so slow.

I gasped, clutching at his shoulder, the stretch of him stealing my breath. He let out a deep groan, his forehead pressed against mine, and I could feel I was about to come undone.

"Kelly…" his voice shuddered. "You feel…incredible.

Every movement was deliberate; we savoured the moment and there was no rush towards the end. Just the deep steady rhythm of connection, every thrust pulling me closer to him, every gasp shared between us. My hands roamed his back, nails digging lightly across his skin, needing him closer, deeper. And then he shifted hitting that spot inside me that made me cry out and his groan followed, low and guttural.

"Don't stop," I whispered, my voice trembling. "Please don't stop."

"I won't," he promised, his lips brushing mine, his thrusts slow but devastating. "Not until you fall apart for me."

Pleasure coiled tighter and tighter inside me, my body arched again, every nerve on fire. I clung to him, needing the steady strength of his body moving against mine and the raw emotion burning in his gaze.

Finally release ripped through me a second time and it was all consuming. A wave that left me trembling as I clutched at him like he was the only solid thing in the world. He followed seconds later, groaning into my neck, his body tensing and then shuddering as he buried himself deep and let go. The sound of him, broken and raw, consumed me entirely.

We collapsed together, tangled in sweat and sheets, our hearts racing in sync. For a long moment, neither one of us moved. Then we lay side my side, as he cradled my body, my head laying on his chest. His hands traced slow circles on my arm, whispering sweet nothings into my hair and grounding me as my eyes began to flutter shut.

Dominic

The first thing I notice when I woke wasn't the sunlight or the faint hum of Sunday morning traffic outside, it was the emptiness beside me. The sheets on her side of the bed were cool, untouched for hours. For a moment, still half-asleep, I reached out with my hand, expecting to find her there. Expecting warmth from the curve of her body, the softness of her hair against my skin. But my fingers brushed nothing but cold cotton.

My eyes blinked open, disorientated, and I sat up too quickly, my heart pumping harder than it should have at such a simple discovery. The room still smelled faintly of her—sweet vanilla, it was intoxicatingly familiar. It lingered in the air, clinging to the pillow, and leaving a ghost in her absence. It's almost felt like she was still here if I just closed my eyes again.

But she wasn't.

The reality sank in like a stone in my chest. She had left. Slipped away like a thief in the night, without so much as a note, a kiss or a message. No sound of the door closing, no whispered goodbye. Just... Nothing.

I ran a hand through my hair and swung my legs over the edge of the bed; elbows braced on my knees. My mind raced at a million miles per second with questions I couldn't answer. What just happened between us? What did it mean to her? Did it even mean anything at all? For me, it had been everything.

The way she looked at me when our lips met, the softness in her touch, the way her body moved in unison with mine—like we were savouring something we had been missing for far too long. It was like a rediscovery, like finding something I didn't realise I'd been searching for all this time.

And she had felt it too. I just knew she had. I saw it in her eyes last night. So why did she leave? I stared at my phone for what felt like an eternity, my thumb hovered over her name in my contacts. Part of me wanted to call her right away, demand an explanation, and ask her what the hell had just happened between us. But the other part hesitated.

Instead, I did the only thing I could think of—I called Peter.

"Mate, Its barely 9 a.m. You better have a good excuse," he answered on the third ring; sounding groggy, slightly agitated and unimpressed.

I leaned back against the headboard, pinching the bridge of my nose.

"I need to talk."

There was a pause, then a heavy sigh.

"Let me guess.... Kelly?"

"Yeah," I admitted quietly.

He muttered something to his wife and then I heard his heavy footsteps and a door shut.

He let out a resigned groan, "Alright Dom, Shoot. What's happened now?"

"She was here, last night." My voice came out hoarse, weighted.

"Oh…did you…?" he ask carefully.

"Yes we did," I swallowed. "But she left before I woke up. No note…nothing."

"Bloody hell." He let out a low whistle. "So…was it that bad, or…?

"It was amazing," I said, dragging a hand over my face. "It was intense, different. It wasn't just sex…. not for me. I don't even know how to describe it. It felt like…like it mattered. You know?"

My voice faltered, quieter now.

There was a thoughtful silence on the other end.

"If it felt that way for you, it probably did for her too. Maybe she panicked."

"Panicked?" I frowned.

"I mean, think about it; she's under a lot of pressure at the moment. Then add in your history with her, maybe it just feels all too much. She probably needed some time away to mull over everything that happened last night."

"So, what am I supposed to do? Pretend it didn't happen?" I exhaled sharply, pacing across the bedroom.

"No," he said firmly. "Don't do that. but don't chase her either. Give her space. Let *her* make the next move."

"So just…wait?" I stopped pacing, my shoulders sagging.

"Yeah. But in the meantime, let her know where you stand. Don't play games or make her guess. Tell her how it felt for you, and that you're open to whatever she wants…or doesn't want. Then leave it there."

I sank onto the edge of the bed, staring at the floor. Peter was right, pushing her now would only drive her further away.

"Alright," I muttered.

"Look, mate. I've known you long enough to tell when something's got under your skin. And Kelly…she's not just under it; she's in your blood stream. So don't mess this up by over thinking and overreacting. Just give her the time she needs."

We hung up, but his words stayed with me. I spent the next hour circling my flat like a restless animal, replaying last night in my head, over and over. Finally, I picked up my phone. Draft after draft got deleted; too desperate, too vague or too clinical. I couldn't afford to get this wrong. In the end, I just wrote what was true.

Kelly. Last night meant everything to me.

I don't know exactly what you're feeling right now,

But I'd like to meet up and talk if you are open to it.

No pressure…just honesty.

My thumb hovered over the send button, and I held my breath, saying a silent prayer. Then I pressed it before I could second-guess myself.

One tick. Two ticks.

I stared at the screen until my eyes burned, waiting for the little speech bubble to appear, waiting for…anything. But there was nothing. She hadn't even bothered to read it. I couldn't shake the feeling that something had shifted, but I wasn't sure if it was for the better or worse. All I knew was that last night had cracked something open between us that couldn't be sealed shut again. And even though she hadn't replied, even though the silence weighed heavier with every passing hour, I knew one thing for certain.

For me, this hadn't been nothing. Something new had awoken in me and I wouldn't rest until Kelly Bamford was mine again.

CHAPTER 28

Kelly

September 2025

Oxford street on a Saturday was a warzone of shopping bags and elbows, and somehow I'd agreed to wade through it with Mia and Kennedy. Mia was already two steps ahead, practically running towards Selfridges like she had shares in the company.

"Right, babes, I need jeans, a jacket, and possibly a new man if they've got any in stock," she said over her shoulder grinning.

Kennedy rolled her eyes, adjusting her crossbody bag.

"You don't need another man, Mia. You need to stop buying the same ripped jeans every time we come here."

"They're not the same jeans, they're an *evolution*," Mia countered, with the kind of drama that made a few people nearby turn their heads.

I laughed, shaking my head, but I felt an uncomfortable pit in my stomach. I hadn't told them yet, about Dom, about what happened between us last week. And I knew I couldn't keep it in much longer. We ducked into the store, the air thick with women's perfumes and the smell of leather bags. Kennedy went straight towards the blazers, Mia for the sale rack, and me? I just trailed along, fiddling with the strap of my bag.

"Alright, spill," Mia said suddenly, peeking at me between two hangers. "You've been weird since we met up. Don't think we didn't notice. What's up?"

"Yeah, Kelly. You look guilty as hell, stop holding in whatever it is and just tell us," Kennedy said, glancing over with a smirk on her face and her brow raised.

Embarrassment almost overcame me. God, I hated how well they knew me.

"Okay…so…something happened last week."

"Something good or bad?" Mia asked, eyes sparkling like she was already anticipating the gossip.

"I…slept with Dom." I hesitated, biting my lip and shutting my eyes.

Mia's jaw dropped so fast I thought it might actually hit the floor. Kennedy frozen with a blazer halfway off the hanger.

"You *what*?" Mia screeched, a few shoppers turning our way. She clapped a hand over her mouth, whisper-yelling now. "You slept with Dom….as in Dominic?"

"One and the same," I muttered, allowing the embarrassment to fully sink in.

Kennedy blinked slowly, then set the blazer down. "Start talking…from the beginning please."

"It just…happened," I said, fumbling for words. "I went to his place after the whole donation thing last week, and we talked, and then one thing led to another and…"

Mia gasped so loud again that the woman beside her flinched and moved on.

"Wait…hold on. You mean the same day I was with you at the office? You didn't *mention* this when we spoke after."

I winced. "Mia, I wasn't exactly going to shout it from the rooftops."

"But you could have at least sent me a message or something. A cheeky 'guess what I did' text!" she said, throwing a top over her arm. "Bestie code violation, honestly."

Kennedy shot her a look.

"Mia, let her explain." Then she turned back to me, voice softer. "Kelly, was it…good?"

The thought made my entire body tense up. Flashes of the last week came unbidden—his mouth on mine, the way he'd held me like I was breakable, the intensity of it. My throat felt extremely dry all of a sudden.

"It was…fine," I lied, shrugging like it hadn't set my whole body on fire. "Just physical. I needed to get him out of my system, and well…I did."

Kennedy's eyes narrowed slightly, like she could see straight through me. Mia rolled her eyes; she obviously wasn't buying the casual act either.

"Babes, you don't risk emotional destruction for just 'fine.' Was it fireworks or not?" she pressed.

"Mia…"

"Answer the questions!"

I groaned. "Yes, okay, it was…intense. Magic even, but that doesn't mean anything."

Kennedy folded her arms, her tone calm but firm.

"Kelly, listen to yourself. You're acting like it was meaningless, but you wouldn't look this guilty if it really was nothing."

"I told you…it was purely physical. I needed the closure. Now I've got it." I crossed my arms, defensive.

Mia snorted and glanced at Kennedy.

"Haven't you noticed he's chan…"

"You two just don't get it. I have *made* my decision. I'm not getting back with him. End of." I shook my head stubbornly and began walking towards the perfume section.

"But you still love him." Mia followed after me, hanging up the dress she was holding.

Her words hit me like a slap.

"No, I don't. That ship sailed a long time ago," I replied, laughing too quickly, too loudly. It didn't sound believable.

"He's been going to therapy," Kennedy cut in, her voice gentler now. "He seems…different now, better. More like his old self. That counts, doesn't it."

"I didn't ask him to do that," I muttered.

"No," she replied softly. "But maybe he did it because he wanted to be better. For himself. And maybe a little bit for you."

I took a deep breath, turning away to pretend I was browsing a rail of shirts. The truth was, I *had* noticed the difference. The way he spoke, the patience in his tone, even the softness in his eyes last week. He wasn't the Dom who used to shut me out. But I couldn't let myself go there. Not again.

"He can change all he wants," I said finally, steadying my voice. "But that doesn't change everything that happened. Maybe we just aren't good together. Last week was…a moment. That's all. Like I said, I've got him out of my system now, and I'm ready to move on to other things."

Mia tilted her head, squinting at me like she was trying to read the fine print on my soul.

"You say that like you're trying to convince yourself, not us."

"I mean it," I insisted, forcing a smile. "When I see him next, I'll tell him straight. It's over. No second chances. No getting back together. Just…nothing."

Kennedy touched my arm, her eyes kind but searching.

"If that's truly what you want, we'll support you. But don't lie to yourself, Kelly. Don't bury what you really feel just because you're scared."

Her words lodged in my chest, heavy and unwelcome. I refused to acknowledge it with a reply.

Mia broke the tension with a dramatic sigh.

"Fine, fine, but can we at least discuss the steamy sex you had with your ex. Give us all the details…spare nothing."

"Mia!" Kennedy smacked her arm lightly and she giggled.

"What? Don't act like you don't want to know. Plus, it was *just physical*, wasn't it. So, detox achieved, now spill." She winked at me. "Though between us, I'm not buying it."

I rolled my eyes and let out a laugh. It sounded hollow in my ears.

Dominic

Wednesday morning met me with a knot in my chest, the streets of Knightsbridge were already buzzing and lined with polished, extravagant cars. Suited men and women in designer attire filled the streets. On any other day, I would have admired it all, the energy of money and prestige filling the air. But today, my thoughts weren't on the multimillion-pound deal that awaited me in one of these buildings. They were on Kelly.

Uncle Antonio, always immaculately on time, was already sat waiting in a café across the jewellers' office. He wore a pressed navy blazer and scarf tucked neatly at the collar. He rose, clapped me on the shoulder, and motioned for me to sit.

"Cutting it fine, aren't you?" he said with a grin.

"I'm on time." I replied, sinking into the chair opposite him.

"On time is late. Early is on time." He chuckled, signalling for the waiter. "But I'll forgive you. You look like a man who hasn't slept."

"I haven't."

"Ah." His eyes sharpened with that irritating uncle-knows-all glint. "Business nerves?"

I shook my head, rubbing my jaw. "It's not business, its Kelly."

"Go on." his expression softened, and he leaned forward.

I hesitated. Talking about Kelly; even to him, felt like I was exposing a raw wound. But it had been gnawing at me since that night and bottling it up wasn't working.

"I…uh…we slept together," I admitted, lowering my voice, though no one in the café gave a damn about me.

"When?" he raised his eyebrows at me but didn't look surprised.

"Last month. The day after I made that donation to her project."

"The one for the school?"

"Yes. She came over to confront me about it. We argued, then we…well, we didn't argue for long."

"Alright, spare me the details." He chuckled under his breath. "I'm old, but I don't need you to paint a picture."

I huffed dragging a hand through my hair.

"She hasn't replied to my text since. I told her what it meant to me and that I wanted to talk, to see where she stood…but nothing. No reply."

"Hmm." He tapped his chin, considering me. "And now you're spinning in circles."

"Yes." I leaned back, exhaling. "I don't know what to do, Uncle."

He studied me for a long moment before speaking.

"Domenico, do you remember when your parents passed, and you went silent for months? Didn't answer calls, didn't look anyone in the eye. I worried about you every day."

"Yes, I remember." I muttered, wringing my palms together under the table. I hated having conversations like this, but I refused to shut down this time.

"You built walls so high, nobody could reach you. Kelly climbed those walls, but eventually she got tired of scraping her hands on the jagged bricks. Can you blame her?"

"No," I whispered.

"Right. That honesty is a start. You can't demand from her what you didn't give before. If she needs space, give her space. Let her feel safe again, not cornered."

The words settled heavy in me. He was right, of course. Kelly had always asked for openness and connection. I'd shut her out instead. And now, when I was finally cracking open, she was keeping her distance. It was fair, but brutal.

He reached across and clasped my forearm.

"Whatever happens with Kelly, today is very important. This deal is the culmination of everything your parents built, everything *we* have built as a family. I know I may not say it enough, but you are all I have. You *are* my son, and we have been on this journey together for a very long time. We have fought hard together, secure this today and the legacy is yours. I think it's time for me to take a step back, I'm getting old now, and I need to let go of the reins a bit. Don't get distracted by anything today."

"You're right." I forced a breath and looked at my uncle, his hair now grey, lines spreading across his face. He never married and never had kids of his own. But he had been a fantastic father to me; he raised me well.... sometimes too strict, but he raised me with love and patience. I would forever be grateful for everything he sacrificed for me.

"I'm always right," he said with a grin, then stood up, straightened his blazer. "I'm off to meet a lady friend, now go make me and your parents proud."

The boardroom was every bit as slick as expected, floor-to-ceiling windows, a gleaming mahogany table, crystal water jugs, leather chairs. Across from me sat the senior partners of Edmund & Co. one of the largest luxury jewellery houses in Europe.

For two hours, I talked, presented and answered their sharp questions. I laid out our ethical sourcing policies, our artisan collaborations and our investment in sustainability.

I showed them sketches of our designs, bold yet timeless, marrying tradition with innovation. And they took it all in.

When the head of their board leaned back finally, a smile tugged at his mouth, and I felt something close to disbelief.

"Mr. Moretti," he said smoothly, "We've reviewed countless potential partners. None have impressed us quite like you. We'd be honoured to work alongside you. Expect the contracts by Monday."

For a moment I just stared back. Then I stood, shook his hand firmly, and felt the weight of years lift from my shoulders. That was it. I did it. My parents…no, our legacy, our name, everything…was secure. The world should have been at my feet, but all I felt was hollow. I would update Uncle Antonio tomorrow; I didn't want to disturb his evening. Peter was definitely not available to celebrate with me tonight—he would be at home with his wife.

As I walked out into the London air, I tried to swallow the ache of loneliness, but it clawed at me relentlessly. My hand drifted to my phone almost without thinking. Only one name filled my mind, I hit call before I could talk myself out of it.

It rang, and when her voice came through, it was soft and cautious. I nearly sagged with relief.

"Hello?"

"Kelly." My throat suddenly felt dry. "Hi. I, uh…I just came out of a meeting. The one I told you about, with Edmund & Co. It went well. Really well."

"That's great," she said. Her tone was polite but cool and distant. "Congratulations, Dom."

"Thank you. I just had to call and let you know. Do you remember how much I stressed about it? And now…its done."

"I'm happy for you," she said simply.

I wanted her to sound excited, the way she would have in the past. she would have screamed down the phone, asked me to pick her up so we can celebrate. I wanted her to sound proud. But instead, it felt like she was reading off a script. She had definitely checked out of this…thing we had between us.

"Kelly," I said carefully, "About what happened last week…"

Silence stretched.

"Last week," I repeated, desperate to fill the void. "Us. What happened between us. I just…I need to know how you feel, where you stand. Because I…"

"Dominic," she cut me off, her voice stern and sharper than I had ever heard it. "I don't want to talk about it."

Ouch. The hollow space inside me widened.

"Kelly, you can't pretend it didn't mean anything."

"Stop." Her voice was like steel wrapped in sorrow. "It didn't mean anything to me. I'm happy for you but its better this…"

"Kelly, no I don't believe…"

The line clicked dead.

I stood frozen on the pavement, phone limp in my hand, the roar of London traffic blurring around me. I had just secured the future I'd been working towards my entire life. And yet, I felt like a man standing in the middle of a crowd, holding everything but having nothing at the same time.

CHAPTER 29

Kelly

I hung up the phone, my entire body trembling so much I had to lean against the desk to balance myself. I felt the start of a migraine forming at my temples and my throat burned. Before I could even think about holding it in, tears blurred my vision and spilled down my cheeks.

My words to Dom hadn't been cruel, not entirely, but they were sharp enough to cut through whatever fragile hope he had left. Hopefully, I had finally severed this bond that held us together. I needed him to get the idea of *us* out of his head; there was no magical reunion waiting at the end of this painful back-and-forth.

And yet, as I pressed my hands to my face and sobbed into the silence of my office, my heart betrayed me. It ached and screamed, and it whispered his name like a wound that refused to heal after all this time. I told myself this was mercy. That letting him go fully was the kindest thing I could do for both of us. He deserved clarity, and I deserved peace.

Still, the ache hollowed me out. I thought about his voice on the phone, scared; unlike the Dom that was always so confident and sure of himself. He sounded so full of hope when I congratulated him on his triumph. God, I *was* happy for him. How could I not be? He'd worked so hard for years, carried the weight of his parent's legacy on his back, rebuilt everything from scratch after grief nearly swallowed him whole. This was everything. For a moment, I wished I could celebrate with him; to give him a hug and—no, I couldn't do that. The line had to be drawn somewhere.

I pressed my palms into my eyes and drew in a shuddering breath, trying to pull myself together. I had no time to fall apart like this; there was still so much work to be done. The fundraiser was in two weeks, my dreams mattered too, my purpose. I couldn't allow my heartbreak to derail me. I let out a shaky breath and paced the length of the office.

I needed a plan, not for the fundraiser, but for me. the truth was, I was so fed up of the pressure in this town. Dom was on every corner; I could never be truly free from him and everyone I knew kept wanting to have conversations about what we were doing and what my decision was. Frankly I'd had enough, it was crushing me. every corner of this town held a memory. I couldn't breathe here; this town I loved so much had eventually become a little prison for me. Each day I got to relive my worst nightmares.

So, I'm leaving.

Not forever, just long enough to clear my head and remind myself of who I am. What my purpose truly was. I would go to Tawenga, spend time with the people, the children, join them in the work and watch our plans take shape. I would remind myself that this mission was bigger than my heartbreak. Yes, that's the plan. After the fundraiser, I'll book the flight and just go.

The thought brought a flicker of relief and my heart stilled, my breath slowing. I was till gathering myself when the office door burst open and Mia's voice rang out.

"Kelly, babe, you will not *believe* the nightmare parking situation outside…oh! Honey what's the problem? Have you been crying?"

Kennedy followed close behind, her expression instantly softening when she saw my face. she shut the door gently behind her, while Mia dumped her shopping bags onto the nearest chair.

"Dom called, I just…" I tried to smile, but it felt brittle. "Why won't he just leave me alone?"

They both looked at each other and then at me.

"What did he say, love?" Kennedy asked, moving to my side and putting her arms around me.

"He called to tell me about his big business deal. You know the one he's been working on for the last year. Well, he got it, its…life changing," I said, swallowing hard.

"That's amazing," Mia said softly.

"Yes, it is," I agreed. "And I'm so happy for him…I told him that. But then he wanted to talk about us, and I just couldn't do it. I didn't want to have that discussion. So, I shut him down…I told him that night didn't mean anything to me."

Silence settled over the room for a moment, and they both stared at me with their mouths hanging open.

"But…" Kennedy started, but Mia placed her hands on her arm, silencing her.

I watched them and felt something similar to anger rising within me.

"He will survive. He has his multimillion-pound deal to soften the blow, right?" I said, turning to walk back to my desk and my long list of unanswered emails.

They followed me, Kennedy sitting across from me, making sure to hold my gaze. She was calm, unflinching and I had no choice but to wait for her to speak.

"Kelly, are you sure this is truly what you want? Because from here, you don't look like a woman who's moved on. you are tearing yourself in two."

"I *have* moved on," I said, a tad too quickly. "I'm fine. I just need to focus on the fundraiser now. And then…I've decided to take some time away. Maybe a few months, maybe a year or so."

"What?" Mia's brows shot up.

"Yes, I'll be going to Tawenga, after the fundraiser. I want to be part of everything happening there. Honestly, I need a break from here. I need to breathe."

"I get it. That might be exactly what you need, love." Kennedy agreed, studying me and nodding slowly.

"Maybe I can come with you. My job is flexible and I…" Mia chimed in, worry etched all over her face.

"…No, no, I can do this by myself. I want to do this alone. I hope you can understand. I love you both and I'm grateful for all your help. But I need to do this alone."

My words lingered and they both looked at me, their eyes filled with tears. I said nothing more, reached for my laptop and begun to reply some emails.

"Right, this fundraiser has to be flawless. Two weeks is going to come by so fast. I've finally got the last of the RSVPs so now we can finalise the details with the caterers and venue decorators."

They both gave me a long look before finally jumping into business mode, busying themselves with logistics and seating plans.

Dominic

I found myself on the familiar path, my feet dragging, as though part of me resisted being there. The evening autumn sun was sinking low, turning the sky a bruised orange and the only sound was the rustle of leaves in the breeze. I lowered myself onto the bench across their grave, it has always been easier to keep that distance, easier to pretend I was just visiting the park and not the place where my parents lay buried.

In my hands I had the antique box my uncle gave to me, on the day of their funeral. It was filled with some of my parents belongings; pictures mostly, and an unopened letter I had tucked away and promised myself I would never open. My eyes rested on the carved stone, on their names and the years that defined their beginning and their end. Too short. I leaned forward, elbows on my knees and rubbed my face with both hands.

Kelly's voice had not stopped echoing since our conversation a few hours ago. *It didn't mean anything.* She'd said with such conviction and…God, did she believe it, even *I* was starting to believe it. There was no point calling her again, everything that needed to be said, had been said. And it was all my fault; I had burned down that bridge with my selfishness and betrayal.

She deserved better than me, that's for certain. I sat across from the two people I desperately needed to speak to, knowing they would never answer me.

"Mum. Dad," I swallowed; my voice came out low, almost foreign. "I don't know if you can hear me, or if this is just me talking to myself like an idiot, but…I need to say this. Its time."

I remained seated, gripping the box so tightly I started to lose feeling in my fingers. Their headstone felt too far away, the weight of what I carried; in my heart and in my hands, felt too heavy. I stayed there for several minutes, staring, fighting against the tide rising within me. Finally with legs that felt like they belonged to someone else, I stood and walked over. I felt weary…worn out by the grief I refused to release.

Their grave looked the same as always; well kept, polished, flowers replaced often. Uncle Antonio and Kelly made sure of that. They wanted to ensure my parent's resting place reflected who they were and how much they were loved. But it mocked me, reminded me of how I carried on with life, pretending this horrible thing didn't happen, locking them away, like the memories locked away in this box. And Kelly carried that weight for me.

I placed the box on the ground, wiping my sweaty palms on my trousers. My mouth was dry.

"Remember how we always talked about our jewellery being in one of those Knightsbridge shops, about how the elite would one day wear our pieces. I signed that deal today." I said quietly, the words almost catching. "Our designs, your hard work, everything you left behind is now secure…. I've made sure it will last."

The silence swallowed me whole.

"I hope you a both proud of me." My voice dropped and closed my eyes. "I hope…I hope I've done ok. And that I haven't let you down."

I took a deep breath, picking up the box and opening it, for the first time ready to face its contents. It was filled with pictures of us, me as a baby being held by my dad. Pictures of my parents wedding day, and multiple pictures of us as a family. We looked so happy, our home was always full of love, and it was painfully evident in these pictures.

Finally, I pulled out the letter, the white paper now a pale-yellow due to age. The ink had seeped into the paper, making the writing appear slightly blurry. But still, I could make out my father's handwriting:

To my brother, Antonio,
If anything happens to me and Lucia,
Please ensure that this letter is given to Domenico.
Love, Nicolas.

My Dearest Domenico,

If you are reading this, it means your mother and I were not granted the chance to tell you these words in person. Life, in all its beauty and cruelty, has taken us sooner than we had hoped. My greatest sorrow is leaving you without the strength of my hand on your shoulder and your mother's warmth beside us

Domenico, you were my pride from the moment I first held you. I have watched you grow into a young man with fire in his spirit, and yet tenderness in his heart. You may feel lost now, you may feel broken, but I need you to stand tall, for yourself, for the legacy of our family, and for the people you will one day guide.

You will hear many things about me, my triumphs, my mistakes, my stubbornness. Take the lessons but do not carry the burdens. I do not ask you to be me; I ask you to be better. Protect what matters. Honour, integrity, family; these are not just words, they are the foundation on which you will build your life. As I have.

Your uncle, Antonio will be at your side. He has his flaws, as do we all, but he is your blood, and he will guide you where I cannot. Trust him when you feel unsure, but do not lose your own voice. Lead with conviction and courage, my son. And above all, be kind. Ambition will carry you forward, but kindness will give your journey meaning.

Remember to love fiercely, to cherish those who stand with you, and to never take for granted the gift of time. Your mother and I adored you with all our being. Carry us with you, as a shield and a reminder that you were, and always will be, deeply loved.

When grief grips you so tightly you cannot breathe, remember this: We are proud of you. You were the brightest part of our lives. Do not let sorrow harden your heart. Instead, let it fuel your compassion and your drive to build something greater than I ever could.

YOU are my legacy, Domenico. And in you, I live on.

Be brave. Be wise. Be better.

And never forget, you are loved beyond words.

With all our heart,

Papa and Mama

The wind rustled the trees again, blowing through my hair, messing it up and something in me broke open.

"I miss you both," I whispered, my eyes burning and I blinked hard. "God, I miss you so much. Every day. And I've been so damn angry about it…about you, leaving me like that. not knowing how I would keep going without you. I shut down and buried myself in work because it kept me occupied and made me numb. And I…"

My jaw clenched and tears slipped hot and fast down my face.

"I've been a horrible man. I pushed away the people I love, Kelly got the worst of me. She tried to love me through it all, but all I did was make her feel invisible." Guilt surged like bile in my throat.

"And last year," I whispered, shaking my head. "The ultimate betrayal. I cheated on her. God, I can't even explain it, but I know you would have both been ashamed of me. I broke her."

I stood there, staring at their names and my chest heaved as though every word I'd choked back for years had just spilled out in one rush. And then I couldn't speak anymore. The emotions I'd fought so hard to bury finally won. My knees buckled, and I collapsed onto the grass, one hand braced against the cold stone. A sob ripped out of me, raw and jagged. Then another. Until I wasn't holding back at all.

I pressed my forehead against their tombstone, my body shaking with the force of my tears. For the first time since they died, I let myself fall apart. I wept for the boy who'd lost his parents too soon. For the man who'd destroyed the only love that kept him tethered. For every mistake, every silent treatment and every selfish choice.

"I'm sorry," I choked out, over and over. "I'm so sorry for letting you both down."

I don't know how long I knelt there, hand pressed against their names, tears soaking into the earth. But eventually, I stilled, something had shifted. It wasn't that the pain disappeared…it didn't, and I doubt it ever would. But a weight had lifted, like the cage I'd built around my grief and guilt had finally opened, and I was set free. I could finally breathe.

And in that clarity I knew I had to try once more with Kelly. I finally understood exactly what I needed to do, I couldn't let her go. Not until I said what needed to be said. Not without showing her that I'd finally faced my demons, that I was ready—able to be the man she deserved. I pulled my phone from my pocket, wiping my tear-soaked face with the back of my sleeve. My hands trembled as I scrolled to Kennedy's number. She answered after two rings.

"Dom?"

"Kennedy." My voice was rough, still thick with emotion. "I need your help."

"My help? Dom, are you being for reals" She paused, "What's going on?"

"I need you to bring Kelly to the park. Don't tell her it's for me, just…just get her there. I'm making my way there now."

"This sounds crazy, she doesn't want to see you Dom, and I certainly don't feel comfortable tricking her. I think you…maybe it's time you just let this go."

"Please," I said quickly. "Please, Kennedy. I know I don't deserve her. I messed up big time and its beyond repair. But I figured it out…how to finally tell her everything I should have said years ago."

There was a longer pause this time and I held my breath.

"Dom…she's planning on leaving. After the fundraiser, she will be going away for a while."

The words hit me like a punch to the gut.

"Then this is it. This is my final shot. I'm begging you. Please. Just bring her to the park. I'll be waiting at the gate."

"Ok, ok." She exhaled slowly. "You'd better know what you're doing. This isn't going to be easy..."

"I know," I cut in, relief flooding me and almost knocking me off my feet. "But I have to try."

When the call ended, I looked up at the sky that had now deepened into twilight. I felt exhausted but lighter than I had in years.

"Mum, Dad," I whispered to the grave. "Wish me luck. I'm going to get my girl back."

And with that, I rose, ready to fight for the only woman I had ever loved.

CHAPTER 30

Kelly

The air was cooler that I'd expected, and I wished I brought my jacket with me. Summer was well and truly over. I folded my arms as we walked, hugging myself against the cold breeze. Kennedy and Mia strolled either side of me, chatting easily, clearly enjoying this so-called "fresh air" that had dragged me away from my desk.

"I really don't have time for this," I muttered, half to myself, half hoping they'd hear and decide to turn back.

"Oh, come on, Kelly," Mia said, her smile far too cheerful for how I felt. "You've been glued to that office chair all day. A walk will do you good."

"And a matcha," Kennedy added with a grin. "Didn't you say you wanted one? We can grab one on our way back,"

I sighed. They were relentless.

"Yes, but I need a sandwich too. Thanks for the offer."

Kennedy rolled her eyes and looped her arm through mine.

"Fine, I'll get all of us a matcha and sandwiches. And we can stay a bit later at the office to make up for the break."

I huffed, though a tiny part of me was grateful they cared enough to pull me out of the rabbit hole I'd been in. But I felt a bit excited, I couldn't wait for the fundraiser; I knew it would be spectacular and then my trip to Tawenga. I would finally be able to breathe and enjoy some time with myself. Peace. That thought kept me moving, step after reluctant step along the path.

As we neared the park, my stomach grumbled, and we all laughed.

"I'll get us some cakes also." Mia said, poking my belly.

We rounded the corner, approaching the wrought-iron gate of the park and I stopped dead.

Dom was standing there like he'd been waiting for us; he saw us immediately and smiled sheepishly. One hand in his pocket, the other held a bunch of flowers, his eyes fixed on me.

My breath caught in my throat.

"No. No, no, no." I froze, jerking my arm out of Kennedy's. My heart slamming against my ribs as heat shot through my body. "What the hell is this? Why is *he* here?"

Kennedy opened her mouth, but I was already spiralling.

"You tricked me," I snapped. My voice sharp and trembling. "You dragged me out here knowing.... Knowing

I didn't want to see him. How dare you ignore me like that?"

Mia lifted her hands defensively.

"Kelly, wait. ..."

"No!" I turned on both of them, fury and betrayal surging in equal measure. "Do you have any idea…what this does to me? After everything? After I t*old* you I needed space from him?"

They exchanged a look, the kind of look friends think you don't notice, full of silent apologies and good intentions that meant nothing when the damage was done. Dom stepped forward then, and my stomach dropped further.

"Kelly," he said voice low, careful, as though he was approaching a wild animal that might bolt. "Please. I just want a conversation. Ten minutes. That's all I'm asking. After everything we've been through...can you give me that?"

His eyes searched mine, and for a second...just a second, the years we've shared, the love we once had, flickered in my chest like a dying flame. But I couldn't.

"No." My voice came out hoarse. "You don't get ten minutes. You don't get *anything* from me, Dom. You made your choices."

He swallowed hard, the flowers in his hand drooping, and desperation etched into every line of his face.

"I know. I know I did. But please, just listen. If you choose to walk away after, fine. I'll accept it. But please just... Hear me out."

"Don't." I shook my head, backing away a step. "You don't get to beg me, Dom. Not after what you did. Not after how long I begged for you to even see me."

My chest began to tighten. The park gates, the people walking by, even Kennedy and Mia's anxious faces, blurred at the edges.

He moved closer, his voice breaking.

"Kelly, please. Just ten minutes. That's all I'm asking. Don't shut me out like this. Please."

And then something in me snapped.

Images in my vision began to darken, my breath short and ragged. The pounding in my chest turned painful, like my heart was trying to claw its way out.

"No," I spat out, clutching at my chest. "No, no, no, I can't...."

My throat closed, the world narrowing. Was this a panic attack? This can't be happening here. Not in front of him.

"Kelly?" Kennedy's voice sounded far away. "Oh my God. Kelly, What's wrong?"

"Breathe." Mia was by my side. Her hand rubbed my back, as she tried desperately to calm me down.

But I couldn't breathe. The air just wouldn't come, my lungs locked tight, and my body began to tremble as I heaved.

"Kelly, baby, it's okay." Dom's face was blanched as he approached me, dropping the flowers. "Just breathe. Please…"

I staggered back out of his reach, desperate to get away from him, to find oxygen. My legs carried me without thought as I turned and started to run. I stumbled out into the street. Then a horn blared. Tires screeched.

Impact.

A white-hot burst of pain shot through me, stealing what little breath I had left. My body lifted and I felt weightless, before I crashed down against the unforgiving ground, with a sickening thud. My world shattered into sound. As cars horned and people screamed. In the panic, I was able to make out Kennedy's screaming and Mia shouting for someone to call an ambulance. I saw their feet racing towards me. Dom got to me first, his raw broken cry tearing through the chaos.

"KELLY!" He roared, his voice cracked and strangled.

Warmth pooled beneath me, my world was tilted, lights and shadows blending together. And then his arms were around me, lifting my head, cradling me against him. His tears felt hot as they dropped on my cheek.

"Not like this," he wept, rocking me. "Please, God, not her. Not her."

I wanted to tell him it was okay, I tried. If I could just breathe, I would be able to tell him that, but my lips wouldn't move. My body refused to obey. Then darkness crept in, heavy and unstoppable. The last thing I heard was Dom's voice, broken and desperate, screaming my name as if the sheer force of his love could pull me back.

It didn't.

Mia

October 2025

Crystal chandeliers threw soft golden light across white-draped tables, the air was fragrant with fresh roses and lilies, carefully arranged in tall glass vases. The guests mingled in muted voices, wine glasses in hand, polite conversation filling the gaps where music should have been livelier. But it didn't feel right.

The fundraiser was a success; everything was beautiful and polished. Exactly as Kelly would have wanted it. But she wasn't here. I stood at the side of the hall with Kennedy, my palms slick with sweat despite the cool air. I kept fiddling with the edge of the note cards in my hand, though I wasn't sure if I would use them.

My stomach churned with nerves.

"She would have hated this," I muttered under my breath.

"What do you mean?" Kennedy glanced at me, her brows furrowing.

I gestured towards the stage, towards the microphone waiting like a spotlight of truth.

"Me. Standing up there. Talking about her while she's…" My voice caught. I couldn't bring myself to finish the sentence.

Her hand pressed gently against my arm.

"She'd be proud. You're doing this for her Mia. We both are."

I nodded, but the knot in my throat didn't loosen.

Across the room, I spotted Kelly's parents. Her mum sat stiffly in her chair, hands clasped in her lap, as if holding herself together was the only thing keeping her upright. Her dad rubbed her shoulder every few minutes, his own face lined with exhaustion.

Beside them was Alexis, her eyes were red and puffy despite the careful makeup she'd applied. She hadn't let go of her phone all evening, glancing at it as if willing for good news to appear. Zara was here last week but only stayed a few days. She was beside herself and had stopped eating when she learned of the accident.

My heart ached for them. For all of us. The plan tonight was simple; a fundraiser to showcase Kelly's work, to gather support for her cause. A celebration of her tireless passion. But now…it felt like a vigil. The event coordinator gave me a nod from the corner, the cue that it was time. I swallowed hard.

"Ready?" Kennedy asked softly.

"Not even a little," I whispered back.

Still, I forced my legs to move, heels clicking softly against the polished floor as I made my way to the stage. Every step felt heavier than the last, as though grief itself were pressing down on me. When I reached the podium, I placed my note cards down, though my hands trembled too much to pick them up again.

The room quieted. A hundred pairs of eyes turned towards me. I gripped the sides of the podium and took a shaky breath.

"Good evening, everyone." My voice wavered, but I pushed on.

"Thank you for being here tonight. For supporting Kelly's vision, her work…her heart."

A murmur rippled through the crowd, soft and sympathetic. I glanced at her parents and sister, and my throat burned.

"Most of you know Kelly. You know how extraordinary she is. When she believes in something, she doesn't just talk about it…she makes it happen. She gives it everything she has. She believed this world can be changed one act of kindness at a time."

My voice cracked, but I pressed on.

"That's what tonight is about. Continuing her work, carrying on her vision, even when she can't be here to lead us."

I paused, blinking against the tears welling in my eyes. The crowd was silent as they waited for me to continue.

"She should be here," I whispered, almost to myself. Then louder: "Kelly should be here tonight, standing where I'm standing, telling you about her passion. But she cant. And right now, she needs our prayers more than ever."

A collective hush fell over the room, the kind that prickled against your skin. I pressed a trembling hand to my mouth, struggling to steady myself. Kennedy's eyes locked on mine from the side, silently telling me it was okay. To keep going. So, I did. Tears blurred my vision. The note cards sat untouched and useless. Every word I spoke came straight from the breaking pieces of my heart.

I gripped the microphone with both hands.

"I'd like to ask for a moment of silence…for Kelly. To pray for her, to think of her, to remember the light she has brought into all our lives."

The room bowed its head. Silence stretched deep and heavy. This silence carried a weight that pressed against the walls. Kelly's mum wept openly into her husband's shoulder and Alexis—phone pressed against her wobbling lips, squeezed her eyes shut as the tears rolled down her cheeks. I stared down at the podium, my heart echoed its own silent plea: *Please, Kelly. Come back to us. Please.*

A sob slipped free before I could stop it. Kennedy was at my side in an instant. She slid her arm around my waist, gently guiding me away from the microphone.

"I'll take it from here." She leaned in and whispered to me.

I nodded, unable to speak, my body shaking as I stepped aside.

She faced the crowd, her voice calm but thick with emotion.

"Thank you. Thank you all for being here tonight, for supporting Kelly and her cause. Please, enjoy the rest of your evening, and get home safe."

Applause rippled through the hall; soft, restrained, nothing like the usual cheer of a fundraiser. It was full of respect and solidarity. As she closed out the evening, I slipped down from the stage, my legs weak and a bit wobbly. Then I found a quiet corner and finally let the tears fall freely. This was meant to be Kelly's night and all I could do was hope she would be with us to see the next one.

CHAPTER 31

Dominic

The hospital room smelled of Kelly's favourite vanilla candle and her mother's lavender perfume, with a hint of despair. Two weeks of being here had caused me to become a bag of anxiety. I sat slumped in the chair beside Kelly's bed, elbows on my knees and my head in my hands. My body ached and my eyes were heavy, but not half as much as my bruised heart.

The machines hummed and beeped softly, each sound reminding me she was still there, still fighting. But she hadn't woken yet, not once since that day. Every morning, I arrived and spent the entire day here, and every day I begged for some kind of miracle. The door opened with a quiet creak. I looked up.

The doctor stepped in; the clipboard tucked under his arm. His face said more than his words would. He came closer, lowering his voice like truth was a secret best whispered.

"We're doing everything we can," he said gently. "Her body is strong, and we are lucky there's no major damages. But right now…we're just waiting on her. She has to decide to wake up."

My chest caved in on itself.

"Sometimes patients surprise us. The human body is complex. They comeback when we least expect it. But we need to prepare…for all possibilities."

His words sliced through me… *All possibilities?*

I turned back to look at her, she didn't look like herself, her face was pale, and her hair fanned against the pillow. Her mum and I had tried and failed multiple times to comb out the knots in her hair. I felt like I wasn't doing enough, and I hoped she was comfortable. She looked like she was sleeping, peaceful in a way that mocked the storm inside me.

"Thank you," I rasped to the doctor, though I hated every syllable. He nodded and slipped out, leaving me alone with her. I dragged the chair closer, so close my knees touched the bed frame. My hands trembled as I reached for hers. Her skin was warm, soft and the contact undid me.

"Amore Mio," I whispered, the words tumbling out instinctively, words I hadn't used in years. My love. My heart. I pressed my lips to her knuckles, tears sliding down my cheeks.

"I don't know if you can hear me. God, I hope you can. Because there's so much I need to say. So much I should've said years ago,"

I drew in a shaky breath.

"I locked everything away and I'm sorry. All my feelings, my fears…my grief. I thought I was protecting myself, but all it did was push you away. You begged me to let you in…and I…" my voice broke.

"I shut you out instead. After my parents died, I couldn't cope with the grief and the pain. And a lot of the time, I wished I had died with them. I refused to process that grief, and it clawed away at me over the years.

"The only person that was ever truly able to reach me…really reach into the dark parts of me, was you. And it scared me to feel so damn vulnerable, so instead of allowing you to love me, I pushed you away and kept you at arm's length. Time and time again. I made you feel like you weren't part of my world, but really, you were the only world that mattered."

I squeezed her hand desperately.

"I stopped caring about the things that interested you, I stopped listening when you spoke about the things you cared about. I made you feel invisible. I was blind and stupid and selfish."

A sob tore through me, but I forced myself to keep going.

"And then…Amber." Her name burned a hole in my mouth. "That was the worst decision of my life. You didn't deserve any of that and I will regret it for as long as I live."

I laid my forehead against her hand, tears soaking her skin.

"If I could take it all back, redo everything, I would. But all I can do is tell you how truly sorry I am. I'm sorry, my love. I'm so damn sorry."

The monitors beeped steadily, cruelly indifferent to my anguish.

I lifted my head, brushing her hand with my thumb.

"Do you remember the house? Your dream home, the one with the wide porch and the big windows you loved. I found one on the market. I…I set up a meeting with an agent before… before this happened. I wanted to surprise you. To show you I was finally listening. Finally ready to build that life you dreamed of."

My throat tightened as images of what our life could be filled my mind; Kelly laughing in the kitchen, sunlight spilling across her face, kids running through the garden. A forever I'd been too scared to give her.

"I can see it now. You, me, maybe a couple of kids…" I choked on the words. "A little girl with your smile. A boy with your stubbornness. A home full of love because that's what you deserve. That's what you always deserved, and I want that life with you."

"Everything I am and everything I have is yours, you are the reason I breathe and when I am with you, my life makes sense. I love you with my entire being, in every way possible and in every possible life I will ever live…"

I leaned closer, brushing a coil from her forehead. "…even when I was too broken, too proud, too stupid to show it. You are it for me. My beginning, my middle, my end. There's nothing else after you."

The tears wouldn't stop. They soaked my face, my hands, the sheets.

"But if you don't want that," I whispered. "If you don't want me anymore, if you can't forgive me…I'll understand. I'll never pressure you and I'll never chase you again. I'll let you go and understand that our time has passed. All I ask…"

My voice cracked, desperation bleeding through.

"All I ask is that you wake up. Be okay. That's enough for me. If you're okay, I'll survive. Even if it means loving you from a distance."

Silence pressed in around me. The machines kept their steady rhythm, and I hated them for not changing, for not giving me a sign. I bent forward, resting my forehead against her hand.

"Please, my love. Please come back. Don't leave me like this. Don't leave the world like this. I can't…" My voice broke into sobs. "I can't lose you too."

And then…as if by some miracle her fingers twitched. Just barely, if felt like a dream but I swear I saw it. My breath caught as I leaned closer.

"Kelly?" My voice cracked.

Her eyelids fluttered, slow at first, then steadier, until her gaze found mine. She was groggy and confused, but she was there. Alive.

"Dom…" Her voice was raspy, like sandpaper, hearing it made my chest cave in.

I pressed the button for the nurse with one hand while holding her hand with the other. "I'm here. I'm right here."

She blinked at me, like she was trying to focus. Then her lips curved into the faintest smile. "I heard…I heard everything."

I frowned. "What?"

"You let it out," she whispered. Her eyes glassy but sharp, piercing me in that way only Kelly could. "All that pain you've been hiding. That's *all* I was waiting for."

My throat burned. "Kel… I'm sorry for everything I put you through, even before Amber. Even…this. It's all my fault and I understand if you never…"

"No." Her voice was still weak, but her words were strong and sure. "The cheating… it hurt. God, it broke me. But I always knew it wasn't really about me. You were running from yourself. And until you stopped running, and sabotaging everything, we never stood a chance."

Her honesty hit me like a punch. My instinct was to look away, to hide, but not this time. I forced myself to meet her gaze. "I don't deserve anything from you, Kelly."

"Maybe not. But I don't think I have given everything yet." She squeezed my hand with surprising strength. "I just needed you to face your demons, for yourself. Not just for me."

I swallowed hard, my chest tight. "I thought if I admitted how broken I was, how weak, you'd never look at me the same. I thought strength meant holding it all in."

"There is strength in being vulnerable," she said softly, her smile widened just slightly. "You're stubborn. Always have been."

"So stubborn I lost the best thing I ever had," I muttered.

"Almost," she said, pausing to catch her breath, "But we still have time."

I looked at her then, even pale and exhausted, she was radiant. Stronger than me by miles. I leaned closer, lowering my voice. "I don't know what comes next, Kelly. I can't promise I won't stumble. But I swear to you, I'll never hide from you again. No more walls, no more silence. Just me. Mess and all."

Her eyes softened, and tears slipped down her cheeks. "That's all I ever wanted. Not perfection. Not some perfect love story. Just you—honest, raw, present."

I reached up and wiped her tears gently with my thumb. We stayed like that, quiet, but not empty. For the first time in years, it felt like hope wasn't some cruel joke. It was right here, between us, fragile and alive.

Kelly shifted slightly, wincing at the tubes. "Dom?"

"Yes, my love?"

"Can I please have my engagement ring back?"

I felt my chest split wide open. I kissed the back of her hand, my tears soaking into her skin.

I dug my hands into my pocket, "Of course you can, It's yours. I've been carrying it with me every day since you gave it back."

And I slipped the engagement ring back where it belonged.

EPILOGUE

Three years later

It has been 3 years since the horrific events that took place. And for the last two years I had been living in Tawenga, personally overseeing the building of the school, the accommodation and also a block of apartments for the teachers. I was so amazing to be able to fully immerse myself in their culture, to build relationships and to see this dream take shape.

I looked at my reflection in the mirror, my face was more flushed than usual, it was likely due to the intense heat… along with other reasons. I splashed some more water on my face and focused on my breathing, shutting my eyes for thirty seconds, and leaning against the cool porcelain of the sink.

"Baby? Are you ok?"

I turned around and chuckled, Dom's floating head was visible at the door, which he held open just enough for him to peak in.

"Yes, I'm coming out now."

"This is a woman's bathroom." a voice called from behind him, and then a woman walked past, making sure she gave him a scowl.

"Oh, I'm sorry…I'm just waiting for someone."

I giggled silently and threw the lady a look of apology. He had been waiting outside for about fifteen minutes now. *Oops*

I quickly dried my hands, reapplied my lipgloss and walked out.

"I got you some water, gum, sprite and…. salt and vinegar crisps." He searched through the bag whilst glancing worriedly at me.

He had been amazing these last three years, truly a changed man. I was so happy when he decided to join me in Tawenga a year and a half ago. Although he was now fully in charge of the jewellery business, he was better at taking breaks and allowing others to carry the weight of all the responsibilities and actually relax for a bit.

"Thank you darling," I said, opening the bottle of sprite and throwing my head back, drinking half of it most immediately.

"Our gate is open; people have already started boarding."

"Oh, thank goodness. I can't wait to get home and see everyone. Put my feet up and just…."

"…nest? I know baby." Dom finished, his palm rubbing my round stomach. At eight months pregnant, I felt like I was already about to pop. Our little one would be arriving very soon.

We got to our gate, the last passengers to arrive. Partially because I moved so slowly these days but also because I had been puking up my guts for last twenty minutes. This morning sickness was kicking my ass; first of all, it lasted all day and second; it didn't get any better after the second trimester. But it was worth it for this little bundle of love.

"Enjoy your flight Mr. and Mrs. Moretti," the attendant at the gate said, waving us off before shutting the door.

Dom squeezed my hand, sometimes I still can't believe everything that took place, but I'm just so grateful it worked out the way it did. And as the plane lifted into the sky, I couldn't help but smile, knowing that whatever adventures awaited, we'd face them together. Home sweet home at last.

THE END

Acknowledgements

First and foremost, I want to give all glory and thanks to my Lord Christ Jesus, who has carried me through this journey with grace, strength, and purpose. To my mother, Loretta Boyo, my daughter, Eliana, and my siblings—your love and support have been my anchor, and I am forever grateful.

To Eden Sunday and my wonderful beta readers, thank you for your honesty, encouragement, and insight. You helped shape this story into something truer and stronger. To Fathima Hakkim, my talented illustrator, thank you for bringing my vision to life so beautifully. To Hunii M. Gray, my dear friend and editor, thank you for every late night, every back-and-forth, and every word of encouragement along the way. I couldn't have done this without you.

To Deborah Jones and Cheyenne Mischewski, my faithful sounding boards—thank you for listening, challenging me, and keeping me grounded when I needed it most. To my ARC readers, your time, feedback, and enthusiasm mean more to me than I can put into words. Thank you for being part of this journey from the very beginning. This book carries pieces of all of you within its pages and I am endlessly thankful.

And finally, to you, the reader: thank you for opening your heart to Kelly and Dom's story. My deepest hope is that their journey touched you, that it reminded you of the resilience of love and the courage it takes to heal. This book was written with love, and I hope you felt it on every page.

HOLIDAY HEARTS

Andrea is just a simple, no-nonsense chef, and Raymond's world of wealth, polished estates, and meddling family drama feels completely out of reach. Yet somehow, he's drawn to her spark, her fire, and her fierce independence. As Christmas draws near and the Bamford wedding chaos reaches its peak, Andrea faces a choice: keep her heart guarded…or risk everything for a love she never expected.

For readers who love The Holiday Swap by Maggie Knox, Christmas at Little Beach Street Bakery by Jenny Colgan, The Twelve Dates of Christmas by Jenny Bayliss and The Hating Game by Sally Thorne.

About the Author

Denise B. Henry is a London-based indie author with a passion for weaving stories that blends heart, culture, and imagination. She has two children's books published: My Little Best Friend and I Have a Rainbow.

Bruised Hearts is her debut novel and the first in the Hearts In Bloom series. When she is not writing, you'll usually find her creating beauty content on social media or curled up with a good book. She is a devoted fan of romance, fantasy, and psychological thrillers—the kinds of stories that make you swoon, dream, or sometimes sit right on the edge of your seat.

Socials
TikTok: @authordenisebhenry
Instagram: @authordenisebhenry
Facebook: Author Denise B. Henry
Website: https://www.denisebhenry.com/

Printed in Dunstable, United Kingdom

72298733R00211